PRAISE FOR ISABELLA MALDONADO

A Different Dawn

"A horrifying crime, cat-and-mouse detection, aha moments, and extended suspense . . ."

—*Kirkus Reviews*

"Maldonado expertly ratchets up the tension as the pieces of the puzzle neatly fall into place. Suspense fans will be enthralled from the very first page."

—*Publishers Weekly*

"A thrill ride from the very start. It starts off fast and never lets up. It's one of the best thrillers of the summer."

—Red Carpet Crash

"*A Different Dawn* is a heart-stopping journey on parallel tracks: police detection and personal . . . Isabella Maldonado has created an unforgettable hero in Nina Guerrera."

—Criminal Element

"A killer of a novel. Fresh, fast, and utterly ingenious."

—Brad Thor, #1 *New York Times* bestselling author

The Cipher

An Amazon Best Book of the Month: Mystery, Thriller & Suspense

"The survivor of a vicious crime confronts her fears in a hunt for a serial killer . . . forensic analysis, violent action, and a tough heroine who stands up to the last man on earth she wants to see again."

—*Kirkus Reviews*

"[In] this riveting series launch from Maldonado . . . the frequent plot twists will keep readers guessing to the end, and Maldonado draws on her twenty-two years in law enforcement to add realism. Determined to overcome her painful past, the admirable Nina has enough depth to sustain a long-running series."

—*Publishers Weekly*

"*The Cipher* by Isabella Maldonado is a nail-biting race against time."

—POPSUGAR

"Maldonado does a superb job of depicting a woman who's made a strength out of trauma, and an even better job at showing how a monster could use the internet to prey on the vulnerable. Maldonado spent twenty-two years in law enforcement and her experience shines through in *The Cipher*."

—The Amazon Book Review

"A heart-pounding novel from page one, *The Cipher* checks all the boxes for a top-notch thriller: sharp plotting, big stakes, and characters—good and bad and everywhere in between—that are so richly drawn you'll swear you've met them. I read this in one sitting and I guarantee you will too. Oh, another promise: you'll absolutely love the Warrior Girl!"

—Jeffery Deaver, *New York Times* bestselling author

"Wow! A riveting tale in the hands of a superb storyteller."

—J. A. Jance, *New York Times* bestselling author

"Intense, harrowing, and instantly addictive, *The Cipher* took my breath away. Isabella Maldonado has created an unforgettable heroine in Nina Guerrera, a dedicated FBI agent and trauma survivor with unique insight into the mind of a predator. This riveting story is everything a thriller should be."

—Hilary Davidson, *Washington Post* bestselling author

THE
FALCON

ALSO BY ISABELLA MALDONADO

FBI Agent Nina Guerrera series

The Cipher

A Different Dawn

Detective Veranda Cruz series

Blood's Echo

Phoenix Burning

Death Blow

THE FALCON

ISABELLA MALDONADO

THOMAS & MERCER

Text copyright © 2022 by Isabella Maldonado
All rights reserved.

No part of this book may be reproduced, or stored in a retrieval system, or transmitted in any form or by any means, electronic, mechanical, photocopying, recording, or otherwise, without express written permission of the publisher.

Published by Thomas & Mercer, Seattle

www.apub.com

Amazon, the Amazon logo, and Thomas & Mercer are trademarks of Amazon.com, Inc., or its affiliates.

ISBN-13: 9781542035620
ISBN-10: 1542035627

Cover design by Christopher Lin

Printed in the United States of America

For my family, whether related by blood or the bonds of friendship: I am forever grateful for your understanding and patience over the years.

Chapter 1

Fairfax County police officer Nina Guerrera's booted feet pounded the pavement as she raced after the shadowy figure fleeing from her. The thirteen-year-old girl she chased was petite—no bigger than Nina—but she was fast.

Nina knew from experience that a blast of adrenaline favored sprints over marathons. All she had to do was keep her quarry in sight and wait for fatigue to set in.

Probably coming to the same conclusion, the girl gripped the edge of a metal trash can as she rushed by, tipping it into Nina's path.

Nina timed her footfalls as the can rolled toward her, hurdling over it without slowing her pace.

"I can do this all night, Bianca," she called out. "How about you?"

Without turning or breaking her stride, the girl raised her left hand, middle finger extended.

Nina laughed loud enough for Bianca to hear, which was the point. She wanted her to know that running was futile.

The second mile proved too much for Bianca, who bent over to rest her palms on her knees and suck in gulps of air. Nina came to a leisurely stop several paces away, knowing better than to crowd her.

When Bianca finally caught her breath, she directed a stream of expletives at her pursuer between gasps. Certain the verbal barrage had been calculated to cover fear, Nina ignored Bianca's rant and focused on her appearance.

At thirteen years old, Bianca Babbage had the haunted eyes, hunched shoulders, and wary demeanor of someone who had lived on the street when she was too small to defend herself.

Nina knew the look. She had seen it in the mirror when she was Bianca's age.

"When's the last time you ate?" Nina asked her quietly. "I can tell it's been a while since you've had a hot meal."

In her youth, Nina had known both physical and emotional starvation. Since she had become a patrol officer, she'd seen the symptoms in others enough times to recognize the deprivation that baggy clothes, heavy makeup, and a defiant attitude could not disguise. Symptoms on full display in the girl before her.

"What are you, the food police?" Bianca licked her lips, putting the lie to the sarcasm behind the question.

"My cruiser's over there." Nina tipped her head in the direction they had come from. "I can take you to get a burger."

Bianca's blue eyes narrowed with suspicion. "As soon as my butt hits the back seat, you'll haul me off to juvie."

Nina stepped closer. "Let me buy you dinner, Bianca. I want to talk to you. That's all."

Silence stretched between them. Nina could feel the girl's penetrating gaze boring into her as she tried to figure out if she could trust a cop.

She had heard her fellow officers talking about Bianca back at the station over the past few weeks. They described her as a serial runner who seemed to prefer life on the street to foster care. The other cops couldn't understand why the girl kept leaving a roof over her head and three squares to take her chances in dark alleys and wooded parks.

Nina understood.

She'd made a promise to herself that she would be the one to take the call the next time Bianca took off. Nina wouldn't simply file a report and put out a BOLO—she would find Bianca and get her to talk.

Nina had taken the runaway report from the middle-aged couple who had served as Bianca's foster parents for the past six months. The husband had been surly and unkempt, with a beer gut and a scraggly mustache only slightly thicker than that of his wife, whose nicotine-stained fingers constantly scratched at a rash on her fleshy neck. Nina had barely managed to hold herself in check when they referred to Bianca as a "problem child" who wouldn't listen.

The same comments had appeared in reports from Nina's foster parents and teachers when she was a foster child years ago.

Nina had combed local teenage hangouts that night, showing around a picture of Bianca until she finally traced her to a parking lot behind a strip mall. She spotted the girl among ten or fifteen kids who scattered in all directions as her marked patrol car came into view.

The cruiser's tires had barely screeched to a stop before Nina had jumped out and started running after Bianca. Rather than tackle the girl to the ground, Nina had stayed on her heels through back alleys and dimly lit streets, never letting her out of sight.

Now that she'd had time to rest, Bianca showed signs of bolting again. Her eyes darted down the street, and her upper body tilted forward like a runner at the starting block. The promise of a meal had clearly enticed Bianca, but Nina was on borrowed time.

How to get her to stay? More importantly, how to get her to confide her secrets? Nina could only think of one way to earn Bianca's trust.

She would open up first.

"Before you take off again," she began, drawing Bianca's startled gaze, "I'd like to share something with you."

Bianca folded her arms protectively across her chest and made no response. The move briefly exposed an angry welt peeking out from under the frayed cuff of her dark hoodie.

"I grew up in the foster system," Nina said. "Never knew my biological family." She let that sink in before continuing. "I was left in a dumpster when I was a month old."

Bianca looked her up and down in obvious disbelief.

Nina knew how she would appear to anyone who hadn't known her as a child. Her crisp police uniform consisted of a gray shirt and navy-blue pants, polished tactical boots, and a ballistic vest that made her look bigger than she was, a far cry from the tattered clothes she had worn at Bianca's age.

"I wasn't born a cop," Nina continued. "Growing up, I bounced from one foster home to another. Sometimes no one would have me, and I would stay in a group home for a while. I'm small, like you, so people took advantage of me. Until I put a stop to it."

Bianca's eyes widened. "How?"

"Come with me and I'll tell you," Nina said, baiting the hook.

She watched an array of conflicting emotions play across Bianca's expressive face until finally, with obvious reluctance, she got into the cruiser and sat in silence while Nina took her to the nearest McDonald's. After ordering burgers and fries for both of them, Nina took up her story.

"When I was sixteen, my foster father offered me to his bookie to pay off his debts," she said, deliberately blunt.

Bianca gaped. "You mean—"

"That's exactly what I mean. When I wouldn't cooperate, they beat me. I have marks, too, only mine are on my back."

Bianca pulled her sleeves down and tucked her hands completely inside them. "What did you do?"

"I lit the bookie's beard on fire and got the hell out of there." Nina popped a fry into her mouth. "Lived on the street for a while, too, but that didn't end well for me. Which is why I'm not going to stand by and watch you put yourself in danger. Not when I can do something about it."

She stopped, allowing Bianca to process her words, to grasp that Nina could understand her as no one else could. Sensing the girl's hesitancy start to break, Nina waited her out.

Finally, Bianca put down her half-eaten burger as her eyes filled with tears. "No one believes me," she whispered.

Nina said nothing until Bianca's gaze met hers. "I believe you."

Three simple words were all it took. Words Bianca had probably never heard from any adult. A single tear slid down Bianca's hollow cheek as she strained to hold her emotions in check.

Nina leaned forward. "Tell me everything."

The dam broke. Over the next twenty minutes, Nina listened carefully as Bianca talked. In the end, Bianca agreed to take off her hoodie, allowing Nina to inspect the angry welts up and down her arms.

Nina pointed to the red lines around her wrists. "Flex-cuffs?"

Bianca nodded, then lifted the hem of her frayed blue jeans to show more marks on her shins and calves.

"That's why I kept taking off," Bianca said, her voice as thin as her frail body. "But I can't go back again. They told me if I ran again, they'd kill me and make it look like an accident when I came back." She swallowed. "I believe them."

While Bianca finished her meal, Nina contacted her supervisor to request someone from Child Protective Services meet her at the magistrate's office in downtown Fairfax to help secure warrants against Bianca's foster parents for felony child abuse.

Three hours later, Nina unlocked the door to her apartment on the top floor of a four-story walk-up in the unofficial Latin corridor of Springfield.

She pushed the door open and turned to Bianca. "It's not much, but it'll do for a couple of days until we can find a new foster home for you."

Bianca wrinkled her nose. "I don't want to move in with another—"

"I'm not going to let you stay anywhere unless I personally check it out."

The next-door neighbor's door opened. "What's going on out here? It's past midnight."

Mrs. Gomez stepped out into the hallway in a pink chenille robe and fuzzy slippers. Mrs. G and her husband had emigrated from Chile thirty years earlier. They had raised four children in the apartment and were now alone after the last one had left for college a year earlier.

Nina waved her off. "Go back to bed, Mrs. G. It's just me."

Mrs. G squinted at Bianca. "Who is this?"

"This is Bianca Babbage. She'll be here with me for a bit until we find her family to stay with."

Mrs. G drew closer, eyes filled with concern. "*Mi'jita*, where is your *familia?*"

Bianca jerked her chin at Nina. "Officer Badass here just locked up the two losers who pretended to take care of me."

Nina recognized the tactic. Hide the pain under a thick layer of snark. Failing that, feign indifference. Children raised without stable families had many means of coping, and Nina had employed them all. Sometimes, she still did.

"No parents?" Mrs. G looked appalled. "No aunts or uncles? No grandparents?"

Bianca looked down at her shoes.

Nina broke the awkward silence. "Child Protective Services took Bianca from her parents a few years ago. I can't go into details."

Mrs. G reached out to Bianca, and Nina almost stepped between them. Her own experiences had made her leery of unsolicited physical contact, and she figured Bianca felt the same way. To her surprise, Bianca allowed Mrs. G to pull her into a gentle hug.

"Come to my apartment tomorrow morning," Mrs. G said, her voice thick with emotion. "I'll make you both a nice breakfast." She smiled. "I'm making *pastel de choclo*."

"What's that?" Bianca asked.

Nina answered, giving Mrs. G a chance to compose herself. "It's a kind of quiche, but it has beef, chicken, corn, and spices."

"Beef *and* chicken?" Bianca looked dubious. "In a quiche?"

"I used to make it for my little ones on the weekends." Mrs. G sighed. Her gaze traveled up and down Bianca's slight frame. "You need good food."

Nina's eyes met Mrs. G's. Clearly Bianca needed a lot more than food.

How many times had Mrs. G lamented her empty nest?

Nina's lips spread into a wide grin as a plan took shape in her mind. She was a protector, but her own dark past had left her unable to provide the warm, nurturing environment Bianca so clearly needed. The kind of home Nina had never experienced.

The two women came to a tacit understanding that night. Nina would keep Bianca safe from harm, and Mrs. G would give her the love Nina couldn't.

Chapter 2

Present day
Arizona Institute of Technology, Phoenix campus

The crisp March air brushed his skin, raising gooseflesh on his arms as he lifted the night vision binoculars to his eyes. He had watched her earlier that evening, walking arm in arm with that bleached-blond, spray-tanned, muscle-headed moron. Now she was crossing the quad with him.

He cursed under his breath and followed their progress as they reached the sidewalk and stopped under one of the overhead lights in front of the student union. She tugged her jacket's hood over her head, laughing as the first fat raindrops plopped onto the sidewalk around them.

What was Spray Tan talking to her about? The best tooth-whitening products? How to keep that fake bronze glow all year round? How much he'd bench-pressed at the gym today?

Spray Tan bent his head down to her. He'd damn well better not, he'd better not—and then he did it. He gave her one of those sloppy, tonguey, noisy kisses. She didn't even try to fight him. She would soon learn what it was like to be kissed in a way that truly fed her hunger. To be in the care of a real man, and not that empty-headed Ken doll.

Spray Tan broke off the embrace and strolled away. He didn't even glance over his shoulder at her as he left. She lingered, making doe eyes at his back as the darkness swallowed him.

Despite everything going on, Spray Tan hadn't offered to walk her to her dorm. Unlike him, Spray Tan had no clue how to use all those gym-rat muscles. Spray Tan was a preening peacock, nothing more. He, on the other hand, was a bird of prey.

He slipped the field glasses inside his jacket pocket, opened a small folding umbrella, and strode toward her.

"How are you doing tonight?" he called out from a few paces away.

She spun around, wide eyes darting in his direction. "Who's there?"

At least her survival instincts weren't totally absent. She hadn't seen his approach from the rainy gloom beyond the glow of the light above her.

He adopted a soothing tone. "Campus police." He stepped into the lamp's halo and let her scan his uniform.

She visibly relaxed. "Nice to see you, Officer . . . um . . . what's your name?"

"Call me Horace." He held out the umbrella in polite invitation. "I've been assigned to escort any lone female students back to their dorms."

She jerked a thumb over her shoulder. "I'm in Verger Hall."

An all-female dorm known as the "virgin vault." Ironic, since he knew she was hardly anyone's definition of chaste. The thought annoyed him briefly, as it had when he had first taken an interest in her. He consoled himself with the knowledge that she would soon care nothing for any other man. Ever.

"I'll let the dispatcher know I'm walking you there." He lifted the portable radio from its belt clip and mashed the "Transmit" button. "Bravo-nine-eight on an escort to Verger Hall."

She had no way of knowing the device was not turned on. He waited a moment, tapped the transmitter in his ear as if he'd received an acknowledgment, and then slid the radio back on his belt.

"You're a freshman?" he asked, falling into step beside her and lifting the umbrella to cover both their heads.

"Is it that obvious?"

"Upperclassmen don't live in Verger."

She nodded and strolled along beside him, relaxed, compliant. Exactly the way he wanted her. When they neared one of the older buildings along the way, he came to an abrupt halt and clutched her arm.

"Hey," she said, trying to tug free from his grasp. "What are you doing?"

"Shhh." He crouched, swiveling his head as if scanning for threats. "I heard something."

She stilled, as he knew she would, and huddled close to him. "What is it?" she whispered.

He raised a finger to his lips to silence her, then released her arm to clasp her trembling hand in his. Still hunkered down, he tugged her behind him and rushed ahead until he reached the side of a nearby dark building. "Someone's following us."

"Who?" she whispered. "Is it . . . is it the one who's been taking students?"

"You can hide in here." Ignoring the question, he pointed at a service door set into the side of the structure. "I'll check the area."

She shook her head. "Don't leave me."

He opened the door and motioned inside. She darted in without hesitation, turned, and beckoned him to follow her. He obliged, shutting the door behind him.

After a long silence, she spoke quietly. "I've walked by but never been in here before."

He kept his voice low. "That's because no one uses it right now. Tanner Hall is one of many buildings on campus that are over a hundred years old. It's scheduled for demolition at the end of the semester, so the classes and offices have been moved to other buildings."

Her eyes traveled to his radio. "Did you call for help?"

"No need for that," he said softly. "I've got you now."

Before she said another word, he yanked her tight against him and clapped a damp cloth over her mouth and nose. She thrashed, panic widening her eyes as she gazed up at him. After a flurry of futile kicks, she went limp in his arms.

Chapter 3

The next day

FBI Special Agent Nina Guerrera stood beside Bianca on the front porch of her aunt Teresa's house in Phoenix. Bianca, now eighteen, had arrived at Sky Harbor Airport half an hour earlier after flying in on a red-eye from DC.

"You sure your aunt is okay with me staying at her place over spring break?" Bianca said. "It's a big ask considering she's never met me."

"Teresa's motto is *mi casa es su casa*," Nina said with a wry smile. "She tried to get me to move in with her while I'm in town on this case, and I only met her a couple of weeks ago myself."

Two and a half years earlier, Nina had left the Fairfax County police to join the FBI, where she'd been assigned to the Washington field office and then a task force near Quantico. Separated from her biological family at birth, she had only recently discovered her parents had died long ago. She also learned she had relatives living across the country in Phoenix, and her mother's twin sister, Teresa, was the unofficial leader of their clan. Since their recent acquaintance, Teresa had made it her mission to make up for twenty-eight years of lost time.

Bianca crossed her arms. "Which is exactly my point. How could she take me in when she doesn't know you all that well?"

"She's a lot like Mrs. Gomez," Nina said. "Latina mothers have ways of making you comply . . . and of making you feel welcome. Teresa insisted you use her daughter's old room while you're in town. Since I'm staying at the hotel with the rest of my team, I think she wants to be sure I'm at her house as much as possible when I'm not working."

"You told her I'll be spending a good chunk of the day at AIT, right?"

Bianca was due to get a Bachelor of Science degree from George Washington University in DC in May. After finally finding a stable and loving home with Mr. and Mrs. Gomez at thirteen, Bianca had flourished. Once she'd stopped cutting classes to hide from school bullies, the teachers spotted her remarkable potential. When an IQ test put her in the top percentile, she had been allowed to take exams to finish high school at fourteen.

Now prepared to complete her undergraduate degree with a dual major in computer science and biology, Bianca was considering three elite tech universities for her master's studies. Among them was the Arizona Institute of Technology in Phoenix.

"Are you sure you want to go to AIT, or are you really just here to check out my bio family?" Nina asked.

"I'm here to see Dr. Dawson," Bianca said. "He got in touch with me after my mentor helped get my thesis study published. He's developing implantable nanotech, and I'm working on a concept that could introduce them into the human body through engineered viruses. It could help people with spinal cord injuries walk again. What could be more important than that?"

"Agreed." Nina felt a rush of pride as she looked at the petite teen who might very well change the world. Dr. Dawson wasn't the only one in academia who had taken notice of her work and seen its potential. "Just make sure you follow the rules."

Bianca looked like she was suppressing an eye roll. "I'll be home before dark." She held up her little finger. "Pinkie swear."

"I'm not kidding," Nina said, knocking on the door. "I'll handcuff you to my wrist if I need to."

Teresa arrived moments later, beaming in welcome. "Come inside, *mi'ja*," she said to Nina, pulling her in for a quick hug before turning warm brown eyes on Bianca. "And this must be Miss Babbage."

Bianca extended a hand. "Friends call me Bee."

Teresa took the proffered hand and held it, leading Bianca into the kitchen, which smelled of hot coffee and cinnamon.

"I know you're in a hurry to get to work," Teresa said to Nina, who had followed. "But there is always time for a quick breakfast."

She laid a platter of churros dusted with sugar and cinnamon on the counter. The aroma of the freshly baked delicacies made Nina's mouth water.

Bianca, who normally would have gone straight for the coffee, picked up a churro, nibbled at the end, closed her eyes, and groaned with pleasure. "These things are amaze-balls."

Teresa beamed. If she had any qualms about Bianca's facial piercings, tattoos, or the blue streak in her hair that perfectly matched her cobalt eyes, she didn't show it.

Nina thought she understood why when she recalled that Teresa's son, Alex, was also eighteen years old and covered in body art.

"So you are here to tour the campus at AIT," Teresa said to Bianca. "My son would like to go there next fall after he graduates high school in a couple months. Maybe you two will be in some of the same classes."

"I doubt it," Bianca said, blushing. "I'm starting my master's program."

Teresa turned to Nina. "I thought you said she was eighteen?"

"She is."

"And going to a school like AIT?" Teresa regarded Bianca. "You must be a genius."

Bianca shifted on her feet. "I'm not comfortable with labels."

Neither was Nina. Labels like "willful" and "headstrong" had gotten her in a lot of trouble as a child. She had learned from Bianca that terms like "genius" and "gifted" could come with problems of their own when it came to harassment from other children and resentment from adults.

"Well, we'll make sure you're safe while you're here," Teresa said. "My son, Alex, will drop you off and pick you up whenever you need to go to campus."

"And she's promised to return to your house before dark," Nina said, as much to Bianca as to Teresa.

"It's awful what's been going on at that school." Concern wrinkled Teresa's brow. "You and the other FBI agents better find this guy."

A predator was on the hunt at AIT, and young women were disappearing.

"That's why we're in town." Nina checked her watch. "First briefing starts in twenty minutes. Time to get to work."

Chapter 4

FBI Phoenix field office

When Nina first joined the Bureau, she had believed monsters who preyed on the vulnerable were unfathomable pits of darkness who could not be mentally dissected or understood. Recent experience had changed her outlook.

A few months ago, she had been selected to join a pilot program developed by Supervisory Special Agent Gerard Buxton of the Behavioral Analysis Unit. Frustrated by the inevitable stovepiping that occurred in massive bureaucratic organizations like the FBI, Buxton believed a small hybrid team consisting of agents detailed from the Cyber Crime, Violent Crime, and Behavioral Analysis units would offer a fresh perspective in the field.

After concluding an assignment in which they had been temporarily based at the Phoenix FBI field office, Nina and her new team found themselves in the PFO conference room once again.

Lieutenant Stan Hazel, who was in charge of the investigative section of the Arizona Institute of Technology's campus police, was here against his will. Hazel had been named acting AIT police chief by the university's chancellor while their current chief took his annual Mediterranean cruise over spring break.

After five female undergraduate students vanished without a trace from the university's downtown campus, the public outcry had been partly directed at the Phoenix police department, even though the AIT police had jurisdiction and were conducting the investigation. When Hazel continued to refuse help from the PPD, they made an official request to the FBI for assistance and convinced the university's chancellor to agree.

"I don't understand why you didn't want to ask for help," Nina said, not sure what to make of the lieutenant's attitude. "You still haven't set up a task force with the Phoenix PD." She gestured around the room. "They should be sitting at this table with us."

Hazel's pale face grew ruddy. "We're not mall cops, Agent Guerrera," he said, indignation tightening his voice. "The AIT police department is a fully accredited law enforcement agency, and we have jurisdiction on campus." His back stiffened. "Besides, I retired from the PPD two years ago, and I know a hell of a lot more than most of their detectives."

Special Agent Dr. Jeffrey Wade, the FBI's most senior behavioral profiler and the unofficial second-in-command of their group, broke the uneasy silence that followed the comment. "Why don't you give us more background, Lieutenant?"

Hazel outlined the steps he had taken since the students had begun disappearing about three and a half months earlier. He explained how their families had formed a close-knit coalition, speaking to the media to keep up pressure and demanding the university enlist the aid of the FBI to find their missing daughters.

"I'm still surprised you didn't request outside resources earlier," Wade said after Hazel finished. "Your department can't have more than forty people, right?"

"Thirty-eight," Hazel said. "And I've been in touch with the PPD and used their assets, but it didn't turn out so well."

He seemed to be waiting for someone to ask, and Nina decided to play along. "How so?"

"I requested one of their K-9 teams to run a track," he said. "We kept the area where the last victim had been clear of any foot traffic. The handler barely got started before his dog vomited and collapsed."

Wade frowned. "The dog was poisoned?"

Hazel nodded. "Rushed him to the vet, who said the animal was exposed to some sort of chemical normally used as an insecticide. The stuff isn't harmful unless it's ingested or inhaled, and this dog was sniffing it straight up his nose."

"Is that poor pooch okay?" Breck asked.

"He recovered," Hazel said. "But that incident put the kibosh on any further tracking requests. No handler has let his dog anywhere near this investigation since."

"I'm sure that's what the kidnapper wanted," Wade said. "Which tells me he's cruel, calculating, and strategic." He turned to Hazel. "What can we do to help, Lieutenant?"

Hazel took a breath before launching into an explanation clearly meant to justify his actions while laying out the particulars.

"The first victim went missing last December second," he began. "Even her parents initially assumed she had run off to Cabo with a new boyfriend." He shrugged. "Apparently, she'd done it before. The second girl disappeared on December twelfth, at the end of the fall semester, right after she took her final exams. When she didn't arrive at her home in Chicago, no one was sure exactly where she fell off the radar. She never boarded her flight, but she could have been snatched somewhere between the campus and the airport." He paused. "There was nothing to indicate she'd been grabbed on university grounds."

"Your department didn't realize there was a pattern right away, then." Nina made it a statement rather than a question.

"Not until a third girl disappeared," Hazel said, "which was on January fourteenth, the day after the start of the new semester. The first two incidents occurred more than a month before the third."

"What did your investigation into that one reveal?" Nina asked.

Hazel rubbed the back of his neck. "The camera system glitched."

Agent Kelly Breck raised a skeptical brow. "Glitched?"

Her background in both video forensics and cybercrimes promised to make her integral to an investigation involving a high-tech environment.

"I should have caught on sooner," Hazel allowed. "The cams were up and running, but the feed during the time window when she went missing was corrupted. On the fourth abduction, the entire video file got deleted somehow. The footage for the fifth incident was intact but revealed nothing."

Wade frowned. "You're saying there are no images of any of the students actually being abducted?"

"That's exactly what I'm saying." Hazel rested his hands on his hips. "We upgraded our entire security system after we identified the pattern, but the cameras still haven't shown us anything useful."

"I'd like to get a look at whatever you have," Breck said.

"No problem," Hazel said. "The computer science department has outfitted a section of their building for us to use as a command center."

Nina moved the discussion away from technology to what she found most important. "Do you think the victims are alive?" She posed the question to the lieutenant, interested to hear his take before any profiling began.

"This isn't a kidnapping for ransom," Hazel said. "No one communicated any demands or threats." He dragged a hand through his chemically darkened hair. "I worked a lot of missing persons cases during my career on the PPD, and I never saw one involving multiple abductions over an extended period that ended well."

Nina couldn't judge whether fatigue or worry had caused the lines tightening the corners of his mouth.

"Without a body, a crime scene, or a witness, we're at a severe disadvantage," Wade said. "We don't know whether an individual is keeping them alive somewhere or if we'll find a mass grave at some point."

"Or they could all be in separate places," Nina added. "Dead or alive."

Breck had downloaded a map of the AIT campus on her computer and shared it on the jumbo screen mounted to the wall. "If they're all alive, who holds five college-age women captive for weeks at a time?" she asked, concern making her southern accent more pronounced than usual.

"Maintaining prisoners takes resources and planning," Agent Jake Kent said, speaking for the first time since the briefing began. "How does he control them? How does he feed them and get them fresh water?" He shook his head. "The logistical problems involved make it more likely he kills his victims and hides the bodies."

Kent had been in the Navy prior to joining the FBI, ending his service as a member of one of their elite SEAL teams. His training in psychology and linguistic analysis had been useful on covert operations, and those skills had now been repurposed to pursue criminals.

Nina considered the facts Hazel had laid out and agreed with Kent's assessment. It seemed likely that the person behind the disappearances killed his victims after they had served whatever purpose he had for them.

Their supervisor, SSA Buxton, turned to Breck. "Can you show us the data points Lieutenant Hazel provided?"

Breck's long auburn curls swayed as she tapped the keyboard. A spreadsheet with names and other information replaced the campus map.

Buxton stood and walked to the monitor. "What do the victims have in common?" he asked the room at large.

Nina pointed out the first things that occurred to her. "They attend a leading tech university, so they're smart," she said. "They're all undergrad students between eighteen and twenty-three years old. They're all white females."

Breck lifted a strawberry-blonde brow. "You're overlooking the most obvious thing, Guerrera. If no one else wants to say it, I will." She gestured at the display of photographs that accompanied each name. "Every last one of these young ladies is beautiful."

Kent frowned. "Eye of the beholder, Breck." He crossed his arms. "There is no objective measure of attractiveness. Beauty standards tend to be culturally driven and change over time."

"Which is why you both have a point," Wade said, joining the discussion. "These women are all of a certain physical type."

Nina looked at Wade. "What does that do for your profile?"

His expression darkened. "I don't like where it takes me. Victim selection is important when it's not a crime of opportunity. There are close to twenty thousand students, faculty, and other employees at AIT. Eliminate the males, which make up more than half that number, and that leaves about nine thousand potential targets. Aside from their obvious intelligence, these women were clearly chosen for their physical appearance."

"Whoever is taking them has also managed to do so without leaving any witnesses or evidence of a struggle," Kent said. "Which indicates a high degree of advanced planning."

"We can tell a lot more from examining the layout of the campus on foot." Buxton glanced at Hazel. "You mentioned that the computer science department made space available for us?"

"We've set up a command post next to the computer lab," Hazel said.

"That's ideal, since AIT is the common denominator in every abduction." Buxton paused. "There is one problem, though. I've been called back to Washington for a meeting with the Director. I'll be gone for at least a week."

Tension filled the room. The head of the FBI didn't routinely call supervisory special agents in to see him in person unless something important was going on. Presumably, a meeting wouldn't keep their boss away for a week. Something else was going on.

"Is it good news or bad news?" Wade asked, voicing their shared concern.

Buxton looked uncomfortable. "His assistant didn't tell me." He focused on Wade. "I'm leaving you in charge of this investigation until my return."

Hazel's cell phone buzzed, drawing everyone's attention to the corner of the table. He spun on his heel and walked over to retrieve it. "Lieutenant Hazel."

They all watched the creases lining his face become more pronounced as he listened.

"I'll be right there." He disconnected and faced them. "We need to get to AIT right away." He slid the phone into his pocket. "Another student is missing."

Chapter 5

Thirty minutes later, Nina arrived at the sprawling modern campus in a black Suburban with her team. After navigating roadblocks and barricades, they parked beside Lieutenant Hazel in the north parking lot.

They got out and joined Hazel, who strode in the direction of a Phoenix police commander speaking to a cluster of officers near the edge of the lot.

"Who called you here?" Hazel said to the commander, interrupting him.

"I did," Wade said from behind Hazel.

Hazel rounded on Wade. "We don't need—"

"You called us for assistance," Wade cut in. "Another student is missing, and you need all the resources you can throw at this while it's fresh. The PPD has nearly three thousand sworn officers and a thousand support personnel. You have a grand total of thirty-eight people."

Hazel's lips pressed into a flat line. He seemed to take a moment to compose himself before turning to face the police commander again. "Where are your officers deployed?" He hesitated a beat. "Sir."

"I've got all ingress and egress points locked down," he responded. "The downtown operations unit is activated, and the helicopter is up." He seemed to choose his next words. "No K-9 units are responding."

Nina didn't blame the PPD. Police dogs were highly valued assets. Exposing them to a toxin would not help find the victim and might prove fatal to a four-footed member of the force.

"Have you started a grid search?" Nina asked. In her own experience as a patrol officer, she had participated in many missing persons cases and knew the standard procedures well.

His response was crisp and efficient. "I've divided the campus into sectors and cordoned off the area where she was last seen."

"What's going on in the downtown ops unit?" Kent asked.

"We've set up a tip line," the commander said. "I've got teams of detectives interviewing the victim's roommate, friends, family, and professors. They're searching her dorm room and social media. Forensic techs are trying to ping her cell phone. She reportedly had it with her. No luck so far."

The commander had clearly been busy. More than half an hour had passed since Hazel had gotten the call from his officers about the missing student. Morning rush hour traffic had slowed their response from the FBI Phoenix field office. Wade's call to the PPD on the way over had allowed them to make substantial headway in the investigation.

"What about security cameras on campus?" Breck asked.

"The video feed was garbled," the commander said. "We can't clean it up."

"I'd like a crack at it," Breck said.

"You can access the system from the think tank," Hazel said to her. "That's where AIT has set up our command center." He turned to the commander. "You're welcome to join us."

"I'm here to handle the immediate response," he said. "That's all at this point."

It appeared the AIT police still had jurisdiction over a student missing from school grounds. The PPD commander was leaving it up to the university to create a task force, and Hazel's comments indicated he intended to keep the investigation under his control as long as possible.

"Do you have an ID on the victim?" Wade asked the commander. "Where was she last seen?"

"Her name is Melissa Campbell," he said. "She was caught on video near the student union around ten o'clock last night. She parted company with her boyfriend after kissing him and started to walk toward her dorm." He glanced at his notes. "She made it to Tanner Hall before the feed went wonky. Last anyone saw of her. We can't be sure whether she entered Tanner or not."

"Was Melissa alone when she got there?" Wade asked.

"It looks like someone was with her, but we can't tell who," the commander said. "We're reasonably sure it's her because she was the only one walking in that part of the campus at the time."

"Who's the guy she was kissing before she went to Tanner Hall?" Kent asked.

"Chad Ames," the commander said after checking his notepad again. "We have him in an interview room at the campus police head-quarters building if you all want to talk to him, but he doesn't seem to know much."

"So this Chad guy leaves his girlfriend to walk to her dorm alone in the dark despite a bunch of disappearances?" Kent scowled. "Yeah, I'd like to have a little talk with him."

Nina hid a smile. She could imagine the kind of conversation Kent would have with Chad.

"My detectives don't like him as a suspect," the commander said, apparently misreading Kent's dark expression. "He's a new student. Transferred here from Arizona State at the beginning of the semester after the disappearances had already started."

"I'll take you to the student union and Tanner Hall," Hazel said to the FBI team, apparently anxious to get away from his former colleague.

After making a mental note to find out what was going on between Hazel and the PPD, Nina fell in step with the others as the lieutenant led them through the grounds.

"This is a beautiful campus," she said when they approached the quad.

She hadn't expected to see so much foliage. Indeed, AIT seemed like an island of greenery in a sea of concrete and asphalt, surrounded by an ocean of desert.

"Our new chancellor is all about minimizing our carbon footprint," Hazel explained. "The dean of horticultural sciences obtained a grant to develop a way to reuse filtered wastewater to maintain the landscaping."

Nina took in the manicured lawn punctuated by lush plants. Rows of towering royal palm trees lined the quad, where the glass-domed roof of the library sparkled like a gem in the center of the campus.

They continued to a massive multistory structure that featured a wide balcony, where Nina saw clusters of empty tables.

"No one's around," she said. "I suppose most students are gone for spring break."

"Classes don't resume for another week," Hazel said.

"Why was Melissa Campbell still on campus, then?"

"A lot of students can't afford a flight home or a vacation on the Mexican coast, so they stay here during the break." He stopped and gestured toward a nearby building. "This is the student union."

Yellow perimeter tape cut across the area in front. He turned and pointed toward an older-looking building on the other side of the quad.

"I'm assuming that's Tanner Hall," Nina said, surveying more yellow crime scene tape around the building, which, unlike most others on the campus, was only two stories tall. Its stone exterior stood in stark contrast to the glass and steel of its neighbors.

Wade squinted up toward the roof. "What's in there?"

"This is one of the oldest structures on campus," Hazel said. "It used to house the cosmology department. They're replacing it over the summer in time for the fall semester. It's supposed to be razed next month."

"It's vacant, then?" Kent asked. When Hazel nodded, he added, "Is it secured?"

"Everyone cleared out at the end of last semester," Hazel said. "We have locks on the doors, but they're nothing special, just ordinary dead bolts."

"At a high-tech university, I'd think you'd have retinal scans or something to access the buildings," Nina said, half joking.

"First, our crime rate is normally close to zero," Hazel said quickly. "Second, our budget mostly goes toward funding cutting-edge research."

Nina figured she'd hit a sore spot. She wasn't judging the lieutenant, who seemed to equate questions with criticism. "Understood," she said. "But the campus is no longer the safe place it used to be, so what is the university doing about it?"

"They're upgrading the entire video system," Hazel said. "There's an audio component now, and motion activation to save energy."

"Has the chancellor considered shutting the school down?" Wade asked. "At least until all the new security protocols are fully in place?"

"She's putting out a statement today," he said. "Instead of returning from spring break as usual, students will go to a remote-learning model until further notice."

"But the campus itself won't be closed?" Nina asked. "There will still be some students and faculty here?"

"We've got multiple projects near completion and a slew of dead-lines to meet, or we stand to lose hundreds of millions of dollars in funding." He lifted a shoulder. "We can't afford a full shutdown."

Nina got the message. Despite what was happening on the grounds, the university had promised to deliver time-sensitive research to various organizations, some involving huge government contracts. In the meantime, someone was hunting in a target-rich environment. If they didn't stop him, more young women would go missing.

Chapter 6

He watched Melissa thrash on the cement floor as she tried in vain to get loose. The hidden pinhole camera provided a remarkably good view of her cell.

Her new habitat.

He saw the perspiration glisten on her bare skin and tamped down a surge of longing. There would be time to indulge himself later. For now, he needed to remain in clinical mode, inspecting her and the surroundings to be sure she was safe and unharmed. He noticed that she kept trying to pull her hands out of the nylon zip ties, bending one of her fingers at an odd angle. He sighed, pulled out his field notebook, and recorded his observations.

Field Notes

Day	Observation	Water 💧	Food 🍎	Strategy 🧭
	Melissa Campbell			
1	Capture went smoothly; nausea from sedation; no other ill effects	None	None	Withhold all stimuli and continue observation
2	Very distressed; may have minor injury to left index finger	None	None	Observe how she moves finger; plan for first contact; attempt drinking

Chapter 7

Nina and the others followed Lieutenant Hazel around the rest of the campus, listening as he noted each location where one of the missing young women had last been seen. He ended their grim tour at a large rectangular building topped with a sloped roof covered in gleaming solar panels.

"This is the computer science building," Hazel said, walking toward the entrance.

Tinted glass doors whispered open at their approach, and Nina crossed the foyer to reach another set of automatic doors, this time made of clear glass. When they slid apart, she had to stop herself from gaping.

"Welcome to the think tank," Hazel said.

A smooth black table surrounded by twelve ergonomic swivel chairs occupied the center of the room. Movement drew Nina's eye, and she turned to stare at a massive floor-to-ceiling aquarium that took up an entire wall of the room. She watched a hammerhead shark glide by, one oddly placed eye trained on her as its powerful tail propelled it forward. Light from overhead cascaded down through the clear water to dapple the sandy bottom, causing brightly colored coral to shimmer.

"Incredible optics, right?"

Nina spun around to see a young man with expressive brown eyes, a pockmarked face, and thick black hair secured in a ponytail that hung down past his shoulders.

"Rick Vale, graduate research assistant." He shook her hand. "I noticed you appreciating our virtual aquarium," he said. "It's on constant display when we're not using the wall for our current project. Very relaxing."

Nina strolled over to follow a stingray's fluid progress across what was apparently a wall-to-wall flatscreen. Looking closely, she could see it was some sort of computer-generated image. She reached out and felt smooth glass under her fingertips.

"This is amazing," she said as Wade, Kent, and Breck joined her.

Kent splayed his fingers against the screen. "It looks so real."

"Because it's a nano-pixel holographic-imaging display," a different voice said from behind them. A burly man in his late forties had joined the group. "I see you've met my assistant," he said. "I'm Dr. Feldman."

Dr. Feldman did not refer to Rick as a partner or collaborator—or even by name—instead choosing words that emphasized his subordinate position. The distinction was not lost on Nina, who had experienced the occasional condescending professor while obtaining her degree in criminal justice.

Wade introduced the FBI team. She noticed he made it a point to include "Doctor" in front of his own name, something he did not normally do. Wade must have picked up on the same subtle arrogance she'd detected and wanted the professor's respect.

Feldman slid a remote from his pocket and aimed it at the wall. An instant later, the fauxquarium vanished, replaced by a virtual map of the campus. Red dots glowed at various points.

Rick edged past Nina to approach Breck. "This is an interactive display," he said, following her gaze. "We've entered the last known locations of each missing student."

Breck turned to him. "I'd be interested to see what each of these young ladies has in common besides attending this school."

Hazel answered her question. "Our briefing was interrupted before I had a chance to review their personal histories with your team," he told her. "But everything we know about the victims is here for you to review. Dr. Feldman and Rick helped create an interactive program with all that information. You can cross-check the contents of our system with any federal databases you like."

"I'll have to create an encrypted mobile hot spot to connect to the FBI server," Breck said. "It's against protocol to link to our server through an outside network. We can't risk opening a back door into a secure system."

"You can use the AIT computer to access what Lieutenant Hazel and I compiled and your own laptop with your hot spot for everything else," Dr. Feldman said, gesturing to Rick. "My assistant can show you how to use the controls on the display."

Rick walked to the black-topped conference table and tapped a spot near the center. A rectangle glowed in front of the chair in the middle of the long side of the table. An instant later, an array of icons bloomed to life inside the borders of what Nina guessed was an integrated terminal set into the gleaming surface. It had been invisible until activated by touch.

Breck quickly snapped her gaping mouth shut. "That'll do in a pinch."

Nina chuckled at the cybercrime specialist. Breck had access to some of the best computer systems available, but AIT's technology had clearly impressed her.

Rick took the seat next to the terminal.

"Let's see if we can catch a scent of our unsub," Breck said, sitting beside him.

"What's an unsub?" Rick asked.

"We use verbal shorthand," Nina said. "We call an unknown subject an unsub. It's how we refer to a suspect we have yet to identify."

"As of now, we have one unsub and six victims," Hazel said. "Unless you think there's more than one perpetrator involved."

"We'll get to that when we start our profile," Wade said. "But for now, we'll work on the assumption that this is a lone actor."

"We might put a stop to this faster if we can evaluate more data points," Dr. Feldman said. "I'm developing a new system using AI and ML to enhance our current predictive-analysis methodology."

When no one responded, Nina spoke up. "Pretend we're not scientists," she said to him. "Or grad students. What do you mean?"

"We have our own verbal shorthand," Feldman said. "AI is *artificial intelligence*, and ML is *machine learning*. Combining the two is at the cutting edge of tech right now. I was working on another project, but the chancellor had me repurpose my research with an eye toward catching whoever is taking these students, locating the victims, or both." He glanced at Hazel. "I've been working closely with the lieutenant ever since."

Wade shifted uncomfortably. "We're grateful for your efforts," he said to Feldman. "But we will need to keep our investigations separated going forward."

"Are you saying you don't want to work with me?" Feldman said, clearly affronted.

"Nothing of the sort." Wade held up a placating hand. "I'm saying that certain portions of the investigation, and some of the data we collect, will be restricted to law enforcement personnel. We cannot disclose sensitive details of the case to civilians."

Feldman did not look appeased. "Lieutenant Hazel had no qualms about sharing information with me. I was able to provide substantive help in his investigation."

Nina considered reminding the professor that however substantive his help had been, the end result was an increasing number of missing students. Tempting though it was to take some air out of Feldman's somewhat inflated ego, she left the verbal sparring to Wade and turned to Breck, who was engrossed in a conversation with Hazel and Rick at the conference table.

"That's how you access the files," Rick was saying to her.

Breck tapped the control panel set into the table's sleek surface. The series of commands converted the wall to a desktop-style display.

"Open that file," Hazel said from the seat on the other side of her.

An instant later, a virtual corkboard filled the wall. Photographs of six young women appeared along a timeline going back months earlier, each beside a bulleted list of information broken down into categories. Nina studied the red lines that connected various data points, the numbered yellow dots spread out over a campus map below the pictures, and digital blue sticky notes containing investigative leads and comments.

"Impressive," Kent said, standing next to her. "Really gives you an overview of the case."

Feldman strode to the wall. "You see what I mean, Dr. Wade. My assistant and I helped fill in this information. We've worked on the case from the beginning."

"And we hope you will continue to help," Wade said in a tone Nina recognized as his most patient. "Within certain parameters."

Nina spoke before Feldman could launch into another argument. "I was under the impression the unsub only struck at night." She gestured to the first victim, Sandy Owens. "But no one's really sure when she was taken."

"True," Hazel said. "But all the others were last seen after dark and discovered missing by morning, so we're assuming he's a nightstalker."

Wade groaned. "Please don't call him that in front of the media."

Nina agreed. A headline-grabbing nickname might attract the attention of national news networks.

"What about the second victim, Cheryl Grover?" Nina asked. "You hadn't identified a pattern yet. How did you narrow the time window?"

"Cheryl was last seen leaving the dining hall around eight at night," Hazel said. "She never made it back to her dorm. She was supposed to fly home to Chicago the next day for winter break. Her roommate had already finished her exams and left, so no one noticed her missing until she failed to show up in Chicago the following night."

"So no one misses her for twenty-four hours?" Wade asked. "She could have been taken during daylight hours."

Hazel shook his head. "We recently went back and interviewed all her friends. She was supposed to meet one of them for coffee first thing in the morning but never showed. The friend just thought she forgot and didn't report her missing."

"You weren't investigating anything at the time," Nina clarified.

"We weren't sure whether she'd left AIT grounds on her own," Hazel said. "She could have disappeared in the city on her way to Sky Harbor Airport. All we knew is she never boarded her flight." He shrugged, spreading his hands. "The trail went cold by the time we started asking questions."

Nina was about to point out that Hazel was contradicting himself, but Wade shot her a repressive look.

"There were no more incidents for over a month until the new semester began," Feldman said, picking up the narrative. "The next one occurred on the fourteenth of January, a day after the students arrived back on campus."

"So far, he only hits when school is in session," Kent said. "Makes sense, since he targets undergrad students, who aren't likely to be involved in grant studies or advanced research projects that would keep them here when there aren't any classes."

Wade addressed Hazel. "Can you find out if there were any abductions in the city during that monthlong break between semesters? I want to be sure he wasn't hunting somewhere else while he waited for school to be back in session."

"I've already checked," Hazel said. "There were no similar incidents in Phoenix or the surrounding jurisdictions over the past year."

Breck tapped the table's gleaming surface, and more data populated the virtual corkboard. Nina was impressed by how much intel Hazel had gathered about each student's background and circumstances. Despite getting a late start in the investigation, he had been diligent about tracing victims' whereabouts and trying to generate leads.

Nina took in the display. "There is no consistent pattern with the timing," she said. "Abductions have taken place on different days of the week and at various locations on campus. They are committed as close together as ten days and as far apart as thirty-three days."

"We've already established the victims don't have anything obvious in common," Wade said. "No classes, employers, relationships, dorms, home states, or hobbies."

"Then how is he selecting his targets?" Kent asked. "We're missing something."

"We can go back through the investigative files from the campus police," Wade said. "But I'd like to interview Melissa Campbell's boyfriend while his memory is still fresh."

"I'll take care of that," Nina said, anxious to get proactive.

Wade gave her a quick nod before turning to Kent. "You go with her."

Nina appreciated the strategy. Her background as a street cop and a criminal investigative agent gave her a lot of experience interviewing people. Kent's training in behavioral profiling enabled him to read body language, verbal cues, and other signs. In short, they would make a good team for the assignment.

Breck reached down to pick up her cell phone and glanced at the glowing screen. "We'll have to table this for later," she said. "I set up an alert to let me know when there's breaking news about our investigation." She pushed up from her seat. "An attorney representing the families called a news conference in front of the administration building. He claims to have an announcement about the investigation."

Chapter 8

Nina surveyed the crowd, grateful she wasn't a supervisor. The missing students' families looked upset, and members of the media were aiming questions at anyone in a position of authority.

She and Kent had decided to interview Melissa's boyfriend, Chad Ames, at the campus police building after the impromptu news conference ended so they would be aware of any major developments before questioning him. She'd been in the spotlight in the past and didn't like news conferences, so she did her best to blend into the background, standing between Kent and Breck while Wade and Hazel took the brunt of the storm.

There was plenty of heat directed at the campus police lieutenant, whom the families blamed for waiting to bring in the FBI until five girls had vanished, Melissa making the sixth disappearance. After taking his turn addressing the group, Hazel had skirted the edge of the crowd to stand directly behind Nina while the chancellor delivered her prepared statement announcing that the school would move to a remote-learning model after spring break ended unless there was an arrest. She emphasized that the campus would remain open for research projects.

After the officials concluded their remarks, a short, expensively dressed man stepped up to the microphone. "We're tired of hearing reassurances from law enforcement that they're doing all they can," he said in strident tones. "We demand action."

A smattering of applause met his words.

According to Hazel's whispered commentary to Breck and Nina, the man was a well-known local attorney representing the families. He had become a fixture, appearing at prayer vigils, fundraisers, and other community events designed to keep the missing students at the top of the news cycle.

Nina figured he planned to represent the families in a joint lawsuit against the university. Today marked another disturbing milestone, and the lawyer was making good use of the exposure.

Every media outlet and internet blogger in the city seemed to be present, further increasing the crowd's growing ranks.

"This morning, another girl is missing," he continued in a somber voice. "I'm here to announce that the families have raised a fifty-thousand-dollar reward for information leading to the arrest and conviction of the person or persons responsible for taking their daughters."

Nina knew what that meant. For every actionable lead, the tip line would receive a hundred crank calls, dead ends, and false accusations designed to send police after someone the caller didn't like.

The lawyer stepped back, and the crowd parted to let someone else come forward.

"Oh hell, not this guy," Hazel muttered under his breath.

"Who?" Nina asked quietly.

"The guy with the bad comb-over sporting the Hawaiian shirt," Hazel said on a groan.

She followed the lieutenant's gaze and spotted a stocky, balding man wearing a purple aloha shirt decorated with multicolored parrots and green palm fronds.

"He calls himself a *psychic detective*." Hazel elaborated. "Goes by Arthur Mage, but his real name is Alvin Scrudd. He's well known in Phoenix."

Nina watched the man, who had his arm around a middle-aged woman with red-rimmed eyes who she assumed was the mother of one of the missing students.

"That lady's leaning on him pretty heavily," Nina said. "Physically and emotionally."

"She's Cheryl Grover's mother," Hazel said. "Cheryl was the second victim. Her mother is a widow, and Cheryl is her only child."

Nina sucked in a breath, imagining herself in the mother's situation, tapping into the fear and grief she must be feeling. She narrowed her eyes as Cheryl's mother accepted a tissue from Mage and dabbed her nose.

"He's taking advantage of that poor woman," Nina said.

"You have no idea," Hazel said. "If he's inserted himself into the middle of this, things are about to get . . . complicated."

Arthur Mage swept his free hand out to encompass the group of relatives behind him. "I've offered my services to the AIT police to help find the missing girls, but they refused my help."

A murmur went through those gathered to listen.

"But the FBI is here now, and perhaps they will feel differently," Mage continued. "I can provide help, but I need law enforcement to interpret the visions I see."

Nina had to admit the tactic would prove effective for Mage no matter what happened. If they spoke to the self-styled psychic detective, he could claim credit for any investigative progress they made. If they didn't locate the missing students, he could explain that they had failed to interpret his visions correctly. Clever.

"I find that working together concentrates mental energy," Mage continued. "But I am prepared to do my own psychic investigation if I must."

Nina glanced over her shoulder to see Hazel's jaw muscle twitching as he ground his teeth. She began to appreciate what he had meant about Mage causing trouble.

Chapter 9

During their brisk walk to the campus police building, Nina and Kent had decided on an interview strategy. She would take the lead, with Kent—the trained profiler—making observations and joining in when he thought it would be advantageous.

Now peering up at Chad, whose impressive height was on par with Kent's, Nina began to have second thoughts about their decision. It wasn't Chad's physical appearance that gave her a sense of foreboding, however. Unlike her fellow agent, Chad oozed the kind of smug superiority that shouted trust fund, elite prep school, and entitlement.

She had run across his kind professionally and personally. With a pretty good idea of what to expect, she braced herself for an interview that promised all the enjoyment of a root canal.

She began by setting the stage for their interaction on more equal footing, eliminating his vertical advantage.

Still standing, she gestured toward the empty chair on the opposite side of the table. "Take a seat, Chad."

She framed it as a command rather than a request, deliberately using his first name without asking. She waited until Chad slouched into the chair before taking the seat directly across from him. Kent eased himself into the seat beside hers, his large frame adding a psychological counterweight to Chad's position.

"I already talked to the cops," Chad said before she could pose a question. "I'm kind of busy. What do you guys want with me?"

So charming.

"Your girlfriend is missing," Nina began. "I'm sure you care about her deeply. We figured you would want to do whatever you could to help us find her." She let that penetrate a moment before continuing. "Even if our investigation cuts into your free time."

"She's not really my girlfriend," Chad said.

"Her roommate seems to think she is," Nina said. "And there are framed pictures of you in her dorm room."

"I have a lot of girlfriends," Chad said, his smile as fake as his tan. "I never told her we were exclusive or anything."

"Can you take us through the last time you saw Melissa?" Kent asked him.

She noticed Kent had used Melissa's name, personalizing her. He had also been careful not to ask what happened the night before, but instead inquired about Chad's last contact with the victim. Chad's subconscious mind would likely pick up on the subtle but important difference, causing him to react in ways that would reveal deception if he had been with Melissa after last night. He might also hedge his response, which would be equally telling.

"It was about ten o'clock or so," Chad said. "We were in front of the student union. It was raining, and neither one of us had an umbrella. I didn't want to get wet walking her to her dorm and then back across to the other side of campus, so I left her there."

Nina mentally added *selfish*, *inconsiderate*, and *lazy* to the growing list of Chad's wonderful traits.

"What do you mean 'left her there'?" Kent said, frowning. "It was dark and rainy, and there had been a series of disappearances involving freshman females on campus. Why the hell would you abandon her like that?"

Kent's protective nature was coming out. Nina noticed his jaw harden and figured Chad was getting to him. She studied Chad closely and watched his expression become calculating. She concluded that he was enjoying himself. Interesting. Most people being interviewed by two FBI agents would be unnerved, but Chad was supremely self-confident.

"I had other shit to do," Chad said, as if that explained everything.

She asked the next question, giving Kent the chance to decide whether he wanted to risk his career by giving this jerk the beatdown he so desperately needed. "Did you say anything to Melissa?"

Chad's tone remained nonchalant. "I told her I was hanging out with some friends, so she shouldn't call me until the next day."

A not-so-subtle way of telling his girlfriend he would be out partying all night. Without her.

"And did you?" she pressed.

"Did I what?"

Nina suppressed an eye roll. Chad was playing dumb. Deliberately trying her patience. "Did you hang out with friends?"

"Sure," he said. "I went over to the frat house. They had a kegger going."

Big surprise. "How long were you at the party?" she asked.

"About an hour."

"Where did you go when you left?"

"Look, I don't have to answer your questions." Chad crossed his arms. "I've been pretty cooperative up to this point, but I'll call my dad's attorney if you keep harassing me."

Hmm. Running to Daddy. Had she hit on something?

"Why would you need a lawyer?" Nina asked. "Do you feel threatened?"

"I didn't do anything wrong," Chad said. "But you guys are all up in my face about what I was doing last night."

Nina and Kent exchanged a look. Chad thought this polite discussion was a hard-charging interrogation. He clearly had little experience with anyone asking questions or holding him accountable for his actions in any way. Nina decided to frame the context of the conversation in no uncertain terms.

"Let me remind you," she began, "your girlfriend is missing. You were the last person seen with her. You understand how we might have a couple of questions regarding your whereabouts?"

"Fine," Chad said. "When I left the party, I took a piece of furniture back to my apartment."

"Did someone help you move the furniture?" Nina asked, wondering if this was his way of establishing an alibi.

Chad met her gaze. "I'm not talking about a sofa, Agent Guerrera. *Furniture* is what we call women who are community property. They belong to the frat." He waved a dismissive hand. "Anyone can use them."

Kent leaned forward, his voice a dangerous whisper. "Excuse me?"

"She was a blonde," Chad said, either oblivious or uncaring about the perceptible shift in the room's atmosphere. "Can't remember her name, but Scott will know. He's our president."

Nina studied Chad's expression, which was equal parts arrogant and defiant. He had directed the comment about furniture toward her, making it clear what use he thought women served. To him, they were objects to be passed around. Most people would not insult the person questioning them so blatantly. Unless they were doing it on purpose as a form of misdirection. She made a conscious decision not to take the bait.

"We'll be in touch with your fraternity president," she told him. "And we'll track down the young lady in question to see if she can corroborate your story."

"Can you give me her number when you find her?" Chad said. "Wouldn't mind seeing her again."

Tired of his game, Nina called him on it. "Are you deliberately screwing with me? Because I can't believe you're so insensitive that your only concern right now is your next hookup."

He gave her a slow perusal. "I think you'd be a lot more chill if you had a good lay." He cut his eyes to Kent. "You should see to that."

Nina laid a placating hand on Kent's forearm before he reached across the table to grab a fistful of Chad's Tommy Hilfiger shirt.

She had dealt with this attitude before, especially as a police officer. Occasionally, men would flirt with her when she tried to assert her authority or accuse her of being frigid if she didn't accept their lewd advances. She had learned to see it for the combination of disrespect and distraction that it was. While Kent's eyes narrowed to icy-blue slits, she handled the overt provocation.

"When I interview someone who's clearly trying to goad me," she said quietly, "it makes me wonder what he's holding back. Are you hiding something, Chad?"

He let out a contemptuous snort. "Other than the salami, I'm not hiding anything."

"Crude, childish, and immature," Nina said, unruffled. "But you didn't answer my question."

"Here's my point," Chad said, smirking. "I don't chase after bitches." He paused. "Why would I bother when they come running to me?"

Nina raised a brow. "So you're giving us the 'I'm too pretty' defense."

Chad shrugged. "Can't help who I am."

"Yes, you can," Kent said. "And you should."

Chad switched his gaze to Kent. "You don't look like you have any trouble with the ladies," he said, studying him briefly. "I mean, other than having a stick up your ass, but I figure that's part of being a G-man."

Kent's voice dropped to a menacing rumble. "To call you clueless about women would be a massive understatement." He leaned forward, invading Chad's space. "One day, I hope you grow up. Right now, you're a man-child."

"I'm done talking to you two," Chad said, appearing nervous for the first time. "If you've got any more questions, you can call my dad's lawyer."

Chapter 10

An hour later, Nina and Kent were back in the think tank with the rest of the team.

"How did it go with Chad Ames?" Breck asked.

"He's a horse's ass," Kent said, summing up Nina's sentiments perfectly. "But he's not a good suspect for this series."

"We confirmed the PPD commander's information that Chad transferred to AIT in January, more than six weeks after the first abduction at the beginning of December," Nina said, lifting a shoulder. "Besides, he's not the type to become obsessed with anyone but himself."

At everyone's confused expression, Kent elaborated. "Chad is a pretty boy who's too self-involved to care about Melissa. His frat president gave us the name and number of another student who can provide an alibi for him during the time Melissa was abducted." He scowled. "Chad claims he could not have abducted Melissa last night, because after he left her at the student union, he was—in his words—taking a piece of *furniture* back to his apartment." Kent went on to explain precisely what Chad had meant by the expression.

"I've seen alley cats with more class," Breck said before pursing her lips.

"The other girl—and several of her friends who saw them together—corroborated his story," Kent said. "Much as I'd like him to be, he's not our guy."

Wade moved the briefing forward. "The PPD commander is standing down their command post," he said. "They've found no sign of the suspect or Melissa. He's turning over all the information his detectives obtained, and the investigation is back in our hands." He gave Hazel a significant look. "I think we should have one of their detectives in here with us going forward."

Hazel shook his head. "The chancellor made it clear she wants me in charge. If we bring in the PPD, they'll take over."

"You invited us in, and we didn't take over," Wade said. "You don't even mind that I run the daily briefings and dole out assignments."

"That's different," Hazel said. "The FBI has no jurisdiction in this case. If there's an arrest, one of my detectives will place the charges and we'll get the credit. On the other hand, I know the PPD. I used to be one of them. Our campus is located within city limits, and they will use that as an excuse to put themselves front and center, given half a chance."

Nina frowned. "And that would be bad . . . why?"

Hazel rounded on her. "The chancellor would lose the ability to control the narrative. This is the kind of scenario that can shut a school down permanently."

"Is it the chancellor who wants to control things?" Nina asked. "Or is it you, Lieutenant?"

Wade lifted both hands in a calming gesture. "Let's work with our current task force for the time being." He waited for Hazel to compose himself before addressing the group. "There are a lot of specifics to follow up, and I propose we divide our time." He glanced at Breck. "Continue trying to clean up the video feeds and find out how they were disrupted in the first place. There may be a digital trail to follow." He gestured to Kent. "Kent and I will flesh out our profile next, and Guerrera can use it to go through the interviews I received from the PPD." Finally, he turned to Hazel. "You've been involved in this longer than anyone else, and you're the expert on this campus. You'll need to work with each of us to fill in the blanks." He met Hazel's gaze. "Are you willing to do that?"

"Of course," he said. "Let's get to work." After a lingering glare at Nina, Hazel took a seat at the conference table. "Over the years as a detective, I was assigned to property crimes, narcotics, and finally robbery," he said. "But never missing persons or homicide, so I'm interested in hearing your profile."

Nina sat down across from him, also curious to know what Wade and Kent had concluded about someone who had now taken six young women and disappeared without a trace.

"I mentioned previously that I believe we're dealing with a lone actor," Wade began. "That's because of his victim selection. The women he takes have a particular look. As Kent pointed out, standards of beauty are not universal, and these victims all bear a strong resemblance to a single ideal of physical attractiveness."

Nina thought she understood. "If there were more than one suspect, the women would vary in appearance due to personal taste."

Wade inclined his head in agreement. "This man—and yes, I'm also saying our unsub is a heterosexual male—is drawn to a certain look, and he's motivated by sexual desire."

"Why do you think it's sexual?" Hazel said. "We don't know what's going on after he takes them. He could be killing them right away without having sex. They could all be in a landfill somewhere."

Kent fielded the question. "He doesn't have to rape the victims for the crime to be sexual in nature. Many serial killers fulfill their erotic impulses with the act of murder, whether or not physical sex with the victim is involved."

A puzzled expression clouded Hazel's features. "You're saying he gets off on the murder itself?"

"That's true in some cases," Kent said. "But not most."

"I believe our guy is sexually frustrated," Wade said. "In many ways, he's the opposite of Chad, who women find desirable. I propose that the unsub is targeting those he feels are beyond his reach under normal circumstances."

"Agreed," Kent said. "He abducts women of a certain type that he finds beautiful. That tells me he's awkward around females and may have experienced rejection in a way that humiliated him in the past."

Nina considered what the profilers were saying. "You think he's eliminating the possibility of refusal by simply taking what he wants." When Kent nodded, she dug deeper. "But wouldn't that make him feel more rejected when they fought against him?"

"We can't be sure until we learn more," Kent said. "He might drug them or otherwise incapacitate them so they're incapable of refusing him, or he might kill them outright."

"Or he may delude himself with an elaborate fantasy that they are secretly in love with him but can't show it for some reason," Wade added.

"Why so many women, then?" Hazel asked. "Why not just one?"

"It's a compulsion," Kent added. "An unmet need drives him, and we have to figure out what that need is because he's not going to stop."

Chapter 11

Several hours later, Nina sat at her aunt Teresa's kitchen table with Bianca. A long day poring through Hazel's investigative notes from the past several months and studying the AIT campus had left her with more questions than answers, and a family dinner had provided a much-needed break. Her uncle and her cousin Alex had finished dinner, helped clean up, and taken their desserts into the living room to watch the Arizona Suns game.

The women had remained in the kitchen, trying to weasel information out of Nina about the investigation.

"You know I can't share," Nina told them. "You're wasting your time grilling me."

"We livestreamed the news conference," Bianca said. "Sounds like you don't have too much to share anyway." She slid Nina a sly grin. "Maybe that psychic detective guy can help."

Nina knew Bianca, firmly grounded in science, did not believe in psychic powers. She was clearly trying to get Nina to open up by needling her.

"Nice try, Bee, but I'm not falling for that."

Teresa sighed. "Then at least tell me I shouldn't worry about you two."

Nina understood her aunt to mean that as long as a kidnapper was stalking AIT, she would consider both her niece and her houseguest at risk.

"I'm way past this guy's age range," Nina said, then gave Bianca a pointed look. "And Bee will never be on campus after dark and won't be alone at any time."

Nina didn't add that, having just abducted a victim, the unsub was unlikely to be on the hunt for another anytime soon.

"I'm meeting with Dr. Dawson tomorrow," Bianca said. "He's going to give me a tour of the campus and go over the grant research he's conducting."

"I'll stop here and pick you up on my way in from the hotel," Nina said. "Then you can text me when you're finished with the professor, and I'll take you back here."

"See?" Bianca turned to Teresa. "It's like she's in the Secret Service and I'm the freaking president. She's practically got me in lockdown."

"Good," Teresa said. "And don't look at me like that. It's for your safety."

Nina, grateful to have backup from her aunt, was not prepared when Bianca launched a counteroffensive.

"Since you won't talk to us about the case," Bianca began in an overly innocent tone, "how about you give us the scoop on what else is happening behind the scenes in that task force you guys have set up?"

Nina struggled with the change in subject. "Scoop?"

Bianca winked at Teresa. "There's this totally hot guy on Nina's team, Agent Jake Kent. I keep telling her she needs to look into that situation."

Teresa smiled. "You never told me you had a man in your life. I would like to—"

"Because I don't," Nina interrupted, cheeks burning. "And I've explained to Bee at least fifty times that agents who work together cannot date." She turned to Bianca. "It's a nonstarter."

Bianca had outmaneuvered her, recruiting Teresa as an ally in the same way Nina had. In the process, she had also neatly diverted the conversation away from herself. The girl was too smart by half.

"So there's no man, then?" Teresa asked.

Bianca answered for Nina. "Zero, zip, *nada*." She squinted thoughtfully. "Or I should say, *nadie*, to be grammatically correct."

Bianca had studied Spanish in school for the sole purpose of eavesdropping on her foster parents, Mr. and Mrs. Gomez. Nina couldn't decide whether that meant Bianca had used her prodigious mental powers for good or not.

"How about Javier, then?" Teresa said, regarding Nina thoughtfully. "He's not married."

During two recent investigations, Nina had been paired with Phoenix police Homicide detective Javier Perez. Teresa and her family had known him for years, and apparently they thought well enough of him to consider him appropriate dating material.

"Oh yeah, I saw him on the news during that last investigation." Bianca leaned forward. "The dude is a total smoke show." She tilted her head in mock coyness. "Tall, dark, and handsome."

"Please don't," Nina said, trying to keep the conversation light to hide what was fast becoming mortification. "I . . . can't right now."

Bianca lifted a pierced brow. They both knew her background. Thanks to a serial killer who called himself the Cipher, most everyone did. Through his social media postings, the world had watched her suffer at the hands of a violent sadist who left her psychologically and physically scarred when she was sixteen.

Nina had gone to therapy after the attack but stopped before she became a police officer at twenty-one. Unfortunately, she had found herself unable to confide everything to her therapist. He had sensed her hiding something and gently probed, but she had walled herself off, unwilling to lay bare her innermost secret, the one that brought with it a deep sense of shame.

She had still never told anyone that part of her story, and until she could trust another person with the knowledge, she would not be ready for anything remotely resembling a healthy romantic relationship.

Thoughts of the time she had spent as the captive of a madman brought their current case to mind. Perhaps more than anyone else investigating the series of disappearances, Nina felt a visceral connection that came with a stab of fear. How would Melissa Campbell spend this night?

Chapter 12

It was past midnight when he reached behind Melissa's head to tug at the binding that held the blindfold in place.

When she flinched, he used his most soothing tone. "Be still." He offered her a promise. "If you're good, I'll consider taking off those flex-cuffs."

She stilled.

With extreme gentleness, he slid the fabric off, allowing it to drift to the hard cement floor. She squinted, even though the lone bulb overhead provided only dim light. She had been blindfolded all day.

Her gaze settled on his face. This was the moment of truth.

"Horace?" Her voice quavered as she spoke.

He was surprised. "You recognize me?"

The drug he had used on her usually caused memory loss, but people reacted differently to chemicals. He hadn't been sure how much of their encounter she would recall.

"You're the campus cop," she said. "Why did you . . ."

Her words trailed off, and he could see dawning comprehension in her expression.

"It's you." Her gray eyes narrowed. "You're the kidnapper."

He could see her breathing quicken as realization morphed into fear. Now she knew the full scope of her predicament. He made no response to her comment and lifted the lid from a portable cooler the size of a lunch box. Her watering eyes followed his movements as he bent to reach inside.

"Do you want what's in here?" he asked her.

"I d-don't know." She took a shaky step back from him, the tether leading from her ankle strap to the bolt on the wall sliding on the smooth floor.

"I think you do." He watched terror bloom on her face and stretched out the tension.

She had no idea what was in the container. Would it be a knife? A gun? A set of electrodes? The possibilities were only limited by the size of the box. This was a critical step in the process. He would make sure she understood who was in control.

Slowly, he lifted a chilled bottle of water from the cooler.

Her gaze darted from the bottle in his hand to his face, trying to read his intent.

He smiled. "Cool, fresh water."

Doubt clouded her lovely features.

He held it out to her. "The lid is still sealed. Look, I haven't tampered with it."

She ran a pink tongue over parched lips.

Aware the sedative and the vomiting would have made her desperately thirsty, he reached out with his other hand to unscrew the top. A discernible snap signaled that he had told the truth. The seal was unbroken until he twisted the plastic cap. He angled the bottle, allowing a bead of condensation to trickle down its side, plopping to the dry floor.

He moved to stand over the drain in the corner and held the container's open top above it. "I'll pour it all down." He tilted his hand, allowing a few precious drops to spill onto the round metal grate.

"No!"

He righted the bottle. "Are you thirsty?"

She could only manage a raspy whisper. "P-please."

"I will always provide for you." He gave her a long, assessing look. "But there are rules."

She shrank back again, shaking her head in silent denial.

He gentled his tone. "You must accept what I offer. Right now, I'm offering a cool, refreshing drink of water."

"I don't understand."

"I will pour the water into my mouth. You will drink it from my lips."

Her whole body shook. "N-no."

He tipped the bottle again, dribbling a bit more into the drain.

"All right," she said, frantic. "I'll do it. Just please don't hurt me."

"I'm giving you what you need," he told her. "The opposite of hurting you."

He lifted the open bottle to his lips and sucked in a generous amount. Holding the liquid inside his mouth, he beckoned her to him.

She crept closer, trembling with fear, a rabbit edging toward a hawk. He remained perfectly still. Finally, she drew near enough to bend her head back and lean into him. Slowly, with infinite patience, he angled his head down to hers and waited. She would have to make the first move. Would have to demonstrate her trust in him. He waited another full minute while she moved her mouth upward in tiny increments.

After what seemed like an eternity, her trembling lips met his. He rewarded her instantly, slackening his jaw to allow the free flow of water directly into her mouth.

She gulped greedily, drinking him dry.

Without hesitation, he raised the bottle and filled his mouth again, then waited.

This time, she came to him quicker, anxious for the refreshment he provided. He closed his eyes and savored the feel of her lush mouth moving against his. This time, he waited an instant longer while her tongue pressed against his closed lips before he parted them.

He wrapped strong arms around her slender frame while she drank, turning the process into an intimate embrace.

A lover's kiss.

"That's enough for now," he said after her fourth drink.

"More." She looked up at him. "Please."

He fought against the arousal building within him. This was always the most difficult part of the training process. One thought pervaded his overheated brain: *To conquer her, I must first conquer myself.*

She changed tactics. "What about my wrists? That thing is digging into them. I've been good."

"Soon." He reluctantly stepped back. "To prove you're ready, you've got to obey the rules."

"What rules?"

"You must come to me willingly," he began. "Do as I command at all times. Show me you're worthy."

"How do I show you I'm worthy?"

She wanted him to tell her. Give away his secrets. Allow her to put on an act and attempt to deceive him. Not a chance.

"It's not something you do," he said. "It's something I sense."

"I don't understand. How can you tell what I'm feeling?"

"I can," he said. "That's all that matters."

Chapter 13

He pulled out his notebook with eager hands. The initial postcapture contact had gone exceedingly well. She had accepted water from him with only a small amount of hesitation. She had to have been thirsty, which certainly helped, but he had high hopes that part of her had wanted to press her lips against his.

He imagined her waiting in anticipation of his next visit, equal parts hungry for what he would provide and hungry for him. Picturing her lovely eyes gazing up at him adoringly almost made his knees weak. She was perfect for him.

He had finally found his true mate.

Field Notes

Day	Observation	Water 💧	Food 🍎	Strategy 🧭
Melissa Campbell				
1	Capture went smoothly; nausea from sedation; no other ill effects	None	None	Withhold all stimuli and continue observation
2	Very distressed; may have minor injury to left index finger	None	None	Observe how she moves finger; plan for first contact; attempt drinking
3	Accepted water from mouth after minimal hesitancy; is learning to trust	8 ounces water	None	Wait another day to introduce feeding

Chapter 14

Nina's eyes began to glaze as she stared at the wall-size monitor. The team had spent the morning combing through video files Hazel had provided from his investigation into the disappearances. Breck was in her element, but Nina found the situation frustrating. Hazel had explained how a system-wide computer glitch on the night of each abduction had compromised the campus security cameras.

"Sometimes, they failed to record hours at a time," Hazel said. "Other times, the video files were corrupted or lost altogether."

"And we don't have an ecard-reader time stamp or a video for Tanner Hall either," Breck said.

Hazel turned to her. "It appears we have some gremlins in our security system. The night Melissa was abducted, we had a problem with our server." He paused for emphasis. "Again."

Breck's brows drew together. "Does AIT have its security system on a dedicated server?"

"Two years ago, we were hacked by foreign nationals looking to steal our latest biotech research," Hazel said. "The FBI agents who came to investigate told us the cyberpirates ended up selling some of our intellectual property to be used by terrorist regimes interested in manufacturing bioweapons. After that, the chancellor tasked our computer science department with creating a completely self-contained internal server with double encryption." He shrugged. "We migrated the security system onto the same platform last year. Everything worked fine until a few months ago."

"Makes me think it's being hacked from the inside," Kent said.

"I'd like to install new video-surveillance cameras that are linked to our FBI server—not the internal AIT one," Breck said. "Should put a stop to the glitches."

"I'll call the Phoenix field office to make the request," Wade said. "We should be able to get it done within forty-eight hours. Hopefully, before he strikes again."

"Tell them we want an Echo-45 system," Breck said. "There won't be anywhere he can hide after I get it up and running."

"I agree with Kent," Nina said. "This has all the earmarks of an inside job. He's affiliated with AIT, but in what way?"

"I might have an answer to that."

They all turned to see Dr. Feldman standing in the doorway that separated the computer lab from the conference room.

"How long have you been there?" Nina said, irritated. "We had an agreement that we would invite you into the briefing after we discussed sensitive matters among ourselves."

She did not add that Breck had scanned the think tank for any microphones, transmitters, or other listening devices despite the professor's assurances that the space was private.

Feldman strolled into the room. "If it'll make you feel better, I'll activate the door chime to let you know when the door opens." He gave his head a small shake as if the idea were ludicrous before continuing. "I've been inputting the new data into my system, and the predictive-analysis model has led the AI program to a conclusion about the identity of the suspect."

He paused, and Nina had the impression he was drawing out the tension before making his announcement. She refused to play into the drama by begging for him to share. As if by tacit agreement, everyone simply waited in silence. They were not a bunch of eager undergrads hanging on his every word.

After a long moment, he finally spoke. "The system predicts a member of the maintenance staff or a groundskeeper at the school rather than a student, faculty member, or administrator."

Wade gave him a skeptical look. "Based on what?"

"Some of the algorithms had to do with a nexus of access and opportunity," Feldman said. "Think about it. Those kinds of workers are everywhere. No one suspects them or thinks twice about seeing them around or going in and out of various buildings." He shrugged. "They're invisible."

Nina was stunned at the professor's comment. He was so arrogant that he didn't even realize what he had just said was beyond the pale. Perhaps he viewed anyone without an advanced degree as invisible, but she certainly did not. The momentary silence around the room spoke louder than words about how the others had received the insensitive remark.

Hazel was the first to recover. "We've been through this before, Dr. Feldman. My detectives have been actively investigating the disappearances since January. They've already interviewed the janitorial staff, groundskeepers, food-service employees, maintenance personnel, and many others who work here. Nothing promising came up, which is why I asked you to include students, professors, faculty, and administrators in the spreadsheet."

"And the program screened them out," Feldman said, voice rising.

"Because you set the parameters," Hazel continued.

Nina was surprised to see the two men at odds. Hazel had expressed support for Feldman's continued involvement in the investigation. They had been collaborating for weeks. Apparently, Hazel's approval did not extend so far as to tolerate a civilian second-guessing him.

"Just making a suggestion." Feldman raised a placating hand. "Not trying to tell you all how to do your jobs or anything."

"And yet . . . here you are," Hazel said. "Telling us how to do our jobs."

"We will definitely look into those individuals closely, Dr. Feldman," Wade said. "We appreciate any input. Now, however, we need to discuss the case privately."

With an air of someone who had been greatly offended, Feldman started toward the door to the computer lab.

"Professor," Nina said, then waited for him to turn. "Activate the door chime."

He shot her a glare before marching out. When the others simply looked at her, she lifted a shoulder. "You all were thinking it. We don't want him barging in here unannounced or lurking at the door. I'm just the one who said it to him."

Wade turned to the group. "We would best use our time by reading through the interviews with the groundskeepers and other employees that have already been done before we consider pulling them all in for another face-to-face. Kent and I will get started on that. Guerrera can help us while Breck and Hazel work on the video."

"What about the students and faculty?" Nina asked.

"The spreadsheet has basic info for about twenty thousand individuals," Breck said. "I can do a fast sort for age, sex, dates of employment or admission, home or dorm address, or position with the university in a couple of minutes."

"No other details?" Wade asked. "Just those categories?"

Hazel's response was defensive. "We didn't have time to include detailed background information about every single person affiliated with the school."

"Then we'll have to come up with parameters to narrow the search," Wade said, then turned to Breck. "Hold off until Kent and I do more analysis."

Wade was in his element, doing what profilers did best. Nina was always amazed at how they took a massive pool of potential suspects police had already contacted and winnowed them down to a manageable number of likely candidates. Identifying key traits and behaviors to look for could shave months off an investigation and save lives.

She was about to settle in with Wade and Kent when her cell phone buzzed in her pocket. She slid it out to see a text from Bianca.

KNOCK, KNOCK.

Smiling, she typed a quick response. WHO'S THERE?

OPEN THE DOOR DAMMIT, IT'S LUNCH.

Chapter 15

Nina walked through the think tank entry door to find Bianca standing in the lobby of the building, holding four large white plastic bags.

"I thought I was supposed to give you a ride back to Teresa's," Nina said, taking two of the bags. "What's all this?"

"Your aunt," Bianca said. "When you offered to take me back last night when we were in the kitchen together, she came up with her own plan. She knows I have to stay here until Dr. Dawson finishes giving me a tour of the campus. Alex got off school early, so she had him drop off food for the task force . . . although this looks like enough to feed the school's marching band. He told me to text him when I'm done with the tour, and he can take me home and save you the trouble." She glanced around. "I mean, you're kind of busy and all."

Nina figured it had been a collaborative effort. Teresa loved cooking and was used to preparing food on a large scale. For her part, Bianca had doubtless wanted a peek inside the place where the task force was doing its work. Her curiosity knew no bounds.

Nina heaved a sigh and led the way inside. "Lunch, everyone."

"Lord, that smells good." Breck motioned toward the conference table. "Just plop it over there."

"That looks like more than we can eat," Wade said. "I'll invite Dr. Feldman and Rick."

He didn't fool Nina. The gesture would serve as a peace offering after their awkward parting earlier. She was starting to unload the bags when she caught sight of Bianca, who had frozen in place, jaw hanging open.

"OMG," Bianca whispered. "I never want to leave this room."

"I know, right?" Breck said. "Guerrera says you're thinking about coming here in the fall. I bet that decision just got a little easier, huh?"

Bianca turned in a full circle, taking in all the glorious electronics. "I wasn't considering computer science at AIT, but I might need to rethink that decision."

"We have the best computer science program in the country," Dr. Feldman said, walking in beside Wade. "I'm Dr. Feldman."

Bianca shook his outstretched hand, then did the same with the younger man beside him.

"Rick Vale," he said, smiling. "Dr. Feldman's graduate research assistant."

"I double majored in com-sci and biology for my undergrad work," Bianca said. "I'm here checking out graduate programs."

Dr. Feldman's expression became calculating. "That's an interesting combination, Miss . . . ?"

"Babbage," Bianca said. "Call me Bee."

Rick shifted on his feet. "Dr. Feldman is always looking for the best research assistants." He blushed, apparently realizing he had inadvertently bragged while trying to pay Bianca a compliment.

They all took seats around the conference table. Teresa had thoughtfully provided paper plates and plastic forks, no doubt from the stockroom at the Mercado Vecino downtown. Nina recalled her recent meal with Detective Perez at the Latin market Teresa's parents had opened decades ago. Meeting her aunt and eating her cooking had given her a taste of many things that had been missing in her life.

As they pulled containers out of the bags, exposing their fragrant contents, Nina's mouth began to water. The intoxicating aroma from *arroz con pollo*, enchiladas, *frijoles*, and street tacos made with the most delectable carne asada Nina had ever tasted filled the room.

Breck let out a moan of pleasure. "I'm going to need a cigarette after this."

Nina smiled with pride. Teresa had a wonderful way of bringing family into everything she did. By cooking for the crew, she had extended her hospitality to them in the most authentic way a Latina mother could—she fed them.

"That's a nice piece of coding," Bianca said, eyeing Breck's open laptop.

"Crap," Breck said, reaching over to close the top. "I didn't mean to leave that open. Got distracted by all this deliciousness." She gestured toward the table.

"I could help you," Bianca said. "I can see that you're trying to—"

"No, no," Breck said quickly. "I've got it."

Feldman's jaw hardened. "I offered my assistance, too, but we're mere civilians. The FBI doesn't want us involved." He stood. "Apparently, we're some sort of security risk and can't be trusted."

The professor was thin-skinned, and the reminder of his exclusion from the investigation had brought his temper back to the surface.

He picked up one of the bags and glanced at Nina. "Thank you for lunch, but it's time we got back to work."

Rick got to his feet and followed Feldman through the interior door into the computer lab.

Bianca's gaze shifted from the closing door to Nina. "What the hell was that about?"

"He didn't like being kicked out of the sandbox," Nina said.

"I wasn't trying to cause trouble," Bianca said. "But I saw the code, realized it was a trapping worm, and wanted to help." She gave Breck a quick grin. "I recognized the subroutines."

"Much appreciated," Wade said. "But we can't talk about the—"

"We can go over computer algorithms without discussing the case," Bianca said quickly.

Wade regarded her a long moment before he gave a curt nod to Breck, who addressed Bianca. "I'm in the process of designing a program to detect a power surge in the AIT's security system and send an alert to my cell phone," she said. "If I succeed, I'll need a way to trace the interference back to its point of origin."

"Can you hitchhike on a virus?" Bianca said. "One that will only attack the surge's interference and nothing else?"

"Thought of that," Breck said. "But the AIT firewalls are robust. They don't allow penetration."

"Then mimic the firewalls by embedding some of the virus code into them ahead of time."

Breck tilted her head in thought. "You want me to pre-infect the firewall with the virus I'll create?"

Bianca shrugged. "It's worth a shot."

"That might just work," Breck said, then turned to Nina. "She's whip smart."

"Tell me about it," Nina said. "I've known her since she was thirteen."

"Actually, my research made me think of it," Bianca said. "I'm manipulating a virus to carry nanotech into a human body."

"I get it," Breck said. "You're piggybacking the biotech."

One corner of Bianca's mouth quirked up. "And just like you, I'm designing the carrier cells to target a certain point and deliver the payload, but in my case, it's nanotech that will heal the damaged nerve tissue." She paused. "At least, that's the theory. Dr. Dawson is interested in my delivery-system concept. That's why he invited me here." She checked her watch and gave a start. "I've got to fly. He's expecting me in five minutes. He went to a faculty lunch, so he put our tour off until later . . . which is now."

"Don't forget to text Alex to pick you up when you're done," Nina called out to her as she left.

Fifteen minutes later, Nina pushed back from the table, pleased with the delicious food and a mental break from the draining experience of investigating a disturbing series of crimes. She felt relaxed for the first time since their initial briefing at the FBI Phoenix field office.

A loud buzz interrupted the moment of respite. All eyes turned to the corner of the conference table, where Hazel had left his cell phone. Another round of vibrations rattled the device against the smooth surface.

He picked up the phone, tapped the screen, and held it to his ear. "Hazel." The color drained from his face as he listened. "Understood," he said. "We'll be right there."

He disconnected and looked around at them. "Bodies were discovered about two hours ago." He paused. "Phoenix police believe they're five of the missing students."

Chapter 16

It took Nina a moment to absorb Hazel's words. Both Wade and Kent had speculated that the prospect of finding the missing students alive was not good, but she had operated on the hope of a rescue rather than a recovery. Six girls had been cruelly snatched, and now five of them would never return. She saw her own shock and anger reflected in the faces around her. Everyone in the room had dedicated their lives to stopping killers. They had failed, and the weight of that failure was profound.

"Where are the bodies?" she asked Hazel as everyone scrambled to gather their things.

"I'll explain on the way." His terse tone did not invite discussion. "You might have trouble finding this place. I'll give you all a ride."

Within minutes, they had clambered into Hazel's assigned campus police SUV and were headed south through downtown Phoenix on Central Avenue. Bluetooth in his ear, Hazel had been busy gathering information and unable to answer any questions as they drove onward.

Nina, who sat in the back seat between Wade and Kent, waited until Hazel had taken two more phone calls before prodding him again. "Where are we going?"

"South Mountain Park," he said, veering through traffic. "Some kids were playing where they shouldn't and stumbled across the bodies."

"They were in a city park all these months?" Kent said. "Hard to believe no one found them until now."

"South Mountain is one of the largest municipal parks in the United States," Hazel said. "It's got over fifty miles of trails and three mountain ranges."

"I see your point," Kent said. "So where were the kids playing?"

Hazel's expression darkened. "In an abandoned mine shaft. From what I understand, they'd been riding their mountain bikes off the trail when they ran across the entrance."

"Sounds dangerous," Breck said, sitting in the front passenger seat with her laptop open as usual. "Don't they put fences around places like that?"

Hazel lifted a sardonic brow. "I've never seen a fence that would stop three fourteen-year-old boys with an overload of curiosity and plenty of time on their hands. They found a way under the chain-link fence. The barbed wire on top wasn't an issue after that."

"Was the area monitored?" Breck asked. "Was the fence alarmed?"

"No and no," Hazel said. "Which the boys discovered after a couple of test runs before getting past the fence. There are hundreds of abandoned mine shafts all over the valley, and this one is pretty remote. My guess is no one saw a need for elaborate security measures."

He continued along Central Avenue to the park's entrance, easing the SUV to a stop in front of a small stacked-stone guardhouse attached to a larger building, and buzzed his window down. A man in a park ranger uniform approached.

"Take Coyote Road to the Saguaro Trailhead. That will connect you to Chaparral Trail," the ranger said after checking each of their credentials. "You'll have to get out and hike about a quarter of a mile in. The PPD will guide you to the scene."

"I was expecting US Park police," Wade said. "Then I recalled you mentioning this was a municipal park."

"Phoenix PD has jurisdiction here." Hazel scowled. "Which is going to make things a hell of a lot more complicated."

Nina gazed out the window, taking in the rocky desert ground covered in brush and mesquite as they bumped along the increasingly rustic roadway. At one point, Hazel stopped to wait for a group of horseback riders to cross in front of him. A gorgeous palomino eyed them curiously, swishing a blond tail before following its companions onto a narrow dusty path.

"It's hard to believe we're inside a major city," Kent said.

"Fifth largest in the US," Hazel said, continuing on to the trailhead, where he parked beside a cluster of PPD vehicles.

Nina was beginning to appreciate how bodies could have gone undiscovered for months in such rugged terrain.

"Shit," Hazel muttered. "They brought out the mobile command center."

She followed his gaze to a hulking white behemoth of a vehicle idling in the center of the parking area. Complete with its own satellite dish and antennae, it had bump outs on either side that had been extended, giving it even more girth.

"Looks like they're setting up shop," Nina said. "I'd guess the PPD plans to take over the whole investigation."

Hazel looked like he needed an antacid. "Let's get in there before they shut everyone out."

They got out of the SUV and walked to the edge of the Saguaro Trailhead. Aware that Hazel had no jurisdiction off campus, Nina strolled to the nearest uniform and held up her creds. "Special Agent Guerrera. Which way to the crime scene?"

Having been a local cop herself, she knew that asserting authority went a long way toward gaining access to sensitive areas.

The officer indicated a dirt path leading uphill. "You only need to go a couple hundred yards," he said. "Can't miss it."

Nina's shoes kicked up plumes of dust as she traipsed up Chaparral Trail. She heard the others behind her. The men's footfalls were heavy, in contrast with Breck, who picked her way through the rocks and barrel cactus strewn along their path.

When Nina crested the hill, she blinked at the sight of yellow perimeter tape strung between palo verde and juniper trees to cover an expanse of terrain half the size of a football field. The site was not easily accessible by foot, but how long would it take before news choppers started circling overhead?

"Wish we didn't have to keep meeting under these circumstances, Agent Guerrera."

Nina turned to see Phoenix Homicide detective Javier Perez approaching. The discussion at Aunt Teresa's house the previous night came to mind, and she felt her cheeks warm at the sight of the handsome detective.

"Not him again," Kent muttered.

Nina realized he had used almost the same words—and precisely the same exasperated tone—that Hazel had used to describe Arthur Mage.

She shouldn't have been surprised to see Perez. The case was no longer a missing persons investigation, which was Hazel's purview. As she had suspected, now that they were dealing with murders, the PPD Homicide Unit would take charge. She had enjoyed working with Perez in the past. Kent, on the other hand, was not a fan. Judging by Hazel's glare, he wasn't either.

"You all know Perez?" Hazel put the question to the FBI team in general.

"We've worked together before," Perez said without elaborating before the others could respond.

"Isn't there anyone else in the PPD Homicide Unit?" Kent asked. "Why is it always you?"

"Some members of my squad are inside with the crime scene techs," Perez said with an air of exaggerated patience. "Two more are interviewing the kids who found the bodies. I've got the lead." He opened the large duffel by his feet and pulled out several plastic bags containing folded Tyvek suits. "You'll need to put these on." He passed them out to everyone. "You won't be able to touch anything until Crime Scene leaves, but you can have a look."

"Five bodies, right?" Nina asked.

Perez nodded. "I've reviewed photos of the missing women, and I was able to recognize at least three of them."

"What about the other two?" Nina said, pulling open the bag Perez had handed her and taking out a white coverall.

"Highly likely they're the first ones taken, but we couldn't be certain," Perez said. "It was hard to tell."

"Could mean he holds them for a while, then replaces them," Kent said, stuffing his muscular arms into the sleeves of his suit. "Or he might have kept them alive and killed them all at one time. We'll know more once we get an estimated date of death for each of them."

"That's going to be tricky," Perez said. When Nina gave him a questioning look, he added, "You'll see."

"How deep in and how far down does this mine go?" Hazel asked.

"SAU has been deployed to explore the shaft," Perez said. "And we're accessing whatever old records we can find."

Nina recalled from her earlier work with the PPD that they referred to their SWAT team as the Special Assignment Unit. She knew they would be thorough in their search.

When they had finished putting on their outfits, Perez led them through a gate and down a steep hill toward the opening of what looked like a cave. He pointed out a detached lower corner near one of the metal posts where the trio of curious boys had bent the chain links upward to crawl through, and the wooden boards lying on the ground that had been pried away from the mine's entrance.

"We spoke to the rangers, who told us they hadn't noticed the bent section of the fence," Perez said to them over his shoulder. "Which would make sense if the killer took a few moments to bend it back into place each time he left."

When Nina followed him into the mine's dark mouth, she was the only one who did not have to duck her head. Soon after they cleared the first section, everyone was able to stand up straight.

"There's a chamber off to the side," Perez said, leading them deeper inside in the dim glow of battery-operated lights dangling from spikes embedded in the stone walls.

Rounding another bend in the shaft, Nina squinted at the sudden blast of illumination from an array of lights perched on tall stands, their wires leading outside to a rumbling generator. She recovered enough to take in a team of crime scene techs in white coveralls moving throughout the open subterranean space. Others, who she assumed were police officials and detectives wearing similar coverings, lined the walls, observing without interfering.

Her gaze finally rested on a massive stone slab in the center, and she sucked in a breath. She had been to many crime scenes during her career as a police officer and a federal agent, but nothing could have prepared her for what she saw.

Chapter 17

Nina stared in growing horror at five human forms laid out shoulder to shoulder in a neat row on what looked like an ancient stone altar. The two on the left were completely wrapped head to toe in strips of white cloth. The next two beside them were clearly the nude corpses of females, but were covered in white granules and looked dehydrated. The one on the right end of the grouping had been similarly treated and also appeared to be dried out, but not as much.

"He's making mummies out of them," Nina said into the shocked stillness around her.

No one responded. Even Wade seemed to be at a loss for words.

She watched one of the crime scene techs taking video as his colleague dusted the white residue from the upper bodies of the three unwrapped bodies. Inching closer, Nina could make out their facial features. "Haley Garrett, Katie Smith, and Emily Macon," she murmured.

"The three taken before Melissa Campbell," Perez said, confirming her suspicions. "I'm assuming the other two are Sandy Owens and Cheryl Grover, but we'll need confirmation from the ME."

Wade pointed at five plain terra-cotta urns, one standing near the head of each body. "If he's followed ancient Egyptian mummification procedures, those jars contain—"

"Their internal organs," Perez finished for him. "The techs already opened the lids to take photographs." He grimaced. "I got a good look inside."

The color drained from Breck's face. "Those jars are full of guts?"

"In ancient times, priests would slice open the abdomen and remove all the internal organs except the heart," Wade said. "They would put the stomach, liver, lungs, and intestines in separate containers." He glanced at the altar. "In this case, it looks like he might have saved time and space by using only one vessel for each victim. The ME will be able to tell us how he divided everything up."

"How do you know this stuff?" Nina asked him.

"There's a fascinating exhibit at the Smithsonian that features mummies," Wade said. "I've been several times. I guess a lot of what I learned stuck."

"You mentioned that they left the heart in place," Kent said. "Why?"

"Because ancient Egyptians believed it housed the soul." Wade was in full clinical mode, offering his analysis without obvious emotion. "The brain, however, was considered unnecessary in the afterlife, so it was discarded."

Nina's lunch roiled in her stomach, but she willed herself to keep the food where it was. "But their heads are still intact." She looked at Wade. "How did he . . ."

Before she could fully form the question, Wade responded. "Traditionally, priests would pull the brain out through the nose using an iron hook. They used the hook to cut the gray matter into pieces they could slide out through the nostrils and—"

"Holy crap." Breck held her hand up, palm out. "I'm getting a super-disturbing visual image in my head."

"What is that white stuff on the unwrapped bodies?" Nina asked, getting off the subject of brains.

"A mix of salt and baking soda," Perez said. "Crime Scene did a quick field test."

"That would dry out the corpses," Wade said. "Along with the arid climate here in Arizona."

"He prevented them from decaying," Kent said. "It's interesting to see the lengths he went to in order to preserve his victims." He looked around. "Just getting them here was a major undertaking, and then he had to return repeatedly to keep working on them."

"We're several miles away from the AIT campus." Nina glanced at Perez. "Are there any traffic cameras or license plate readers that might have captured his tags on the way here or footage of him carrying a large sack into the park?"

Perez shook his head. "Nearest traffic cams are in the downtown portion of Central Avenue. We'd have no way of telling which cars entered the park."

"Do the rangers take down visitor information?" Breck asked.

"They open the gates in the morning and close them at night," Perez said. "That's all."

"Wait," Nina said. "If the gates are closed at night, he would have to take the bodies here in the daylight. Probably in the trunk of his car."

"What if they were alive when he brought them here?" Hazel asked. "Maybe he made them walk in at gunpoint."

"There are no signs indicating he killed them here," Perez said. "For now, we're working off the assumption that they were murdered elsewhere and transported to this location after they were deceased."

"Why would he take so many chances of getting caught by reenacting an ancient ritual?" Nina asked no one in particular. "He must have come back here on a regular basis."

"Because preserving the bodies was more important to him than the risk of capture," Kent said. "He's driven by a compulsion."

"Whatever compelled him will be tied in with how he selected and subsequently murdered his victims," Wade said. "Understanding what that is will lead us to our unsub."

Wade's comment drove the point home to Nina as she contemplated delving into what was surely a warped mind. They had begun the day searching for a kidnapper. Now they were hunting a serial killer.

Chapter 18

Nina edged closer to peer at the nearest unwrapped victim over the shoulder of a crime scene tech taking photographs. Scanning the girl's still form, she noticed something clutched in her folded hands, sticking out from the white particles covering the body.

"She's holding a black feather," she said to no one in particular.

Wade stepped beside her. "Looks like an ostrich plume."

"All of them have one," Nina said, noting that the wrapped bodies also had their arms folded over their chests with what appeared to be a very dried-out feather tucked beneath their cloth-covered hands.

She turned her attention back to what appeared to be the most recent victim. Her gaze traveled down the length of the girl's partially dehydrated body to her feet. "What's with the leather anklet?"

"Judging by the placement, I'd guess it's some other kind of restraint," Perez said.

An identical leather strap appeared on the other unwrapped bodies in the same place, just above the left foot.

Nina pointed. "Do you see there's a steel ring attached to the strap as well?"

"That reminds me of the kind of ring you see on a dog's collar," Perez said. "The killer could have chained the victims to something by their ankles. That way, he could control their movement."

Nina was outraged at the thought of this monster chaining young women. Unbidden, memories of her own captivity rushed into her mind, and sweat prickled her scalp. Distractedly, she rubbed at her wrists as she recalled the feeling of having her hands and ankles bound to a table. Naked and terrified, she had been completely vulnerable to the twisted desires of a madman.

She noticed Kent watching her with a concerned expression and willed herself to focus on the present.

"I wonder if the other two have the same leather ankle strap under their wrappings," Hazel said.

"I strongly suspect they will," Wade said. "Looks like someone purchased or made them custom for the three most recent victims. After killing them, he did not repurpose the ankle bracelet for the next girl."

"Why do you say the three nude bodies are the most recent?" Perez asked Wade.

"I'm not an expert on ancient Egyptian culture," he said, "but I recall a docent at the Smithsonian explaining that the practice of preserving the bodies took at least a couple of months." He waved a hand toward the stone slab. "It appears the killer began the process as soon as he murdered one of the girls, which would explain why they are each in a different stage of mummification. Once he finished and wrapped them, the decomp would virtually stop."

Nina considered the remains before her and agreed with Wade's assessment. "He spent time posing each body," she said, turning to Kent, who appeared lost in thought as he stared at the eerie tableau. She was curious to hear his take on the scene. "He made sure the feather was positioned so it wouldn't fall out of their hands throughout the course of the ritual."

"The killer laid them out, most likely in order," Kent said, studying one of the other girls. "The way he arranged the victims shows attentiveness and deliberation. They do not appear to be damaged in any obvious way."

Kent and Wade exchanged a meaningful look. Clearly, the two profilers were reading the scene on a deeper level.

"What does that tell us about the unsub?" Nina asked them.

"He's organized and meticulous," Wade said. "He doesn't abuse the bodies or treat them with contempt. He doesn't throw them away or leave them to rot. He carefully preserves them using a complicated method designed to keep them intact for centuries."

"Some offenders leave bodies lying around," Kent elaborated. "Some hide them. Very few treat them with such extreme care. This unsub arranges them on what looks like an altar with their hands folded over their chests clutching a feather."

"What's the significance of that?" Breck asked.

"Whatever meaning the killer gives it," Wade said. "We'll look into it, but it might be highly personal to him. It's certainly worth running through ViCAP."

Nina agreed. The massive Violent Criminal Apprehension Program database maintained by the FBI would tell them whether any other murders had occurred in which victims were mummified or feathers were placed on them.

"According to the crime scene techs, an initial inspection of the bodies did not reveal any immediate cause of death," Perez said. "There's no obvious trauma, which makes me wonder if they were poisoned. The ME's report and the toxicology results will provide definitive answers, but a preliminary screening can offer some clues."

"Until we know differently, we'll work under that assumption," Wade said. "He already poisoned a K-9 tracking dog, which means he's comfortable working with toxins. He would know enough to choose something that wouldn't contort his victims' features or accelerate decay."

"While we wait for the autopsies, the techs will take the evidence they collect to the Phoenix crime lab for analysis," Perez said. "They'll forward all their photos to me, and I'll upload them to the task force system so we can analyze the scene."

Perez would be joining them inside the think tank, which made sense to Nina. The PPD Homicide Unit would be front and center in the investigation going forward. She was pleased to see that they wanted to work with the existing task force already in place rather than go solo.

"You and the FBI team can head back to the on-site workspace you've set up," Perez said to Hazel. "I'll meet you there later."

"What will you be doing?" Wade asked him.

Perez jerked his chin at the five silent forms lying on the stone. "I'll finish up with the evidence techs and get the bodies transported to the ME's office." He blew out a sigh. "And I have to contact the families. Three of the girls can be identified by next of kin." He hesitated. "The others may have to wait for DNA."

Nina had performed her share of death notifications. Informing family members of tragedy was one of the worst parts of the job, and she knew the toll it would take on Perez.

"They look like pictures I've seen of ancient mummies," Nina said. "He took his time re-creating the same conditions, like he wanted them to remain here undisturbed for thousands of years."

She contemplated the scope of what the killer had done. For reasons of his own, he had deprived the world of five young women who had bright futures—who were smart and successful and had things to contribute to the world. Their loss could never be measured.

"I've investigated hundreds of deaths," Perez said, breaking into her thoughts, "and I have to admit, this is one of the most bizarre scenes I've ever witnessed."

Chapter 19

Nina walked along the path toward the computer science building, deep in discussion with Breck, while Kent, Wade, and Hazel strode behind them. Rounding the corner of the building, she spotted Dr. Feldman and Rick standing outside, talking to a tall man, fortyish, wearing a tweed jacket and blue jeans.

Rick, apparently hearing Nina and her team approaching, turned toward them. The movement revealed another person standing beside him. A small person.

Bianca gave Nina a finger wave.

"What are you doing here?" Nina asked as soon as they were close enough to talk.

"This is Dr. Dawson," she said, gesturing toward the tweed-jacketed man. "I went to meet him in his office."

"I had planned to give Miss Babbage a tour of our facility," Dawson said. "Some of the research she is interested in would be conducted on human remains, and she wanted to see the cadaver-storage unit at the medical sciences building."

"I've been using virtual cadavers because I'm not into animal studies," Bianca said. "But actual human bodies would give me better insight. Clinical trials on live volunteers are probably years away."

Nina swept a hand out to indicate the computer science building in front of them. "And you're here because . . . ?"

"Well," Bianca said, dragging the word out and averting her eyes from Nina's piercing gaze. "We were walking across the quad toward the med-sci building when I got a Google alert with a breaking news story about a bunch of bodies found in a park." She colored. "So I changed course and came over to make sure you knew about it in case it has something to do with your investigation."

Nina wasn't fooled. "You wanted to see if the reports were true." She crossed her arms. "And to worm your way back inside the think tank."

"That is so hurtful," Bianca said in mock indignation. "You'd think I was all up in your business on a regular basis or something."

Nina snorted. "You and Dr. Dawson should get on with your tour of the cadaver-storage unit. We're a bit busy here."

"At least tell me if it's true," Bianca said. "Were the missing students discovered in a park?"

Nina lifted her chin. "I can neither confirm nor deny—"

"Oh, please," Bianca said, then turned to the professor. "Let's go back to the med-sci building. We won't get anything but the company line here."

Dawson glanced at his watch. "Actually, my next class starts in ten minutes. This little detour took up all my free time. Can we reschedule?"

"Sure," Bianca said. "I'm here for the whole week."

"Good to hear." Dawson looked relieved. "Because tomorrow I'm on a panel to hear doctoral candidates defend their dissertations. It might spill over into the following day."

Dr. Feldman spoke up. "I'd be happy to show you around the computer lab now since you're here. You only got to see the think tank during lunch."

Dawson gave his fellow professor the side-eye, and Nina got the distinct impression he was concerned about Feldman poaching his top prospect.

"Bianca was just leaving," Nina said to Feldman, determined to keep her at arm's length from the investigation. "She's going to text my cousin Alex to pick her up."

"Fine." Bianca slid out her cell phone. "I have other ways to find out what's going on."

She turned and sauntered away, head down, thumbs tapping her screen.

"You can stop by the computer lab tomorrow if you want," Feldman called after her. "I'll be here."

"Let's get to work," Wade said, heading up the steps leading to the main entrance of the computer science building. "Did you get the photos from Detective Perez?" he asked Breck over his shoulder. "I'd like to start analyzing the scene."

Everyone stopped when Breck didn't answer.

"Uh, you guys." She looked up from her phone. "Just got another Google alert. The reporters and families are back at AIT. That so-called psychic detective told them he received a message from the girls' *spirits*." She air-quoted the last word. "Which means he already knows they're the ones who were in the mine, and he's announcing it to the public."

Chapter 20

Nina and the others picked up the pace, starting toward the quad to hear what fresh hell Arthur Mage was unleashing into their investigation. They reached the gathering within minutes, quickly making their way toward the outer edge of the crowd where they could listen.

Nina recognized the attorney who represented the families standing in front of the group.

". . . murder victims found only a few miles from AIT grounds," he was saying in a carrying voice. "According to one family member, psychic detective Arthur Mage went into a trance in which he channeled several of the victims."

Kent swore.

Hazel groaned.

Nina settled for a massive eye roll.

"How did he find out so fast?" Breck said in a low voice so no one outside their group could hear. "Even if he got the Google alert about bodies discovered in a park, he couldn't have known that two of them matched the description of the missing AIT students." She huffed out an irritated breath. "I mean, how could he confirm their identities to the public?"

"Because he's a money-grubbing, attention-seeking, self-serving prick," Kent said. "And a fraud."

"I just got off the phone with Perez," Wade said, putting his cell back in his pocket. "He only cleared the scene fifteen minutes ago, and he couldn't locate the families. When I told him it was because they were all on their way here, he assured me Mage didn't get his information from anyone at the scene. All the evidence techs and the other detectives are still there."

"What about the boys who found the bodies?" Nina asked. Bianca's social media addiction had taught her how quickly a teenager with a cell phone could spread news.

"They've been with detectives the whole time," Wade said. "They couldn't have texted anyone or posted about what they saw or made any calls to their friends. The detectives would have also made sure they hadn't sent anything out before the police responded. They would have warned us if they had."

Nina considered other sources of information. "Any lookie-loos watching from outside the perimeter tape or a news helicopter wouldn't have known what was inside the mine."

"Mr. Mage wants to tell the public what he has just shared with the families," the attorney continued, then stepped aside.

"It's obvious Mage had the attorney stall until the media had time to set up," Nina said, motioning toward several crews shouldering cameras and aiming them toward the front.

"I felt a chill rush over my body," Mage, visibly trembling, said to the onlookers, making sure he directed a glance at the cameras. "It was so intense. I felt claustrophobic, then everything went dark, and I don't know what happened after that."

A woman who Nina recognized as the mother of one of the missing girls clutched Mage's arm. "Mr. Mage went all weird," the woman said. "Then he started swaying, and he spoke in a soft voice, like my daughter's." She sobbed. "He told us she was gone."

"He said our girls were dead." A man on Mage's other side spoke next, emotion clogging his throat. "We need answers, but we're not getting any from the police." He pointed at the Phoenix police commander Nina had met in the aftermath of Melissa Campbell's disappearance.

Standing nearby in a dark blue uniform with gold scrolls decorating his hat and a gleaming gold badge, he was easily identifiable as a ranking official.

One of the reporters who had arrived pivoted toward the commander and called out to him. "Is it true that you've located the bodies of the missing students?"

"We need to speak with the families privately before making a public statement," the commander said.

"Mr. Mage already broke the news to us," the father who had pointed at him said. "You may as well admit it."

"We have located five bodies," the commander added after appearing to choose his words. "They were hidden inside an abandoned mine located in South Mountain Park."

Nina figured the commander was safe giving up those details. News choppers had already begun circling over the site according to what Perez had told them.

"Six students are missing," the mother shouted. "Which five did you find? Is one of them my daughter?" She covered her face with her hands.

"I regret that you and everyone else who has a missing loved one are going through this difficult time," the commander said in a sympathetic tone. "I cannot imagine the pain and grief you must be feeling, but our procedures require us to have family members make a positive identification before we confirm what we've found and announce it to the public."

"I'm going to see for myself," the father said. "Right now."

The commander turned his attention to the distraught man. "You can't enter the crime scene at this time. Within the next hour or two, we can meet you at the Medical Examiner's office, where you can view the deceased."

"I have to wait and pray I don't see my little girl when they . . . when they . . ." His shoulders shook as tears overtook him.

Another angry parent stepped forward and gestured to Arthur Mage. "If he hadn't told us about this, when were you planning to?"

The commander's gaze rested on the psychic. "Actually, we would be interested in speaking to Mr. Mage about the . . . source of his information."

Mage smiled. "I will be happy to help with your investigation. In fact, I've assisted police from all over the country in various—"

"That's not what I meant, as I'm sure you know," the commander said, then glanced at the reporter. "I have no further comment at this time. Our public affairs office will provide an update soon."

Apparently sensing he was about to lose his audience, Mage spoke to the group. "I will hold a private séance for the families tonight in an effort to make direct contact with the victims, who might be able to tell us who did this."

Breck motioned for the others to gather around her. "I can't take any more jack-jawing from that carnival barker," she whispered. "While he was running his mouth, I did a little online research. Seems Arthur Mage has made quite a name for himself over the past ten years. Claims he was struck by lightning on a golf course in Scottsdale, and ever since, he's been able to channel spirits . . . for a fee."

"Do the spirits accept credit cards?" Nina asked.

"Don't know, but he sure does," Breck said. "He put out a shingle in downtown Phoenix, where he gives readings and offers classes."

"Classes?"

"Yeah, for a couple thousand bucks, he'll teach folks to speak to the dead."

"I want to know how he found out about the bodies right after we did," Kent said.

"The same way the media probably did." Hazel looked annoyed. "By monitoring police-scanner traffic. I'm going to tell Perez to put in a request that all future dispatches involving this investigation go out using in-vehicle mobile data terminals or on a secure radio channel."

"We'll know if that's what Mage did soon enough," Kent said. "Sounds like the PPD commander wants to haul him in for questioning. Hope he does it before Mage's so-called séance."

"I asked Perez to drop by the computer science building when he comes up for air," Wade said. "We'll need whatever information he can give us from the PPD crime scene techs. We've got to catch this guy before he . . ."

He trailed off, but everyone knew what he meant. Nina reflected on the grieving mother's words. Only five bodies had been found. In her heart, Nina knew which girl was missing. Where was Melissa Campbell?

Chapter 21

Nina sat at the conference room table, looking at the wall screen in astonishment. "How did you find all this so fast?"

She and Kent had been on a video chat with the PPD command center for the past twenty minutes, which was apparently all the time it took for Breck and Wade to make headway in the criminal profile.

Breck's cheeks dimpled. "Research is my superpower." She divided the screen into sections. "We'll cover the more exotic stuff after Perez gets here. First, let's talk feathers. I captured a few images at the crime scene on my cell phone, so we didn't have to wait for the techs to finish and send us their photos before getting started."

"My first impression was right," Wade said. "Each victim was holding a black ostrich plume."

"Any idea where it came from?" Kent asked.

"We checked," Wade said. "Ostrich feathers are not rare. They're used widely in everything from feather dusters to fashion."

Nina was disappointed. "He could have gotten the plumes from a duster at Walmart or a feather boa at a vintage shop."

"And there are ostrich farms in Arizona," Wade added. "Trying to source that particular piece of evidence is a dead end, so I switched my focus to the meaning behind what is clearly part of the unsub's signature."

"A quick check on ostrich feathers and dead bodies led to some strange places." Breck tapped the tabletop, opening another screen, this one featuring a gold statue of a young woman kneeling. Her outstretched arms were lined with feathers, and her headdress consisted of a single upright plume. "This is the ancient Egyptian goddess Maat," Breck said. "She helped determine the destiny of human souls after death."

Nina straightened in her chair. "Ancient Egypt again. This guy has a serious fixation."

"How did she decide a soul's destiny with a feather?" Hazel asked, folding his arms.

"According to what we found in the mythology, when someone died, their heart was placed on one side of the scale of truth," Wade said. "Maat's ostrich feather went on the other side. If the heart weighed less than the plume, the deceased was allowed to move on to the afterlife. If the heart was heavy with bad deeds, the person would be eaten by a fierce goddess with the head of a crocodile and a body that was a combination of a hippo and a lion. The soul would then cease to exist."

Nina considered what she had seen in the abandoned mine. "Each victim held a feather directly over her heart."

"Exactly," Wade said. "It's possible the unsub believed they had all been judged and found unworthy."

"Is there any other significance to an ostrich feather on a dead person?" Kent asked. "Could it be something besides this Maat goddess?"

"I'll grant that it's an obscure reference," Wade said. "But we haven't found anything else that matches the evidence at the scene and also links to ancient Egypt."

That connection had been enough to convince Nina they had found the correct explanation for the ostrich plumes.

"I had some luck researching the leather anklets," Breck said, switching the screen to a close-up of a thick band around a shriveled ankle she had managed to take at the crime scene before they left. "I kept googling *leather ankle straps*." She gave her head a small shake. "You wouldn't believe how many bondage emporiums popped up before I put enough filters on the search parameters to eliminate all the kink. That's when I finally found a match for what was on those two victims."

"How come you ruled out the fetish paraphernalia?" Hazel asked. "There are plenty of shops in town that sell all kinds of leather restraints." He cleared his throat. "If you're into that sort of thing."

The corner of Breck's mouth twisted into a wry smile. "First, I don't want to know how you're aware of those stores, and second, nothing looked exactly like what was on the victims' ankles," she said. "Until I stumbled across this site."

"I'm convinced Breck found a match," Wade said as Breck clicked on a different icon. "And it adds a whole new level of complexity to the profile."

The main door of the task force room slid open, drawing Nina's attention away from the images displayed on the wall screen.

Detective Perez walked in, his head swiveling as he surveyed the space with widened eyes. "I feel like I'm on the bridge of the USS *Enterprise*."

Nina could relate. The massive screen surrounded by banks of high-tech equipment resembled a scene from *Star Trek*.

"How's the crowd out there?" she asked him.

"Dispersed," Perez said. "Two detectives from my squad are at the morgue with the families, going through the formal identification process." He grimaced. "It's going to be a brutal, horrific process for their loved ones. My sergeant sent me here to start collaborating." He paused for a beat. "And I've got news about the mine and an update on Arthur Mage."

"We have some developments to share as well," Wade said. "You go first."

"I'll start with the mine," Perez said. "Our SWAT team went through every part of the area. The entrance we went through was the only access point. There were no more bodies inside, and no evidence left behind in any place other than the stone altar."

"Sounds like he stumbled on it during a trail hike," Nina said, "then realized it was long forgotten and he could use it without being disturbed."

"We reached the same conclusion," Perez said. "There are signs he cut through the chain-link fence to reach the entrance, and I'm sure that would have made him even more convinced he had the mine to himself."

"What happened with Mage?" Wade asked.

"When we got him in the interview room, Mage tried to pull that woo-woo psychic bullshit," Perez said. "Once we explained how we would make it our mission to expose him for the fraud that he is, he spilled his guts like a piñata at a birthday party."

Nina chuckled. "What was his game?"

"A combination of technology and Scam 101. He told us he has a police scanner, which is what we figured. That's how he knew about the bodies."

"What's the rest of his act?" Nina asked.

"He explained how he makes educated guesses while he pumps the friends and families for information," Perez said. "They fill in the blanks without realizing what they're doing."

"Cold reading," Wade said. "A con artist classic."

"And he also does hot reading," Perez continued. "He researches his subjects ahead of time. Looks at their social media accounts. You'd be surprised how much personal information you can get about people if you dig into their posts, likes, tweets, stories, and comments."

"The sonofabitch was preying on those families," Hazel said. "He should be in jail."

"Mage promised to make himself scarce, and we cut him loose," Perez said. "Charging him with obstructing justice would have been a long shot. He certainly interfered, but not necessarily to the point of criminal behavior."

Nina would rather be rid of him than have to deal with the spectacle and distraction of a perp walk and the media frenzy that would surely follow a local celebrity's arrest.

"Now that the Arthur Mage show is over, let's get back to the real investigation," Wade said. "Breck dug up a solid lead."

"I figured there was a reason you all were looking at wildlife," Perez said, turning to the wall screen, which showed a photo of a red-tailed hawk in flight.

"Breck was just telling us about the leather strap around the victims' ankles," Nina said.

"According to this site, it's called a jess," Breck said. "An essential piece of falconry equipment."

Perez frowned. "I've never heard of falconry."

"It's an ancient sport," Wade said. "Dates back thousands of years in civilizations throughout the world." Perez gave him a dubious look, and he continued, "The trainers are called falconers or hawkers. There are clubs around the country. I'm sure there's one in Phoenix."

An idea struck Nina. "Did the ancient Egyptians practice falconry?"

"I had the same thought," Wade said. "Breck and I couldn't get a definitive answer, but they mummified many birds of prey, included depictions of them in their hieroglyphics, and even worshipped a falcon-headed god, so I'd say the odds are good that they trained birds for hunting."

"Obviously I need to learn more about this," Nina said. "Maybe visit one of those clubs."

"Way ahead of you," Breck said, tapping on the table's surface. The official website for the Arizona Game and Fish Department popped onto the screen. "Turns out in Arizona, you need a license from the state to keep birds of prey or to hunt with them."

"Please tell me their headquarters is in Phoenix," Nina said. "I don't want to drive five hours to have this conversation."

"It's here," Breck said, "but on the far side of the city. There's not enough time to go today, but it'll be open tomorrow."

"Kent will go with Guerrera tomorrow, then," Wade said. "He can incorporate any new information into our suspect profile."

"I'd like to get in on that," Perez said. "Maybe learning something about how falconers control their birds can shed light on what this guy does with his captives."

"Control." Wade stroked his jaw. "That's what it's about for him." He turned to Kent. "Are you tracking with me?"

Kent nodded. "This guy is an expert in training. Conditioning. Manipulation."

Wade grew more animated. "That's why the victims didn't show any signs of abuse. No broken bones, lacerations, or even a hint of what killed them. He controlled them in other ways."

"But they're not birds," Nina said. "They're human beings."

"Who are also subject to behavioral conditioning," Kent said. "Especially if they're being held prisoner." His expression darkened. "I've seen it done, Guerrera. It's effective, and it's devastating."

Chapter 22

They had discovered one of his secrets. Watching the news to see overhead shots of the police crawling all over the park had been unnerving. For a moment, he had been afraid they'd found out everything, but he reassured himself that they still hadn't figured out how he had done it. Or who he was. The loss of the sacred death chamber had been a severe blow, but it would not interfere with his plans.

He had laid their bodies out with such care. They had each deserved their fate, but he'd worked hard to preserve their beauty. Looking back on it now, he supposed burial or cremation might have been more prudent, but he had not been able to bring himself to do it.

He reflected on each of them, one at a time, considering how he had selected them. How he had developed the perfect snare for each one. How he had spent time patiently working with them, tailoring his approach to suit their personalities. He had even determined what each one's favorite food was, making sure he could tempt her with what she craved most. He had done everything he could, but they had all disappointed him in the end, earning a black plume from his collection.

But now he had Melissa Campbell, and he felt confident he would not have to find a new place to lay her to rest. She was everything he had hoped for. She was perfect.

He used the controls to adjust the camera so he could watch Melissa struggle against her bindings. He contemplated her progress through each stage of her training. First, she'd been separated from everything and everyone she knew. He had bound her wrists behind her back and blindfolded her, rendering her vulnerable and totally dependent on him. He'd put a jess on her ankle and tethered her to the wall before leaving her to wait.

After a long time in darkness and isolation, he had returned to her, removed the blindfold, and given her the chance to quench her thirst. She had taken his offering. Now the next phase had begun.

Deprivation. A powerful tool he wielded with precision. Loud noises jarred her if the motion sensors detected lack of movement for more than ten seconds, preventing her from getting any rest or sleep. He had kept her in a windowless cell, a single overhead bulb the only—and constant—source of light.

He preferred finesse to brute force, which was a blunt instrument wielded by weak-minded men who knew nothing else. He had a better way. He would not physically touch Melissa again until he judged her ready and willing to feel his caress.

And she was close. So close.

He could see the last light of hope flicker in her eyes. After her brief taste of water, she had gone a long time without sleep, clothing, or food. When her ability to think rationally and regulate her body temperature deteriorated, she would be anxious for his return.

That would be the time to consummate their love. He thought back to the one before Melissa. Her name was Haley Garrett. More than food, Haley had begged for warmth and sleep. When he had finally come to her after days of deprivation in the cold cell, she had practically thrown herself into his arms. He recalled her icy skin pressing against his, seeking his body heat, which he gave her willingly. She had known the price she would have to pay, and did so willingly, opening herself to him in every way.

They had made beautiful love that night. She had returned his kisses, stroked gentle fingers along his flesh, whispered his name as he surged into her.

And then she had revealed her true nature.

At the moment of his climax, Haley had smashed the heel of her palm into his nose. She fought like a thing possessed, and it had taken all his strength to subdue her. It had all been an act. She had not loved him. And she never would. She had deceived him. Another pretty face speaking pretty lies.

And so, Haley had taken her place among the others whose hearts had been judged and found wanting.

He turned from dark thoughts of the past to watch Melissa again. Very soon, he would literally and figuratively have her eating out of his hand.

She paced the small cell as far as the cord on the jess allowed. Without warning, she stopped, tilted her head back, and shouted into the empty room around her, "What do you want with me?"

After hours of silence, she had become desperate.

He spoke into the transmitter. "I want all of you."

She jumped, clearly startled, spinning in a circle as she tried to locate the source of the disembodied voice. He knew she would not find it.

"Where are you?" Her question reverberated against the cinder block walls surrounding her.

He responded with his own question. "Are you hungry?"

This time, her response was faint and weak. "S-starving."

"Cold?"

"Freezing."

"Tired?"

"I don't even know what day it is," she said. "Why don't you let me sleep?"

"You will have rest when you earn it. The same goes for food."

Body shaking, Melissa slumped to the floor. He realized she was weeping, her hopes gone; her will broken. He licked his lips in anticipation of tasting hers again.

Tonight, he would tame his newest bird.

Chapter 23

Nina looked at Breck. "You mentioned that you had more findings you were waiting to share until Perez got here."

"Here I am," Perez said. "What have you got?"

Breck fairly vibrated with excitement. "While Guerrera and Kent were on a video chat with the command bus and Perez was doing his detective thing, Wade and I did a deep dive on ancient Egypt."

Wade took up the narrative while Breck brought up an image of Tutankhamun at the newly built Grand Egyptian Museum near the Giza pyramids. "Depending on the social class of the deceased, mummification time varied," Wade began. "Each step in the process involved priests—usually dressed as Anubis, the jackal-headed god—who performed sacred rituals and said prayers over the body as they worked." He gestured toward the screen. "It took seventy days to mummify King Tut."

Breck tapped the smooth surface of the table again, bringing up an image of a deep brown, wizened body with sunken features. Nina recognized the figure as an unwrapped mummy, based on what she had seen in textbooks.

"As I mentioned before," Wade said, "after death, priests pulled the brain out through the nostrils. Internal organs were removed, and the abdominal cavity was cleaned with wine and aromatics, then filled with spices—including natron, which was also heaped over the entire body. In later centuries, the organs were wrapped and placed back inside the belly area."

Nina was surprised to see that Breck's previous revulsion at the description of the burial rites had evaporated in the face of online research. Breck had managed to compartmentalize the horror of what had happened to the victims in order to objectively evaluate the facts.

"The white granules we saw on the bodies were a substitute for natron," Breck said. "Which is a naturally occurring sodium carbonate used in ancient times for embalming and helps the dehydration process. It's similar to the salt-and-baking-soda mixture the unsub used."

Nina considered the timeline. "If the killer based the process on King Tut—which seems likely because it's so well documented—he would have worked on the bodies for seventy days."

"Then he would have washed them and wrapped them in linen," Wade said, following her train of thought. "So we can assume the fully wrapped victims were deceased for at least two and a half months."

"Can we source the fabric used at the scene?" Kent asked.

All eyes turned to Perez.

"I spoke to the lab director on the way over," he said. "She told me they would try to get more specifics, but initial indications were that the wrappings were cut into six-inch-wide strips from plain white cotton top sheets you could buy at any department store." He shrugged. "There were no tags or markings and nothing distinguishing about them."

"I thought the bodies were at the ME's office," Hazel said.

"Crime scene techs took samples of the fabric before transporting the victims," Perez said. "They needed to get started on the analysis."

Nina appreciated their efficiency. "It looks like the wrappings and the ostrich feathers will be hard to trace," she said. "Apparently, he knew better than to use unique sources for those items."

"He's nutty as peanut butter pie," Breck said. "But he's not stupid."

Wade pulled the discussion back to the evidence at hand. "Given the mummification schedule, the fully preserved remains on the left were probably those of his first victim, Sandy Owens, who was last seen on December second of last year, and Cheryl Grover, who went missing on December twelfth. Emily Macon wasn't abducted until January fourteenth, the day after all the students returned to campus to start the new semester."

"That makes sense," Nina said. "He would have kept Emily alive awhile to play his sick mind games. Assuming he held her at least a week or two, that wouldn't have given him enough time to fully mummify her remains. He was probably planning a trip out there soon, though. He could finish the process with Emily while he checked on Katie Smith and Haley Garrett."

Nina pictured a nameless, faceless man hauling the corpse of a young woman over his shoulder across the rocky ground of the mine. "He was risking exposure every time he went," she said. "Despite what the rangers told you about how remote the area is, I have to think he would know it was a gamble."

"What happened to the bodies next?" Perez asked.

"Ceremonially, nothing," Wade said. "In ancient times, the priests would seal them in their tombs after they were wrapped and blessed."

Nina frowned. "I can't imagine what the autopsy is going to be like."

"Speaking of which," Perez said, "I pulled some strings and managed to get our best ME on the case. He'll be examining Haley Garrett first thing in the morning."

Wade thanked him before turning to Nina. "You and Kent need to be there," he said. "I want as much direct information as possible about what happened to the victims. This will give us the best clues about what he might do next."

"Do you think he'll act out now that we've found the mine?" Nina asked.

Wade nodded. "Discovering a place that is of crucial importance to him—that he may even hold sacred—will have a profound effect on the killer. I'm assuming the only victim who's still missing is Melissa Campbell. And now she's in more danger than ever."

Chapter 24

The following morning, Nina peered through the viewing window at the withered body on the cold steel table. She had been there for nearly two hours with Perez and Kent, who stood on either side of her. They had watched the ME carefully and methodically autopsy Haley Garrett, who had disappeared on February twenty-sixth. The most recent victim before Melissa Campbell's disappearance, Haley's body was more recognizable than the others.

Perez had introduced them to Dr. Pendergast, whom he described as the best and most experienced ME, at the beginning of the procedure.

"We were lucky to get our cases pushed to the front of the line," Perez had told them. "I normally have to wait a few days, if not a week."

A big city would certainly have its share of violent and suspicious deaths, but Nina wasn't surprised an active serial killer had taken priority.

They had spent the next hour and a half in comparative silence, answering occasional questions from Pendergast and trading theories about the bizarre rituals performed on the bodies and what they might signify.

Perez pulled his buzzing cell from his pocket and glanced at the screen. "Better take this," he said. "It's Dr. Ledford at the crime lab. She promised to let me know as soon as she got any results."

He moved to the corner of the viewing room, speaking in an undertone into the phone at his ear.

"I wonder how much Dr. Pendergast will be able to determine, considering all the tissue damage that must have occurred," Nina said to Kent.

Pendergast, who could hear their conversation through the intercom, glanced up at her. "I've been in touch with the lead forensic anthropologist at the Smithsonian," he said from behind his glasses and face shield. "I haven't autopsied a mummy before, and he's going to walk me through some of the more intricate steps." He gestured to Haley's body before returning to his task. "I have, however, done my share of examinations where victims have been found after spending several months deceased in the desert, so I can give you some preliminary findings in a few minutes."

Nina had attended enough autopsies to know this one was almost over. "Can you confirm the identities of the two fully mummified remains?" she asked Pendergast.

This time, he responded without looking up. "I was able to extract DNA. We're comparing it with a sample taken from each of their parents. We'll have an answer shortly."

Her heart went out to the families, who must have been appalled to hear what had become of their daughters. She imagined their profound grief had further magnified when they had to provide DNA to make a positive ID.

Perez disconnected the call and rejoined them. "The crime scene techs analyzed the jesses they had removed from the three unwrapped bodies and found hidden tracking devices sewn into the leather," he said while they waited for Pendergast to finish.

"Were any of them functional?" Kent asked. "Maybe we could intercept the signal and trace it back to the source."

Perez was already shaking his head before Kent finished the question. "They were all pulverized. Looks like the suspect deliberately crushed them to avoid exactly what you're suggesting. They appear to be homemade too," he added. "So we can't hunt down the manufacturer to look for a bill of sale."

Nina was puzzled. "Why didn't he simply take the jess with the tracker off each victim's foot? He wouldn't have had to keep replacing the equipment."

"This was no ordinary rig," Perez said. "Apparently, the killer wanted to make sure his victims didn't remove the anklet with the hidden device, so he used kangaroo hide." At Nina's raised brow, he elaborated, "According to the lab, it's the toughest leather in the world. Crime scene techs had a hard time getting it off the bodies without causing tissue damage."

"He used something flexible but strong," Kent said.

"And he didn't want his victims to remove it," Perez said. "Dr. Ledford told me the straps appear to be sewn together using braided fishing line, which is more than ten times stronger than steel cable. In addition, the metal ring attached to each ankle strap is made of tungsten carbide."

"So that's why he left the anklets on each victim," Nina said. "It was easier to replace them."

"I don't believe that's the main reason." Kent shook his head. "I did some reading on ancient Egyptian funereal rites last night. They believed that the deceased would need many things in the afterlife, and that's why they were entombed with all sorts of objects—as well as the internal organs that had been removed. I think he wanted each girl to wear the special gift he created for her. She would be bound to him forever. Even in death."

Nina considered the level of possessiveness that implied, and the contradiction. "He killed them, so in a way, he rejected them, but he still wanted to control them?"

"That's my take for now," Kent said. "I'll have a better feel as we go forward." He seemed to consider a new thought. "I will say this, though. Egypt is fascinating. I can see how he could become engrossed in its rich history, culture, and achievements."

"The lab also analyzed extraneous black fibers from the final three victims," Perez said, bringing the discussion back to the evidence recovered at the scene. "They weren't from the same cloth as the strips of white sheets the other two were wrapped in. And they confirmed the feathers were ostrich."

"Those three women were nude," Nina said. "Where did they locate fibers?"

"In their hair," Perez said. "The crime scene techs collected tiny strands of black thread."

"Are they unique?" Nina asked. "Can they source the fibers, the fishing line, the ostrich feathers, or the kangaroo hide?"

"They're trying," Perez said. "But they haven't had any luck so far. They're also attempting to source the tungsten ring, which might provide a better lead, since it's more unusual. They'll keep me posted if anything crops up."

Nina thought about the database at the forensics lab in Quantico with thousands of materials from around the world stored for comparison. It might be a long shot, but it would be worth a try.

"Can Dr. Ledford send samples to the FBI lab too?" she asked Perez. "I'm grasping . . . I realize that." She caught movement out of the corner of her eye and noticed Dr. Pendergast had straightened. "What have you got for us?"

"I did a quick preliminary scan of the three unwrapped bodies before I began this morning," Pendergast said, then gestured to Haley Garrett. "The good news is that the preservation techniques used by the perpetrator prevented most tissue decay, insect intrusion, and scavenger predation. The bad news is that those same techniques caused a certain amount of desiccation, which may have altered the outcome of certain tests I attempted to perform."

"In other words," Kent said, "the bodies were dried out."

"Which caused the skin to darken," Pendergast said. "This is due to the melanin in the tissue concentrating as it dehydrates. To put it plainly, the flesh loses plumpness without water and shrivels. Despite this, I was still able to locate discoloration to the left ankle where the leather strap had been affixed," Pendergast continued. "In addition, I found very slight indications of wrist binding in both tarsal areas, as if her hands had been flex-cuffed for an extended period before she died."

"Interesting," Kent said. "He restricts their movement in several ways." He appeared to be forming an opinion about the motives behind the killer's actions.

Nina was more interested in the objective facts of the case at this point. "Were you able to come up with a time of death?" she asked.

"The skin of a mummified body becomes dry and rigid," Pendergast said. "Although shrunken, the preservatives used—in this case, salt and sodium bicarbonate—delayed putrefaction and managed to preserve enough tissue for me to postulate that this victim died between four and six days ago."

Nina pulled out her cell phone and tapped on the calendar feature. "Today is March nineteenth," she said to the others. "That would mean Haley died somewhere between March thirteenth and fifteenth."

"Melissa Campbell was abducted on the sixteenth," Perez said. "He didn't wait long to find a replacement."

"Can you tell how Haley died?" Nina asked the ME.

"I'm going with homicide for the manner of death," Pendergast said. "But as for the cause, I'll need to wait on the final results of a tissue analysis. It seems this victim was poisoned, but I haven't identified the substance used yet."

"How did you arrive at poisoning?" Perez asked.

"All of her internal organs except her heart were removed, salted, wrapped in the same fabric as the others, and placed back in her body cavity," Pendergast said. "According to the expert from the Smithsonian, that was done with the mummies from more recent dynasties. In earlier times, they left the organs in canopic jars and filled the body cavity with natron and sand so it wouldn't appear sunken." He appeared to catch himself. "Didn't mean to go off on a tangent. What I meant was that the liver was preserved enough that I was able to take samples, along with hair and skin, that gave me an initial indication of toxicity."

Kent had a question of his own. "Does she show signs of sexual assault around the time of death?"

"Fortunately, this victim has been deceased only a short period of time, and the preservative mix used on her body was not inserted into her vaginal tract," Pendergast said. "I was able to conclude that she had sexual intercourse shortly before death."

Nina bristled at how the ME characterized what had occurred. "You mean she was raped," she said. "Not sexual intercourse." She enunciated the word. "Rape."

"Yes, she was raped," Pendergast said quickly. "But my findings were unusual." He paused, apparently searching for the correct words. "Visual inspection of the genital area did not reveal obvious injury, so I used colposcopic magnification and toluidine blue staining to detect microtrauma."

Nina pressed for details. "What did you find?"

Pendergast shifted uncomfortably. "The examination did not reveal typical indications associated with forcible sexual penetration, and there was no residual semen present. What I did find, however, was a blend of lubricant and spermicide commonly found in prophylactics."

"I'm not following." She couldn't get a read on his discomfort and had no idea what he was tiptoeing around. "Why don't you spell it out, Doctor?"

"In my experience, some sexual assault victims show clear signs of injury or microtrauma, and others do not," Pendergast said. "If I were put on the stand as an expert witness in this case, I could not definitively rule out consensual sex with someone wearing a condom based on what the autopsy revealed."

"Consensual sex?" Nina said, anger building. "People under duress cannot consent to sex. Under the law, if a victim is subjected to force, threats, or intimidation, it's rape. If a victim is incapacitated, underage, or otherwise unable to give consent, it's rape. Full stop."

Pendergast had touched a raw nerve. As a sex assault survivor, Nina had dealt with the utter dehumanization of being under someone else's physical control. As a law enforcement officer, she had taken statements from victims who had felt judged by society. She recalled one woman whose husband had left her after she'd been raped. He'd reasoned that if she was still alive, she hadn't fought hard enough against her attacker.

"Agreed." Pendergast nodded vigorously. "What I'm trying to say, and obviously doing a bad job of it, is that they may have been coerced—or perhaps rendered incapable of understanding what was going on—but I cannot find any signs of physical force."

Perhaps sensing Nina's agitation, Perez spoke before she could reply. "So this suspect finds ways to make the women comply?"

"Still sexual assault, that's for sure," Nina said.

"My thoughts exactly." Pendergast looked relieved that they appeared to understand him. "In fact, this woman's tissue indicates signs of starvation."

"Another form of control," Kent said, disgusted. "He restricted their movement, starved them, and may have even used narcotics on them to gain compliance." He looked at Pendergast. "Were you able to run a routine drug panel?"

"Samples were sent out for a detailed analysis," Pendergast said. "My preliminary tox-screen results should be back within the hour."

Perez checked his watch. "We should get going if we're going to catch our ride to the Game and Fish Department." He looked through the glass at Pendergast. "Can you text me when you have results?"

"Ride?" Nina said. "I thought we were driving."

"It's the height of morning rush hour right now," Perez said. "HQ for Game and Fish is on Carefree Highway."

Nina and Kent stared at him in silence.

"I keep forgetting you guys are from the other side of the country." Perez blew out a sigh. "It will take an hour to get there and another to get back to AIT in traffic. If we spend an hour or two there, it'll kill the whole day. I made a few calls and got us a ride that will get us where we need to be in about ten minutes."

"You have a magic carpet?" Nina asked.

"Even better." Perez lifted a brow. "How do you feel about helicopters?"

Chapter 25

Twenty minutes later, Nina was airborne in the back seat of a police air unit beside Kent while Perez rode up front with the pilot. The PPD had an impressive air fleet, and one of its helicopters was always up on routine patrol. Given the high-profile nature of the investigation, Perez assured them he'd had no trouble hitching a ride.

A five-minute walk from the ME's office had taken them to the police-headquarters building on Washington Street, where a helicopter waited on the rooftop helipad.

Nina had ridden in a PD chopper only once before, and it had been while she was on a special assignment in Fairfax County during her days as a patrol officer. She would never forget the pilot's words just before takeoff. "This is not a luxury aircraft. It's basically a gravity-defying bucket of bolts that wants to fly apart in every direction at all times." He slid her a grin before turning to face the controls. "There's a barf bag by your seat if you need it. I'm not landing until the mission is over."

Despite a rush of adrenaline as the whirring blades took them straight up, then barreling ahead at top speed, she'd managed to keep her cookies down back then. She figured she could do the same today.

Gazing below, she saw the Phoenix skyline give way to beige desert terrain. The city appeared like an oasis, a mirage left behind as they flew onward with dizzying speed. They circled ever lower while the pilot positioned the craft to put down in the vast desertscape beside a squat brown building situated by itself among the washes and chaparral that constituted the farthest reaches of the city limits.

"Every time I climbed aboard a chopper in the past, I left on a fast rope," Kent said. "Landing rather than jumping out will be a new experience for me."

The pilot landed smoothly and assured them he would be back to pick them up within ten minutes of Perez's call, barring any critical incidents.

Nina gave Perez an appreciative look. "I have to admit, this was way better than inching along in bumper-to-bumper traffic for an hour."

His teeth were dazzling white against his tan skin. "I aim to please." He swung down from the open door.

Kent jumped out and thudded neatly on his feet beside the landing skids.

Nina clambered to the ground with much less grace than her counterparts, pointedly ignoring their outstretched hands as she did. Being only five feet tall had serious disadvantages, but she'd be damned if she would admit it to her peers.

They scrambled out from beneath the maelstrom created by the rotor wash as the pilot readied for liftoff. Perez led them to the building's main entrance.

A man clad in green tactical pants, a tan shirt, tan boots, and a matching ten-gallon hat approached with an outstretched hand. "Director Grant," he said. "Call me John."

After everyone introduced themselves, he showed them into the conference room, which looked like a taxidermist's paradise. Stuffed wildlife of every kind adorned the walls.

Kent studied the various animals. "That's a bighorn sheep," he said, pointing out the massive ram's mounted head. "I didn't think those were native to Arizona."

John followed his gaze. "Bagged that one at the Grand Canyon." He gestured toward an antlered creature beside the ram. "That elk is from Flagstaff."

Nina was anxious to get to business. "We're here to learn about falconry in the area."

"Have a seat," John said, indicating the conference table in the center of the room. "It's not every day two FBI agents and a PPD Homicide detective fly here in a helicopter." His expression grew calculating. "I've seen you on the news. You're investigating that serial killer case, aren't you?"

Nina didn't confirm or deny the assumption. "We hope you can provide information that would help us," she said.

"One thing I can tell you about falconers," John began. "They're a tight-knit community. Most of them are conservationists." He leaned forward. "They brought a couple of species back from the brink of extinction." He chuckled. "Love their birds more than people sometimes."

Nina and Kent exchanged glances. She could tell he was also wondering how that tidbit would fit into the unsub's profile.

"Is the sport popular in this area?" Perez asked.

"Not as much as bowhunting, shooting, or fishing," John said. "Hawking takes years to master, a lot of patience, and enough money to buy equipment and care for the bird."

The mention of equipment piqued Nina's interest. "Where does someone buy equipment around here?"

"Mostly online these days," John said. "And from other falconers, which is also how someone new to the sport obtains a license." Apparently sensing the question before she could pose it, he continued, "You have to be an apprentice before you're allowed to capture and keep a bird of prey in the state of Arizona."

"Do you maintain a database with that information?" Nina asked.

John pulled a flash drive from his front shirt pocket. "When my assistant told me you were coming, I had him prepare an Excel spreadsheet with the names of everyone who has obtained a sport-falconry license in Arizona for the past ten years." He handed the drive to her. "You can sort by name, date of birth, occupation, type of raptor, or date the license was obtained."

Nina recalled that birds of prey were also called raptors and wondered what species the unsub would favor. She handed him her business card in exchange for the drive. "Can you also email it to me?"

Hazel had agreed to supply them with a downloadable spreadsheet containing the names of all AIT employees and students going back ten years. She planned to forward the email to Breck, who could compare the two files for matches in a matter of minutes.

"I'll have George take care of it right away," John said, standing up to cross the room and poke his head through the conference room door to call out for his assistant.

She saw him hand over her business card but couldn't make out what the two men were saying.

John turned to face them. "Good news, our visitor is here early."

They exchanged glances.

"What visitor?" Perez asked.

"I could sit here and continue to answer your questions as best I could," John said. "Or you could watch a live demonstration and ask the falconer yourselves." He opened the door. "Follow me."

Chapter 26

Nina stood between Kent and Perez in the open desert behind the Game and Fish Department headquarters. All their gazes were locked on the man standing before them, who held a majestic gray-and-white bird perched on his gloved arm. John had escorted them to the waiting falconer, who went by Connor. In turn, Connor had introduced his female peregrine falcon, Diana.

"Ancient Roman goddess of the hunt," Kent said after the introductions were made.

Connor inclined his head in acknowledgment. "And of wild animals and wilderness."

Taking in Diana's fierce eyes, sharp beak, and lethal talons, Nina figured the name was appropriate.

"The peregrine falcon is the fastest animal in the world," Connor said. "When they spot prey from the air, they go into a dive called a stoop." He glanced at Diana with admiring eyes. "They've been clocked at speeds over two hundred miles per hour."

"How do they not crash straight into the ground?" Perez asked.

"Peregrines mostly hunt other birds, so they strike in midair," Connor said. "They'll take a rabbit if there aren't birds available, and if they do, they plunge down and level out into a swoop at the last second, scooping their prey up in their talons rather than do a purely vertical attack."

Connor indicated Diana's tucked wings and sleek body. "They are aerodynamic," he elaborated. "Built for speed and maneuverability. They have total control."

Nina tried to understand. "You're saying they dive-bomb other birds?"

Connor lifted his arm. "Let me show you."

Diana launched herself with smooth flaps of her mighty wings. Within seconds, she was circling high above.

"Her vision is keen enough to spot a field mouse even at that height," Connor said. "But I imagine she'll be hunting for a pigeon."

"I noticed the jesses on her legs," Nina said, trying to sound conversational. "How are they used?"

Connor kept his eyes trained on Diana as he responded. "Many raptors used in falconry are not bred in captivity. They are caught in the wild when they are juveniles."

"How do you capture a wild bird?" Kent asked.

"You lay a trap," Connor said, flicking a glance in their direction before returning his gaze to the sky. "You put out bait in the form of their favorite prey, depending on what type of bird you're after and what part of the world you're in."

"What kind of trap will snare the bird without injuring it?" Nina asked.

"I drop a net over it while it's eating," Connor said. "It's important to be extremely careful during that process."

"Can you give us a brief overview of your training techniques?" Kent said. "We're particularly interested in conditioning."

Connor swiveled his head and raised his hand to his forehead to shield his eyes from the sun as he spoke. "The most important thing to have is patience," he said. "You have to keep in mind that you're dealing with a wild animal, and a supreme predator. You don't train a raptor in the same way you'd train a dog. It's a gradual process."

Diana was high enough to be almost out of sight, but Connor seemed to be aware of her progress through the sky as he spoke. "After catching a bird, you secure its leg with a jess immediately to be sure it can't fly away."

"What material is it made from?" Perez asked.

"I use kangaroo leather." Eyes upward, he missed the meaningful glance Nina gave her colleagues. "But some people choose synthetic materials, which can be even stronger. It's a preference."

Nina divided her time between watching Diana climb ever higher above them and listening with rapt attention to the falconer's explanation.

"Do you use a tracker?" she asked.

"Most falconers use a telemetry device, which is usually attached to the jess."

Another hit.

"Would it be possible to intercept the signal and trace the location of someone else's bird?" Nina asked, thinking of Melissa Campbell. The trackers found on the victims in the abandoned mine had been crushed, but perhaps Melissa's was still operational.

"Unlikely," Connor said. "Each device is on a different frequency. You have to program the correct one to your receiver. It's done that way to prevent getting signals crossed if two or more falconers are hunting in the same area."

"What's the next move after tethering the bird?" Kent asked him.

"You've got to cover its eyes as soon as possible," Connor said, glancing down from his observation of Diana. "There's a special hood designed for that purpose. This takes away their sight, which is their greatest sense. Puts them at a complete disadvantage and gives you control."

Nina must have shown her dismay, because Connor shook his head. "It's not like that. Covering their eyes with a hood settles them down. It's done to prevent injury to the bird."

"The fibers," Nina said, unable to elaborate in front of the falconer.

Kent and Perez both gave her knowing looks. They clearly understood her reference to the fiber samples collected from the hair of the victims. Nina now assumed the black fabric found by the crime scene techs was most likely a blindfold placed over the girls' eyes.

Connor pointed. "Watch."

Nina glanced up to see Diana tuck her wings and plummet toward the ground at an incredible speed. She couldn't stop a small gasp from escaping as Diana changed her trajectory, aiming herself like a tactical missile toward a hapless bird flying below her. She slammed into the other bird in a deadly midair collision and flew in a spiral with its limp body clamped in her talons.

Connor raised his arm in a silent signal, and Diana banked, making her way toward them. "Part of the conditioning process involved getting her to willingly give her food to me."

Diana came in at a low arc, and Nina felt the air rush through her hair as the falcon's wings flapped with powerful strokes. She had an almost irresistible impulse to duck her head. After another pass, Diana landed gracefully on Connor's outstretched forearm.

With his free hand, Connor pulled a piece of glistening raw meat from a leather pouch attached to his belt and held it out in front of the bird. After Diana took the offered food from Connor's hand, he detached a dead pigeon from her claws and put it in another pouch attached to his belt. He rewarded Diana with a second chunk of meat.

"I'm careful how much I feed her," Connor said. "Every gram of food is measured out. I must make sure she gets proper nutrition for her health, but not so much that she's unwilling to hunt."

"So you give her food in exchange for what she hunts for you?" Perez asked.

"In the beginning, as soon as I caught her, I began a process called 'manning the bird,' which meant getting her used to me handling her."

Kent looked intrigued. "How did you do that?"

"With constant physical contact," Connor said. "The key was to touch her as much as possible. Like all predators, she viewed me as either something to eat or something to avoid. At first, she wanted to escape or attack. I had to make her understand that I had no intention of hurting her and that I could become her partner."

That particular choice of words took on an entirely different meaning in the context of the killer, and Nina saw her own dawning comprehension reflected in Kent's expression. The man they sought had clearly used similar conditioning to manipulate his captives.

Sensing this was important for understanding the unsub's MO, she pressed for details. "What's next after you man the bird?"

"Another critical part of the process is getting her to eat off the glove. Let me demonstrate."

Connor lifted another piece of meat from his pouch and placed it in the closed fist of the gloved hand on which Diana was perched. Only a small portion of the food was exposed, and she bent her head down to tug at it.

"Notice that when she lowers her head to eat, she's exposing the back of her neck to me, which every self-preservation instinct within her screams not to do."

It was true. Nina realized Diana was vulnerable to attack when she tore at the meat.

"How do you get her to trust you with her life?" Nina asked.

"At the very start, I must withhold food for a bit. Finally, her hunger will overcome her fear, and she will take what I offer because her self-preservation instincts also won't let her willingly starve herself when there is food present. That's the first step. After that, I will require her to make small adjustments. I'll hold the food a short distance away, and she must hop to get to it. Then I put it farther away, and she will have to fly to get it."

"How come she doesn't fly away at that point?" Perez asked.

"This part of the training takes place indoors," Connor said. "And when we go outside for the first time, she's on a tether."

Nina thought she understood. "You had her tethered with the jess around her leg so she couldn't fly away and hunt for herself. You were her only option."

"Exactly. You can't beat a raptor into submission. You must work with its natural behavior to bend it to your will."

Nina was certain the killer had set out to do the same with the young women he captured. Both fascinated and horrified by what they had learned, she was anxious to discuss the implications with the profilers.

After thanking Connor and John for their insight, Nina, Kent, and Perez strolled toward the place the helicopter had landed an hour earlier. Perez had already called for the pilot to pick them up, and Nina made sure they were out of earshot before addressing the two men.

"I'm convinced our unsub is an experienced falconer," she said. "His name has got to be on the list we got from John."

"We'll probably have an answer by the time we get back to the think tank," Perez said. "As long as Hazel got the AIT database for Breck to compare it with."

"I agree with you," Kent said to Nina. "Whether or not his name pops up, he's got a background in falconry. There are too many similarities with what he did to his victims based on what we learned at the autopsy and from the crime lab."

"The way Connor described catching young birds," Nina said. "He could have been talking about young women."

"And kangaroo leather for the jesses," Perez said. "Including tracking devices. It also looks like he blindfolded them."

"I wonder why he needed to track them," Kent said. "I had assumed he had them in a cage or locked in a room or something."

"I assumed he put the telemetry device on as a way to catch them if they managed to escape," Nina said. "If they somehow withstood all his head games, that is. The ME said their stomachs were empty," she added. "I'll bet he controlled their water too."

"Deprivation has been used for centuries with prisoners and entire populations to control people," Kent said. "It's an easy way to break their will, make them too weak to fight, keep them confused and squabbling among themselves."

"The killer abducts them and takes away their food, water, and sight by blindfolding them," Nina said to Kent, curious to hear the thoughts of someone with combat experience as well as psychological training. She knew he had undergone realistic exercises to prepare him for being a POW, but she often wondered if he had ever actually been held captive. If so, he hadn't admitted it. "What's his next move?" she asked him.

"He begins to erode their individual identity," Kent said. "Isolates them so they can't communicate with anyone except him. He might literally keep them in the dark even if he removes the blindfold, only providing light when they do as he asks."

"Mental torture," she said. "What happens to the victim?"

The lines in Kent's face hardened. "Someone living under those conditions could fall victim to Stockholm syndrome after a while."

Nina recalled learning about the syndrome during her training. Those in law enforcement were taught that hostages could turn against their rescuers if they had been held captive for an extended period. After learning to depend on their captor for everything, an abductee could eventually identify with their abductor. One of many survival mechanisms the human mind was capable of adopting.

Nina took the next logical step. "He would continue to torment his victims until—as Connor put it—he bent their will to his own."

Perez had his own question for Kent. "What if the victim never complied?"

"Eventually, he'd kill them," Kent said quietly. "Unlike a falconer, he couldn't release them back into the wild, or they would go to the police."

Perez pulled his buzzing cell phone from his pocket and tapped the screen. After listening for a long moment, he thanked the caller and disconnected.

"That was the ME's office," he said. "Dr. Pendergast identified what killed the victims." He gave his head a disbelieving shake. "Whoever this suspect is, he's full of surprises."

Chapter 27

An hour later, Nina rushed into the think tank ahead of Perez and Kent. "We know what killed them," she announced to the rest of the team. "And you're never going to believe it."

Breck glanced up from the conference table where she sat beside Hazel. "I'd love some definitive information to work with," she said. "Because I'm having zero luck with the list of licensed falconers from the Arizona Game and Fish Department."

"No matches?" Perez asked, ambling in behind Nina.

"We went through the entire database." Breck blew a long red tendril from her face. "It went back ten years without a single match. Of course, he could be doing it illegally. It's not like he's big on following the law."

"Let's hear about something we can work on," Wade said to Nina. "I'd like to know how the victims died."

"Jimsonweed," Nina said, fresh from her online research after Perez provided the name of the toxin. "Also known as devil's trumpet because its blossoms are fluted. It's a flowering plant that grows all over Arizona and in most of the continental US."

"Weed?" Hazel said. "Did they smoke it?"

"The ME believes it was ingested by mouth," Nina said. "But it can be smoked or snorted as well."

Kent, who had followed behind Perez, tapped the screen on his cell phone. "Its scientific name is *Datura stramonium* or *Datura wrightii*, and it contains scopolamine, which is classified as an anticholinergic medication and belladonna alkaloid."

"I'll stick with jimsonweed," Breck said.

"Where would someone get it?" Wade directed the question to Perez, who would have better knowledge of local narcotics suppliers.

"I checked with our department's Drug Enforcement Bureau on the way over," he said. "The plant is uncontrolled in the US and can be purchased online, but it's highly dangerous."

"How so?" Wade asked.

"The dosage is important," Perez said. "According to the narcs I spoke to, the right amount can make you docile, but too much can be deadly, as it was in this case."

"Sounds like it takes skill," Hazel said. "Who would know how to distill it and dose it properly?"

Nina thought she knew the answer. "We're at a tech university. I imagine there are plenty of Bunsen burners, crucibles, beakers, and other lab equipment needed to make a concoction."

"And I'm sure Dr. Google could tell anyone how to brew it up," Breck added.

"What happens when someone is exposed to the stuff?" Wade asked Perez.

"Apparently, if the dose is right, it can cause hallucinations, make you highly suggestible, and cause confusion."

"Couple that with starvation and other kinds of manipulation, and the victims would be easy to control," Kent said.

Perez nodded. "The full tox panel will reveal more, but from what the ME could tell, it looks like the unsub overdosed them when he wanted to kill them. As little as fifteen grams could be lethal, and they would have died within an hour of ingesting it."

"Does it have a rapid onset?" Wade asked. "Could it be used to quickly overpower a victim?"

"Not according to the narcs or the ME," Perez said. "If the perp wanted to knock out his victims, he could have used something like ketamine or propofol. Then he could switch to jimsonweed later to help control them."

"Did the ME find any sign of other narcotics?" Breck asked.

"Not so far," Perez said.

"Which would make sense if he used something to capture them," Nina said. "A fast-acting drug would have left their systems. Either way, final lab results will take longer."

Perez filled them in about the black cloth fibers found in the victims' hair.

"The Phoenix crime lab is sending samples to Quantico along with strips of the white sheets and one of the feathers, but I'm not optimistic," Kent said. "I think our best bet will be to get inside this guy's head."

Nina concurred. "Which we should do fast. There's no specific pattern, so he could strike as soon as tomorrow or as late as a month from now." She turned to Kent. "You were right about his awkwardness around women. He's found a way to take the possibility of their refusal out of the picture by abducting and manipulating them into having sex with him."

"Agreed," Wade said. "In fact, now that the ME has confirmed that he sexually assaulted at least one of the victims, I would put him in the category of a power-reassurance rapist as well as a serial killer."

"I'll bite," Hazel said. "What the hell is a power-reassurance rapist, and how is that different from any other kind of sex offender?"

Wade thought a moment before launching into an explanation. "There is plenty of debate about this, but my studies and observations have indicated four types of rapists. Power assertive, anger retaliatory, anger excitation, and power reassurance. The power assertives rape to validate their masculinity. They're the over-the-top macho types who need to prove something. The anger-retaliatory rapist wants to punish his victims. He was often abused as a child, which created hostile feelings. He expresses his hostility through sexual violence. The anger-excitation rapist is everyone's worst nightmare. He will torture his victims and ultimately murder them. He's the one with the rape kit and the serial killer van. He's smart, resourceful, and often doesn't get caught for a long time."

Wade stopped short, glanced at Nina, and cleared his throat. She held his gaze a moment before dropping her eyes as the unspoken communication passed between them. Wade knew about her past better than anyone else.

She had never heard it described in such clinical terms, but it was clear to her that the Cipher—the man who had tried to kill her, and later destroy her—had been an anger-excitation rapist. She had attended classes at Quantico in which Ted Bundy had been described in those terms. That had certainly been an accurate depiction of the man who had held her captive when she was only sixteen. She recalled gazing into the fathomless depths of his ice-blue eyes. He had debased her in every way imaginable, coming within moments of ending her life. She had looked into the face of evil and lived to tell the tale, but not without deep scars that disfigured her body and tormented her mind.

Wade continued after an awkward pause. "The last is the power-reassurance rapist, which I now believe describes the unsub we are currently dealing with." Deliberately looking away from Nina, he sat down heavily in his chair and turned to Kent. "Why don't you give them an overview?"

Kent hesitated a beat, glancing from Wade to Nina before taking up the narrative. "The power-reassurance rapist has something to prove, both to himself and to the world. His behavior is rooted in a deep lack of self-esteem. He has lived with—or still lives with—a domineering female, which makes him feel emasculated. He doesn't have friends or a girlfriend and is seen as the opposite of an alpha male. He tends to stalk his victims, finding ways to watch them prior to the attack, which will invariably occur by surprise when his target is alone."

"Geographically," Wade added, "he doesn't venture far from his work or home. His attacks are usually close to his base of operations or his comfort zone."

"With everything we've learned now," Kent said, "I think this unsub deludes himself into believing his victims desire him, that they are in love with him."

"Which makes him all the more deadly when the victim does something that shatters the fantasy," Wade said. "It creates cognitive dissonance that he resolves by killing his victims."

Nina summed it up. "They can't reject him if they're dead." She considered the people she'd seen on campus, given the new suspect parameters. "Despite what Dr. Feldman's AI says, I'm not ruling out students, faculty, and administrators. If we're looking for a guy who's more comfortable with computers and calculators than he is with attractive women, we're in the right place. This school is full of them."

"We need to make it more specific," Perez said, glancing at Wade, then Kent. "What else have you two got?"

"He'll have some sort of challenge," Kent said slowly. "Maybe a speech impediment, a skin condition, a nervous tic, a limp, or something else that sets him apart. This may have resulted in his being the victim of bullying behavior as a child. He suffers from low self-esteem."

Nina had learned enough from the profilers to know the next question to pose. "What would be the precipitating stressor for him? What would have started him killing instead of just fantasizing?"

"Anything that reinforced his insecurities," Wade said. "A bad breakup. Someone teasing him about whatever he perceives as his disadvantage. It could also be a loss, like the death of his mother or someone else who emotionally or financially supported him."

"Sounds like the kind of thing we would only know after the fact," Hazel said. "You haven't given us anything we can use to filter through the spreadsheet. I want to know how we can find him."

Nina, who had done her time as a local cop on the receiving end of information from profilers, answered for them. "You use the information to narrow down a pool of suspects," she said. "Putting people in that pool is our job."

"I can help with that," Breck said. "I figured out a way to upload the corrupted footage from the night of Melissa Campbell's abduction to one of the FBI's video-forensics programs without risking introducing a virus into our system."

This had been one of the main impediments Breck had been dealing with. Nina had heard muttered curses and colorful southern expressions from her fellow agent over the past two days as she repeatedly tried different work-arounds.

"Explain," Wade said.

"The program will take a data-rich file and reconstruct the missing pieces using predictive algorithms," Breck said.

Wade looked like he was suppressing a sigh. "In plain English."

Breck gave it some thought. "It could take hours or maybe even days, but the program will gradually put the video back together." She smiled. "If it works, we'll be able to see exactly what happened the night Melissa disappeared."

Chapter 28

Evening had arrived, and he thrummed with anticipation as he reached out to brush a knuckle against Melissa's pallid cheek. "You are so lovely."

And she was. Not only did she meet his high standards but she also exceeded them in every way. His heart soared with the knowledge that she would be his. He had planned the perfect evening. After a nice dinner, they would consummate their love.

"Thank you, Horace."

The smile she gave him was wan. Vacant. Not adoring. Perhaps her hunger had gotten to be too much. He reached into the pouch he had attached to his belt and lifted out a single chicken nugget. He had seen Melissa eat them during the preselection phase. They were among her favorite foods.

Her eyes widened as she followed the progress of the morsel up to his mouth. He placed it between his teeth and waited. She should know by now what to do next, what was expected of her.

Slowly, she raised up on her tiptoes, craning her neck to angle herself forward. His heart ratcheted up as she drew close. He inhaled deeply, drawing in the scent of her shampoo. He longed to run his fingers through her silken tresses but held himself in check. This stage of the process was critical.

Her soft lips finally touched his as she gently nibbled at the offering. He forced himself to remain still, then relinquished the nugget. As she chewed, he selected a second piece, this time placing it completely inside his mouth.

She came to him a bit faster than before, pressing her lips against his until he finally opened his mouth and let her tongue plunder inside for the reward he offered.

The third time she came to him, he opened his mouth wide and pulled her lithe body tight against him, this time hungrily devouring her as she took sustenance from him. Thoroughly aroused, he kept kissing her, crushing his lips against hers with primal need. Surely, she felt it too. Felt the urgency of the heat between them.

But she didn't.

After she swallowed the last bite of chicken, she tried to pull away from his embrace. Even after all he had done. All he had offered. She recoiled slightly. Just a fraction, but enough for him to sense an undercurrent of revulsion. All she had wanted was the food. Not him.

The movement spiraled his mind down into a dark past. A place he never wanted to go but often did.

He was sixteen years old. His older sister, Tabitha, was with her pretty friends in her bedroom. He knew they were in there smoking cigarettes. Mom wouldn't be happy if she found out. But that wasn't likely. He rarely saw his mother. Since she'd started working that second job, she was hardly ever home. She would tell them both to be good and warn him to listen to his sister, who was in charge.

As soon as the door had snapped shut behind his mother, Tabitha's innocent smile turned nasty as she faced him. "Did you hear that, you little prick? You have to do whatever I say." Her smile grew wider. "And you can start by scrubbing all the toilets and mopping the floor."

Their mother had instructed them to share cleaning duties.

"What are you going to do?" he asked her.

She crossed her arms. "My nails."

"But you're supposed to—"

"What part of I'm in charge don't you understand?" She cuffed him on the side of the head. "Get to work." She looked at him thoughtfully. "And if you're thinking about crying to Mom, I'll make you pay. You know I will."

He did know.

Two hours later, she had come downstairs to inspect his cleaning. After granting him a passing grade, she looked him up and down, disdain evident in her features.

"My friends will be here in five minutes," she said. "And I want you to be invisible. You'd better stay in your room; don't come lurking around, listening at my bedroom door, you little freak."

"I'll just get a sandwich first; then I'll go to my room and—"

The doorbell rang.

"No sandwich," Tabitha said, heading to answer it. "Just go to your room."

He started down the hallway but could not resist glancing over his shoulder. He saw Kara walk in. Gorgeous Kara with her long blonde hair and even longer legs. She was a senior and a cheerleader, like his sister. All the cheerleaders hung out together after school. Of course his sister wouldn't want him anywhere in sight.

He was the smallest kid in his class. His mother had taken him to a pediatrician, who had called it "delayed pubescence." He called it advanced humiliation. His high-pitched voice squeaked when he talked. The other kids called him Mickey Mouse. No amount of pumping iron seemed to result in any lasting muscles. To the contrary, the extra demand on his thin frame had only made him skinnier. His upper lip had no sign of peach fuzz, nor did he have much hair anywhere else. His sister told him he had the body of a ten-year-old girl.

Raucous giggling from the front door hastened his steps toward his room, where he stayed half an hour until he worked up the nerve to sneak down the hall to eavesdrop at her bedroom door.

They were whispering. The floor creaked beneath his bare feet as he inched closer. Suddenly, the door swung inward, and Tabitha was there, hand on her jutting hip, glaring at him.

"Look who's spying on us," Tabitha said, latching on to his arm so hard her brightly painted nails dug into his flesh.

"No, I wasn't— I just—"

She yanked him into the room. "What should we do to punish him?"

"I thought your brother was a sophomore," Kara said.

"He is," his sister said, giving him a hard shake. "He just looks like he's in elementary school."

Kara's pretty lips parted in surprise. "No shit, are you sixteen?"

His answer came out at an even higher pitch than usual. "Y-yes."

"No way," one of the other girls said. "Do you hear his voice? I bet his nuts haven't even dropped."

His sister's eyes narrowed. "Let's find out."

"No!" He tried to pull away, but her grip was like iron.

"Oh, come on," another one of the girls said. "It'll be the biggest thrill you've ever had. Bet you'd love to get naked with a bunch of cheerleaders, wouldn't you? Of course, you'll be the only one dropping trou."

He began to fight in earnest.

"Grab him," his sister said, clutching his other arm. "Stop squirming, you little perv."

He was no match for six athletic young women. They wrestled him to the ground and stripped him, then slowly scrutinized every inch of his body . . . and found it lacking.

"Look at those tiny little balls," Kara said, laughing. "They're the same size as the zits on his face."

They taunted him until they became bored with their game, then finally twisted their mouths in disgust and ordered him out. Slamming his bedroom door did not block out their braying laughter as he retreated to his bedroom.

Now he looked at Melissa Campbell and saw that same twist of the lips that should have been parted to receive his kiss. The hooded eyes that should have gazed upon him with adoration. But she did not want him. He could see it plainly now that the heat of his passion had cooled.

Like so many other beautiful women, she had tricked him. In that instant, he weighed her heart on the scale of truth and found it to be as heavy with deception as his own was with heartache. He had been sure she was the one, but he'd been wrong.

Again.

Chapter 29

Later that evening, Nina parked the black Suburban by the curb in front of her aunt Teresa's house. Teresa, who had seen the news conference, had called to let Nina know she'd prepared dinner for the team, insisting they stop by on the way back to their hotel.

"You and the others cannot work on an empty stomach, *mi'ja*," Teresa told her.

When Nina had explained that they had no time for a sit-down family dinner, Teresa swiftly changed tactics, promising to prepare a to-go meal they could pick up and take with them. Then she had promptly disconnected, effectively ending all debate on the matter—a strategy Nina was coming to recognize.

Wade had headed straight to the hotel, where he could provide a video briefing for their supervisor, SSA Buxton, in private. Kent and Breck opted to tag along with Nina, and she had the impression they were curious to meet her newfound relatives.

"Who all is here, anyway?" Breck asked.

"I think it's just us, my aunt Teresa's immediate family, and Bianca," Nina said, opening the driver's door. "A small gathering, by her standards."

They walked to the front porch as a group. The sound of laughter and loud conversation drifted from the house, as did the intoxicating aroma of rich food. She had been desperate to spend time with Teresa, who so resembled the mother she would never know.

Duty, however, pulled her away, as it always would. Whenever she thought of the missed time with her family, her fatigue, or her hunger, a vision of Melissa materialized before her. Melissa would be going through all that and so much more. Nina could only hope her aunt would understand.

Still not comfortable walking inside unannounced, she rang the doorbell.

Moments later, Teresa pulled the door open and reached out to grasp both of Nina's hands in hers. "I'll have everything ready for you in less than ten minutes," she promised. "Bianca is on a video chat with her foster family. She'll be done in a minute."

Nina followed Teresa to the kitchen, where she introduced Breck and Kent.

"Hi, Nina." She turned to see Teresa's eighteen-year-old son, Alex, walking toward her.

A feminine voice called out to her. "Someone wants to see you, Nina."

Her cousin, Selena, strolled in, holding her newborn daughter.

"*Hola*, little Tori." Nina bent to see the adorable pink face with bright eyes looking up at her and was rewarded with a toothless grin.

"She's a happy baby." Selena glanced at her husband across the kitchen. "We're lucky."

"I need some sugar," Breck said, holding out her arms. "May I?"

An odd sensation filled the pit of Nina's stomach as she watched Selena hold the baby out to Breck, who cooed and gently lifted her from her mother's arms. Breck, who was not a mother, looked completely natural holding Tori. Nina, who had never spent much time with babies and had not experienced much nurturing in her life, felt like a stranger in a foreign land.

"You want to hold her next?" Breck asked Nina.

"I—I couldn't." She imagined herself dropping Tori, who seemed as delicate as a porcelain doll.

Kent stepped forward. "It's easy, Guerrera." He extended his arms, and Breck settled the baby into them. "You just have to support the head and body at all times." He arranged Tori's legs near the crook of his elbow and rested her head in his palm. "Kind of like holding a football."

He tucked the bundled infant against his broad chest and smiled down at her. Tori snuggled against him, her eyes drifting shut. Something about seeing the brawny former Special Forces operator cradling a tiny newborn made Nina's heart turn over. For the millionth time, she wished she had the ability to express love and tenderness.

"Part of your SEAL training?" she asked, lightening the moment.

"Part of being raised with three sisters, all with babies of their own," he said. "I'm an uncle eight times over." His gaze rested on Nina. "Why don't you give it a try?"

It might be easy for him, but Nina was terrified she would somehow hurt little Tori, or frighten her, or make her cry.

She took a step backward. "I, uh, I don't think—"

"Do you want both red and green sauce?" Teresa asked.

Nina, certain her aunt had deliberately rescued her from the awkward moment, shot her a grateful look. "We'll take both. Do you need help packing everything up?"

Teresa declined the offer, and Selena took Tori from Kent and went into another room to put her down for a nap.

Nina took in the crowded kitchen with its brightly colored ceramic tiles. The ocher-painted walls and vibrant-green plants in the wide picture window gave the house a Southwest vibe she liked.

Teresa picked up a cast-iron skillet filled with sizzling meat and veggies from the stove and tipped its contents into a foil container. Her husband, John, pulled a stack of fresh, warm tortillas from a round terra-cotta warmer and wrapped them in tinfoil.

"Fajitas," Teresa said as she scooped rice from a steaming pot into a tall Styrofoam container. *"Con arroz."*

Nina's mouth instantly began to water as she contemplated sharing the food with her teammates in the hotel room while they worked.

Bianca strode into the kitchen and looked at Teresa. "Mr. and Mrs. G asked me to thank you again for hosting me." She turned to Nina. "And they wonder why you haven't called lately."

When they had learned she was alone in the world, the Gomez family had taken her under their wing, even though she was an adult. Apparently, finding her biological family hadn't changed their feelings about her.

"I'll call Mrs. G in the morning before we head back to campus," Nina said.

"Speaking of which, what's the latest at AIT?" Alex glanced at each of the FBI agents in turn. When none of them responded right away, he explained. "I just got my early-admission acceptance letter. That's where I'm going next fall."

"Alex is class valedictorian at South Phoenix High." Teresa gave her son a fond gaze. "He's already working on his speech."

Bianca's cheeks colored. "We might end up at the same school."

Nina realized they were both the same age. She narrowed her eyes, watching the interaction between them closely, not sure how she felt about it. She noticed her aunt's speculative expression as she followed the discussion as well.

"I'm checking out Dr. Dawson's program," Bianca said. "But I'm pretty sure Dr. Feldman is trying to recruit me too."

Alex leaned forward, excited. "Dr. Feldman is the reason I applied for early admission to AIT. He's one of the best software designers in the country. I'm developing a program that gamifies machine learning technology to submit for a competition he's judging. He selects only two freshmen to work on his team." Dimples creased his cheeks. "I intend to be one of them."

"I'm curious about your game," Bianca said. "How does it work?"

"Your avatar is locked in a room and must choose one of five items to use to escape," Alex said. "The objects are in a toolbar you can only access once. No changing your mind."

As someone who had literally been locked in a room several times as a child, Nina didn't find the concept of being imprisoned entertaining.

"Sounds like a blast," she said, her tone flat.

Kent's gaze met hers. She was certain he had undergone similar experiences during his SEAL training, or in live combat. Or both.

Alex went on, apparently oblivious to the underlying tension in Nina's remark. "No one's ever defeated the newest version of the program." He wiggled his brows. "Though many have tried."

"Is there an actual solution?" Bianca asked, clearly intrigued. "Or are you punking everyone?"

Alex smirked. "There's a way out. You'll just never find it until I show you."

Bianca's blue eyes lit with the prospect of a challenge. "Bet I could escape in under ten minutes."

Alex shot to his feet. "You're on."

Everyone watched as he abruptly left the kitchen, Bianca close on his heels.

"Looks like Bee found a kindred spirit," Nina said. "And Alex has no idea who he's messing with."

"I have some fresh *galletas* to add," Teresa said, opening the pantry to bring out three plastic bags.

"Oh lord," Breck said. "What are those?"

Teresa smiled, then described each type of cookie as she placed them into the open carryout bag. "Mexican wedding cookies, cinnamon shortbread, and dark Aztec chocolate."

"My stomach will think I died and went to heaven," Breck said.

"Escaped," Bianca announced, striding back into the kitchen. "In less than five minutes."

"But you cheated," Alex said, following close behind her. "You hacked in and changed the code."

Bianca grinned. "Consider yourself schooled," she said to Alex. "That lesson was free of charge."

"You didn't follow the rules," he said to her. "You can't just create a portal to get out."

"Apparently, I can," Bianca said. "I'm not big on rules." She gestured to Nina. "Learned how to get around them from the best."

"I always encouraged Bee to think outside the box," Nina said. "Now she doesn't even see the box at all."

"Damn," Alex said, turning back to Bianca. "I'm going to have to patch that back door before I submit the program."

Bianca responded with exaggerated sweetness. "You're welcome."

"Food's ready," Teresa called out.

Nina realized her aunt had once again deftly changed the subject before the situation became uncomfortable. She had a lot to learn from Teresa.

"We should get back to the hotel," Kent said. "Agent Wade is waiting to fill us in on any updates to the investigation."

His comment dissolved all thoughts of a pleasant family meal, of warmth and sharing, of any sense of normalcy. Somewhere out there, a predator held Melissa.

And Nina could not shake the feeling she was running out of time.

Chapter 30

Field Notes

Day	Observation	Water 💧	Food 🍎	Strategy ✦
	Melissa Campbell			
1	Capture went smoothly; nausea from sedation; no other ill effects	None	None	Withhold all stimuli and continue observation
2	Very distressed; may have minor injury to left index finger	None	None	Observe how she moves finger; plan for first contact; attempt drinking
3	Accepted water from mouth after minimal hesitancy; is learning to trust	8 ounces water	None	Wait another day to introduce feeding
4	Feeding by mouth initially successful. Subject displayed overt signs of rejection.	8 ounces water	3 chicken nuggets	

Chapter 31

The following morning, Nina maneuvered the black Suburban through the streets from the hotel to the AIT campus while she listened to Wade and Kent trade theories on the psychological underpinnings of the profile they were refining in the back seat. Breck sat in the front passenger seat with her omnipresent laptop open and a touch screen stylus clamped between her teeth.

"Damn," Breck said around the stylus. "These records only go back fifty years."

Nina cut a glance at Breck before returning her focus to the road. "What kind of research are you doing?"

Breck slid the pen from her mouth and tucked it behind her ear. "Lieutenant Hazel gave me a passcode and ecard to access the campus library system online. I've been going through historical data on the school to see if I can find anything that might shed light on our investigation. I started by cross-referencing ancient Egypt and AIT."

Nina was impressed. "Did you find anything?"

"A clandestine group called the AIT Sphinx Society," Breck said. "Unfortunately, that's all I could dig up." She blew out a sigh. "One stinking mention. No details."

Her comment had drawn Kent's and Wade's attention. "That sounds like the kind of group our unsub would be interested in if we read the ostrich feather–Maat connection correctly," Kent said. "But why go back fifty years?"

"The search result I found claims the society was founded over a hundred years ago, and was considered to be both prestigious and mysterious," Breck said. "But there are no membership lists because it's secret and all. I figured I could go back to the beginning and find a charter or something. Then I could follow the breadcrumbs going forward to the present."

Wade looked thoughtful. "If they incorporated or filed as a charitable organization under a different name to hide their secret origin, you could research them through public records to see if they have any current members. It's a long shot, but there's some potential."

Nina pulled into the AIT parking lot. "The AIT Sphinx Society might be a secret club, but I don't see why it's not listed in the school's archives."

"I'm sure it is," Breck said. "The problem is that when you go back more than fifty years, the archives are either on microfiche or contained in original documents that haven't been scanned yet. Many of the older texts and papers haven't been converted to downloadable files."

Kent sat up straight. "Are you saying it's going to take a hand search in the school library to find it?"

"The original society charter might never have been transferred to microfiche," Breck said. "It could still be in a dusty old tome somewhere."

"I love dusty old tomes," Kent said. "I can help you search."

Nina almost did a double take. She had trouble imagining a former Navy SEAL sitting at a library study carrel, poring over scholarly volumes. Then she considered his black plastic–framed glasses and remembered that he had an advanced degree in psychology and had mastered four languages. Perhaps Kent, like her, had a touch of nerd buried deep down.

Breck grimaced. "Hazel's already waiting for me at the think tank this morning. He's supposed to bring in a memory chip from one of the AIT cams so I can put it through one of the readers I brought with me."

Nina glanced at Kent in the rearview. "I'll help you at the library. It'll go faster if we work together."

"Perfect," Breck said to Kent. "I'll send you a link to what I found so far. It'll give you a place to start."

Kent pulled out his cell and began scanning his screen while they planned out their morning. A few minutes later, Nina pulled into a parking space near the computer science building. After they got out, Breck handed over the electronic library card Hazel had provided before hoisting the shoulder bag with her laptop and heading for the think tank with Wade.

"Give me a holler if you turn up anything interesting," Breck called out to them.

It took Nina and Kent only five minutes to get to the library at the center of the quad.

"This is such a beautiful building," Nina said, looking up at the glass ceiling as they made their way into the expansive foyer.

"Breck suggested we try the physical volumes first," Kent said. "There's a floor map that should tell us where the archives are located."

Scanning a freestanding interactive map posted near the entrance, they spotted the archives on the lower level in the southeast corner of the building.

Kent gestured to a sign indicating food and drinks weren't allowed. "Good thing we had our coffee at the hotel."

"Guess they don't want spillage and crumbs on their irreplaceable antique books," Nina said, pushing through a set of double doors with a placard indicating they had reached the physical archives. "Understandable."

They were greeted by a sight Nina hadn't seen in a long time. Row upon row of towering floor-to-ceiling shelves, filled with books of every size and color. When Nina pulled a volume out at random, she noted its yellowed pages and cracked binding.

"I feel like we should be wearing gloves or something," she said to Kent.

"Because we should," he said wryly, holding up two pairs of white cotton gloves. "They were in a box by the door."

Feeling a bit sheepish for missing the small table holding containers of gloves, she pulled on the smaller of the two pairs. "Do we look under *s* for *secret societies*?" she asked Kent. "Or how about *e* for *Egypt*?"

He pointed over her shoulder. "We look there."

She turned to see four shelving units filled with black leather volumes. "They're in chronological order, one for each year." She walked over to the shelf, pulled out the first one—dated 1916—and carefully opened it. "The school was still under construction," she said, making her way to a nearby table to sit and read.

"The society may not have formed until after the university officially opened," Kent said. "So I'll take 1917, and we'll keep alternating after that."

They read in silence beside one another for a quarter of an hour, each occasionally rising to get another volume.

"I've got something," Nina said, tapping a paragraph in one of the books.

Kent leaned sideways to look. "That's it. The Sphinx Society was formed in 1919 by a group of five professors."

Nina read the caption underneath an iconic photograph of the Sphinx on the Giza plateau. "Funny. There are no pictures or names of the founding members. Their stated objective was to determine how the pyramids were built."

"Makes sense," Kent said. "AIT has always been a tech school, and the ancient Egyptians were highly technologically advanced. There are many theories, but no one is a hundred percent sure how they managed to construct the pyramids thousands of years ago."

"It's called slave labor," Nina said, not troubling to hide her disdain.

"Hundreds, if not thousands, of people were involved in various parts of the process," Kent said. "But many academics and scientists still debate exactly how they quarried, transported, cut, and placed megalithic stones so precisely with the tools available to them at the time."

"I thought they used ramps and pulleys."

"That's been the prevailing theory," Kent said. "And archaeologists have uncovered evidence of that at other sites, but not on the Giza plateau." He paused. "I've been reading up on ancient Egypt every chance I get, and I ran across another hypothesis that they covered the pyramid with sand as they laid the stones, building up the ground to make slopes for the next layer, then excavated the entire structure when they were finished."

"Smart," Nina said. "That would also leave no trace behind."

"We need to think like the Sphinx Society's founding members," Kent said, his expression thoughtful. "Back in 1919, scientists and historians knew even less about pyramid construction than they do now. There's been a persistent theory dating back more than a hundred years that arcane physics were used to accomplish the task."

Nina raised a brow at him. "Arcane physics?"

"Some theorists still believe the builders had the ability to alter the mass of objects by manipulating their subatomic structure, allowing enormous stones to be moved in a way we can't today."

She gave him a dubious look. "That's . . . interesting."

Kent seemed to share her skepticism. "Apparently, some people don't want to believe the pyramids were constructed using ordinary means—and extraordinary effort."

"Don't they wonder why no one builds them anymore?" She blew out a frustrated sigh. "It takes massive amounts of resources and time. If it could be done by manipulating matter, I don't think they'd have let the knowledge die."

"You can imagine how the idea of that kind of secret would interest a group of elite scientists from the turn of the last century. If they could replicate the process, it would invalidate foundational theories from Newtonian physics to quantum mechanics."

"You act like it was some sort of noble quest for wisdom," she said. "I have a more cynical view. These original professors announced their intention to study the science and engineering behind the pyramids— which, as you pointed out, made sense for a tech university. But if they really believed in the arcane physics theory, I think they wanted to keep their names and any progress they made secret for a more worldly reason."

He seemed to catch on. "Money."

She nodded. "If they figured out a way to defy the laws of physics, they would be at the Patent Office within the hour. Everyone would have to pay them to use the new technology."

"So it was a race," he said. "Their plan was to solve the mystery before anyone else and become the richest men on the planet."

"The only mystery I'm interested in solving right now is the identity of our unsub." She glanced back at the book. "Let's get this information to Breck and let her chase it down. The bad news is that there seems to be no other mention of the society or any name change for the group, so I'm not sure what she'll be able to find in public records."

She took out her cell and took a picture of the page to text to Breck, making sure to include the volume number and location of the original source.

Kent looked thoughtful. "Now that we know where to look, maybe we can find some of the later volumes on microfiche. The Sphinx Society's scheme obviously didn't work out for them, so perhaps they quit after a few fruitless decades. If we learned they disbanded in the fifties, we could end that line of investigation."

Nina saw his point. "It would be a hell of a lot faster than going through the physical books page by page." She glanced around. "Are the microfiche terminals somewhere in here?"

"According to the library map, they're down the hall," Kent said.

They carefully placed the books back on the shelves and strolled down the hall, glancing at the placards on the closed doors in the silent space.

"This has to be it," Nina said when they reached the end of the corridor. Kent looked over her shoulder at a sign that indicated digital archives. She twisted the knob, walked inside, and came to an abrupt halt.

The scene before her stole the air from her lungs.

Kent bumped into her from behind.

They both froze.

The body of a nude young woman lay stretched out on a meeting table the size of a standard door. Her pale hands were folded over her chest, clutching a black feather, and a leather jess circled her ankle.

Nina had no trouble recognizing Melissa Campbell—even in death.

Chapter 32

Within minutes of Nina's phone call to the think tank, waves of law enforcement personnel had rushed to the scene. Perez had made an announcement over the intercom to evacuate the library without specifying the reason. His fellow PPD officers scanned the student and employee ID cards of everyone as they left the building. Fortunately, only a handful of people had chosen to spend an early Thursday morning during spring break in the library.

Nina had left Kent to watch over the body while she guided her fellow agents, crime scene techs, and PPD detectives from the eerily deserted atrium down the stairs to the bowels of the building. She ushered them inside the digital-archive room, where Melissa appeared peaceful in death—Sleeping Beauty waiting for a kiss that would never come.

PPD technicians in white coveralls immediately started to take photographs documenting the placement of every item before disturbing it. Nina could go no farther without risking contaminating the scene. Instead, she and the rest of the task force members lined the walls inside the room to study the evidence from a distance.

"Definitely Melissa Campbell," Kent said to no one in particular.

"Look at her left ankle," Nina said. "Same leather jess as the others. And the same ostrich plume over her heart."

"Melissa's body looks fresh, and not preserved in any way," Wade said, looking at the supine victim with a trained eye. "We'll get an approximate time of death soon enough, but I'm guessing she was alive until quite recently, which is why she wasn't lying on the altar in the mine with the others."

The weight of responsibility that always came with investigating murders descended on Nina. If they had been able to make headway faster, perhaps they could have saved Melissa. Now another family would receive the news everyone dreaded. She recalled Mrs. Campbell at the press conference. The woman had been so miserable, so distraught. Nina did not envy Perez for having the task of making the official death notification.

The thought brought her attention to the detective. "Did you make sure no one is talking about this over the police radio?" she asked Perez.

"Already done," he said. "The protocols have been in place since the last bodies were found."

"I know the coroner is still working through the other autopsies," Wade said. "But can we move Melissa to the front of the line? We can get fresher evidence from her at this point."

"I'll put in a request," Perez said.

Nina turned to Hazel. "When is the last time we can verify this room was empty?"

"We have an officer assigned specifically to the library," Hazel said. "He does a sweep through every room at midnight when the building closes. This room was empty at that time."

"When does the library open?"

"Eight in the morning," Hazel said.

Nina glanced at her watch. "We found the body at eight thirty, so that narrows down the window to eight and a half hours."

"One of the detectives on my squad will take your official statements," Perez said, looking from Nina to Kent.

Nina mentally added writing a report to document the discovery of Melissa's body and everything else they had learned this morning to her list of things to do.

"Time to pose the biggest question," Kent said, addressing the group. "How did he get her in here without anyone noticing?"

After a few beats of silence, Hazel spoke. "Stuffed her in a crate and rolled her in using a dolly?"

"Lowered her down through a hole in the glass ceiling?" Breck said, sarcasm evident in her tone.

Breck's comment reminded Nina of their previous discussion about surveillance. "Did we get those new cams up?"

"Not all of them," Breck said. "But we definitely got the ones around the quad installed, which means we'll be able to see everything that went on last night from every angle around this entire building."

"Can you access it from your laptop right now?" Nina didn't want to wait to get back to the think tank for answers.

"On it." Breck left the room to set up her laptop in one of the study carrels outside the door.

Within minutes, Nina heard Breck cursing, and she went in search of her colleague.

Breck, who had taken a seat at the partitioned desk, glanced up from her screen. "I've checked every video feed going back to midnight."

"And?" Nina pressed as the rest of her team gathered around behind her to listen in.

"And no one entered or left the library after the campus police officer secured the doors," Breck said.

"The video files weren't corrupted or tampered with?" Nina asked.

"These are FBI cameras." Breck tapped her chest lightly. "I personally oversaw the installation and set up the safeguards. They were not compromised."

"Which means the killer was already in the library with the victim before closing," Kent said. "He must have hidden inside until after the body was discovered, then left during the evacuation process." He glanced around. "Or he could still be hiding in here somewhere. We'll have to keep the building sealed and search the premises."

Perez slid out his cell phone and tapped the screen. "I'm texting the commander to request more personnel."

"I'll expand the timeframe on the video," Breck said. "I can start reviewing footage six hours before and after the window to see who came and went and what time."

"Make it twelve," Wade said. "We don't want to miss anything."

"That'll take a while," Breck said. "I'll get on it right away."

Satisfied the surveillance system hadn't been hacked, Nina looked at Hazel, who had left the digital archives room to join the group. "Does the library have motion detectors inside?"

"There's never been a need," he said. "Like I told you before, this has always been a safe school. The crime rate is almost zero."

"Until now," Perez said. "Is the campus police officer who checked the building last night still on duty?"

"His shift ended this morning," Hazel said. "He's at our headquarters building writing his report right now. I told him not to go home until dismissed. Assumed you all would want to interview him."

"We'll split up," Wade said. "Kent and I can speak to the officer while Guerrera goes back to the think tank to review the video with Breck. There could be something we missed."

"I'll compare our video to the AIT feed to see if there are any discrepancies," Breck said from her seat at the carrel. "If the unsub used a power surge to interfere with their cam system last night, I might be able to trace the source."

"Good idea," Wade said. "Dr. Feldman and his team maintain the cloud that stores the video. Have him lock down the files so only law enforcement can access them or view them going forward." He paused as if considering his next move. "And put a new encryption on the system that keeps everyone out, including Feldman. He's not going to like it, but I don't want anyone messing with the cyber portion of our investigation."

"While you all are doing that, I'll notify the next of kin before they hear about it on social media," Perez said. "The students don't know why the library was evacuated, but it's been my experience that word always gets out somehow."

"I'll make arrangements to secure this building as a crime scene until the search is over and PPD detectives advise me they're finished here," Hazel said. "Then I need to brief the chancellor."

Nina started to leave, then paused to ask Wade a question. "Didn't you say you believed the murders were serial in nature?" When he raised a questioning brow, she clarified, "That he didn't keep the first five alive and kill them all at the same time?"

Wade nodded. "From the decomp rates of the bodies, it appears the women's deaths were spread out over a period of weeks or months, but we can't be sure how much time passed between their murders until the autopsies are complete."

"I agree," Nina said, not liking where the conclusion took her. "Now that he's killed Melissa, does that mean he's selected a new target?"

Wade regarded her a long moment before he spoke. "If he hasn't already found his next victim, he's on the hunt."

Chapter 33

Nina stood in the think tank, studying the virtual pin map that took up half the display wall. She reviewed the physical evidence while Breck sat at the table, working with Dr. Feldman and Rick on the digital aspects of the investigation.

They had already locked down the AIT cloud and provided the passcode, but Breck had chosen to wait to inform the professor he would be excluded from the system until after they received final authorization from the chancellor.

"Look at that," Rick said, pointing at the other side of the display wall. "He did it again."

Nina's gaze shifted to where Feldman's assistant had indicated. A grid of thirty video feeds had turned from pictures of the AIT campus to gray static.

"What's the time stamp on that interference?" Feldman asked.

"One o'clock in the morning," Breck said. "On the dot."

"Like maybe it was preprogrammed for the top of the hour," Rick said. "Which means it could have been a worm set to activate at that specific time."

Nina looked at Breck. "Can you source the origin of the surge or the virus?"

"I sure as hell intend to try," Breck said, tapping the controls on the panel set into the table in front of her. "Dammit," she said a few moments later. "This trail of breadcrumbs is going Hansel and Gretel on me. Virtual crows are gobbling them up before I can follow them anywhere."

"Let me try," Feldman said, edging closer to Breck, who refused to move.

"I'm sorry, Dr. Feldman," Breck said. "I can't let you do that. We're restricting access to the AIT server and cloud storage until I have a chance to run this lead down."

"I can't access a system that my department maintains?" he said. "We'll see what the chancellor has to say about—"

"The chancellor is already on board," Nina said, bluffing. Hazel was supposed to get her approval during his briefing.

"This is an outrage." Feldman shot to his feet. "I've been helping with this investigation long before you all showed up, and suddenly I'm not welcome. It's tantamount to an accusation." He started for the door to the computer lab and turned to Rick. "Let's go."

Breck heaved a sigh and got back to work, her hands flashing with blurring speed as she spoke. "This trail disintegrates faster the more I go. There's no way to follow it, so I'm going to find out whether it was a virus or a surge that interfered."

Within minutes, Breck had confirmed her initial diagnosis. The camera system had been briefly disrupted by a surge, then reinstated an hour later when the power pulse stopped. It had not been caused by a Trojan horse virus or a worm.

"Now we know he placed the body between one and two in the morning," Nina said. "I know what Wade told you to do, but can we focus the feed from the FBI cams during that hour and thirty minutes on either side of it before we go through twelve hours of raw footage?"

Breck was on her laptop an instant later. "I can't put it up on the AIT system without compromising our internal server, but you're welcome to look at my screen while I run through a high-speed scan."

Nina took her up on the offer. "There's no sign of anyone approaching or leaving the library during that time window," she said, peering at Breck's screen over her shoulder. "I'd love to believe they've perfected a teleportation device or cloaking technology at AIT, but that can't be the case. We're going to have to go through half a day's worth of material on all the cameras."

"Here's a random question," Breck said. "If he had the ability to come and go without appearing on surveillance equipment, why would he bother to scramble the feed?"

Nina took a stab at an answer. "He didn't want us to know he wasn't showing up on camera."

"Exactly," Breck said. "And why wouldn't he want us to be aware of that?" When Nina failed to respond, she answered her own question. "Because it would eliminate certain possibilities, focusing our efforts and bringing us closer to the truth."

"Which is what?"

"I don't know yet, but I can finally lay a trap." Breck seemed to relish what she clearly perceived as a challenge. "Last night, I managed to create a subroutine that will send an alert to my cell phone when a surge goes through the system. I can't trace the origin after the fact, because the artifacts of the code are erased when I try to detect them." She frowned. "Unfortunately, I haven't installed it yet, but I'll stand a much better chance of following the trail in real time while the surge is going through the system from this point on."

Nina caught her excitement. "And we could flood the campus with boots on the ground if we knew precisely when he took down the cameras. We could catch him in the act . . . and save his next target." The idea was brilliant. "Can you install the program now?"

Breck slid her a look. "Yes, as soon as I have unfettered control of this server."

Unwilling to wait any longer, Nina pulled out her cell phone and tapped in Lieutenant Hazel's number.

"Hazel here."

Nina got right to the point. "Did the chancellor authorize us to take over the AIT server and cloud storage and lock it down?"

"When I told her about Melissa's body in the library, she got pretty upset," Hazel said. "She agreed without hesitation. She's already announced that students won't return from spring break," he added. "Now she's considering shutting down the entire university and sending everyone home immediately."

Nina had mixed feelings. She didn't want another student taken, but she felt they finally had a way to capture the suspect before he carried out his next crime. She also figured he might simply shift to abducting young women in the city, which would be exponentially more difficult to prevent or detect.

"When will she decide?" Nina asked.

"She's got a virtual meeting with the board in twenty minutes," Hazel said. "I'm waiting outside her office now to provide a final update before she goes online. I should have an answer within the hour."

Nina disconnected and gave Breck a thumbs-up. "Lock it down."

Breck began typing commands. "Hostile takeover complete," she said a minute later.

Watching her colleague's computer maneuvers reminded Nina of an earlier conversation. "You mentioned a program you had running in the background," she said to Breck. "The one that's supposed to reconstruct the AIT video from the night Melissa Campbell was taken. Is it finished?"

Breck's head popped up. "Finding Melissa Campbell distracted me a bit." She minimized the screen she was working on, and the wall screen shifted to another view.

"Well, I'll be," Breck said. "It's done."

Nina held her breath as Breck clicked on the file icon. A moment later, grainy footage of the campus filled the screen.

"Why is it blurry?" Nina asked. "I thought the program was supposed to clean it up."

"It was raining that night," Breck said. "That could be part of the problem. Give it a sec," she said, then pointed. "Look at that."

Melissa entered the frame, walking under an umbrella with a man.

"Freeze it," Nina said.

Breck clicked the mouse and sucked in a breath.

The man was an AIT campus police officer.

Chapter 34

Nina stared at Breck. "Our unsub is an AIT cop?"

Breck grimaced. "That would explain a few things."

"Like how he's been getting away with it for so long," Nina said. "He knows the campus and has full access to every building." She put a hand on her hip. "And who wouldn't trust a police officer to walk them back to their dorm after dark?"

"He can also mess with the security system." Breck paused. "Or at least, he could before. He's locked out as of now."

"I couldn't make out his face enough to recognize him," Nina said. "Can you clean up the feed a bit more?"

"We're lucky to have isolated this single image from all the static." She shook her head. "Between the hat, the umbrella, and the rain, there's never a clear shot of his head. If I try to use algorithms to fill in missing pieces of his facial features, I might inadvertently cause the program to misinterpret the data and create an inaccurate depiction."

"Don't do that," Nina said. "For now, it's enough to know we're dealing with a cop."

"What cop are we dealing with?" Wade asked, walking into the room with Kent.

Nina jerked her chin at the wall screen. "Breck was able to get a partial visual of the person who was with Melissa right before she disappeared," she said.

"There's no record of a campus police officer marking out on an escort that night," Kent said. "We checked."

"Which means he intentionally didn't call in his whereabouts to the dispatcher because he didn't want it on record," Wade said.

Another thought occurred to Nina. "Or he was only posing as a cop."

"We should start with the assumption that he was an officer with the AIT PD," Wade said. "That will give us a limited pool of candidates to work with. If it doesn't pan out, we start over."

Breck dragged a hand through her hair. "How do we investigate an entire police department?"

"We use our profile to narrow the field," Wade said. "But first, we need to know exactly who's in that field." He glanced at Breck. "Does that list of AIT employees and students you ran against the falconer database break the names down by position?"

She nodded. "I can isolate everyone affiliated with the campus police."

"We've got a problem," Nina said. "Hazel is with the chancellor. It won't be long until he comes back here. Do we loop him in?"

"Hazel's the acting chief of police right now," Wade said. "Who better to inform us about the personnel in his department?"

"You've made my point for me," Nina said. "When someone he supervises falls under suspicion, he could take it as a direct reflection on his leadership."

"I get it," Breck said. "Someone in charge—especially a seasoned investigator like Hazel—should know if a murderer is working for him."

"Not necessarily," Wade said. "Law enforcement agencies around the world have faced the same issue. It's rare, but every so often, someone who has no business with a gun and badge manages to commit crimes without anyone noticing."

"I agree with Guerrera," Kent said. "Judging by his personality, Hazel is the type who would take offense."

"And what if he's bucking for the chief's job?" Nina added. "It certainly wouldn't improve his chances if it turned out he overlooked a serial killer in his unit."

"Interesting you mention the chief," Kent said. "Too bad he's away on vacation. His position makes him several levels removed from the line officers Hazel works with every day. It's not that different from the military. Being in the trenches together forms bonds."

Nina, who was the only one in the group with a background as a street cop, appreciated the point. "Hazel might try to defend his colleagues or let his personal feelings color his perceptions. He might not be able to give us a totally accurate and unbiased opinion about them."

"Let's say Hazel gives us the straight scoop on his people," Breck said. "He still might inadvertently tip off a potential suspect by acting differently around them."

Wade raised his hands in mock surrender. "Okay, I'm outvoted. We won't show all our cards to Hazel for the time being. When he gets here, I'll ask him to go back to the library to meet with the PPD detectives. He can verify that the building was searched in case the suspect is still hiding inside. When the PPD supervisor tells him they're ready to release the scene, I'll suggest that he might want to personally go through and check for any materials that may have been left behind by the crime scene techs before taking down the yellow perimeter tape and opening the building for general use."

Nina appreciated the ploy. "That should keep him busy awhile. In fact, Kent and I are supposed to give statements to members of Perez's Homicide squad."

"And we still have to fill out our Bureau paperwork," Kent added.

"We'll take care of that and keep working until Hazel reports back here," Wade continued. "At which point I'll call it a day. We can go to the hotel and continue to review the files privately."

"What about Perez?" Kent asked.

Wade stroked his jaw. "He's not with the AIT police, and he's the lead detective on the case. We need to share what we have with him."

Breck nodded. "I'll text him to come to the Phoenix Royal Suites as soon as he's finished meeting with Melissa Campbell's family."

"This investigation has taken another bizarre turn," Wade said. "And I'm determined to be ahead of the curve for the next one."

Chapter 35

Three hours later, Nina crossed the room to answer the knock at the door between the interconnected suites. As they had planned, Wade closed up shop as soon as Hazel returned to the think tank to report that the library had been reopened. The team had gone straight to the hotel to prepare for a long night's work.

Expecting to find Kent or Wade on the other side of the door, she was surprised to see Perez looking down at her.

He raised a dark brow. "Based on that cryptic text Breck sent, it sounds like the FBI has been holding out on me."

He stepped aside and Nina walked past him into Wade and Kent's suite, Breck close on her heels. Wade and Kent were seated at a grouping of furniture surrounding a coffee table. Nina noticed several take-out bags piled in the middle.

"Figured we'd be working through dinner," Perez said, taking a seat on the sofa. "Brought some grub from my favorite Thai place."

Until that moment, Nina hadn't realized they'd worked straight through lunch.

"That's a safe bet." Wade, who was sitting in the lone wingback chair, leveled his gaze on Perez. "We weren't deliberately keeping you in the dark, Detective. In fact, we only made this discovery a few hours ago while you were at the morgue with the family."

"What did you find out?" Perez asked, opening a bag and lifting the containers out one at a time.

"Hold on a sec and I'll show you," Breck said.

While she perched on the love seat beside Kent and rested her laptop on her knees before opening it, the others picked up white cartons at random. Nina opened hers and was pleased to see that she had scored some tasty-looking pad thai. She picked up a set of chopsticks and plunged them into the mass of noodles.

She noticed Kent seize a piece of chicken covered in peanut sauce from his carton while Wade dug through a steaming pile of vegetables.

While they were foraging, Breck had been busying herself with her computer. After another minute, she placed it on the coffee table, turning it toward Perez.

"Recognize anyone?" she asked him.

Perez put down his carton and squinted at the screen. "That's Melissa Campbell." He leaned closer. "Wait. This is from the night she disappeared, isn't it?" He got confirmation from Breck and studied the image again. "Shit. That's a campus police officer with her." He looked up at them. "Who is it?"

"That's the problem," Nina said, sitting down next to Perez on the sofa. "We don't know."

Breck gestured to the laptop. "This grainy picture is the only image I could recover. The uniform and shoulder patch are clear enough, and the body structure indicates it's a man. Unfortunately, he's not wearing a nameplate, and his face is obscured by the hat, the umbrella, and the rain."

"It's also nighttime," Nina added. "And no campus cops marked out on an escort that night. We checked."

"Wait a minute." Perez looked at each of them in turn before he posed his next question. "You all believe the killer is with the AIT police, so why isn't Lieutenant Hazel here with us, going through his employee roster?"

"Breck already has a spreadsheet with all university employees sorted by job description," Wade said, skirting the question. "We were about to start going through their police department."

"I take it you'll use profiling to narrow the list?" Perez asked.

By way of an answer, Wade turned to Breck. "Eliminate all females from the pool." After waiting for her to enter commands, he continued, "Take out everyone who was hired or left their position after the disappearances began."

Nina appreciated the logic. The suspect would be actively working throughout the entire series. He would draw too much attention if he was lurking around the campus after he was let go or before he was employed.

"Next we'll go through their schedules and take out anyone who was traveling out of town during one of the abductions," Kent said.

Nina considered this. "I'm guessing you can't eliminate officers who were either on or off duty, because they could have come to the campus outside of their scheduled shift without attracting attention."

Kent shrugged. "Or they could easily come up with an excuse for being there if questioned."

"That leaves us with three candidates," Breck said a few minutes later, turning the laptop to face the group with a flourish.

They all looked at the names, which were in alphabetical order.

"I can tell you who should be at the top of that list," Perez said quietly. "Lieutenant Stan Hazel."

Chapter 36

Nina studied Perez, whose handsome features had discernibly hardened. "Why do you think Hazel is a good fit?" she asked him. "Don't tell me he's a closet Egyptologist."

"Not that I've heard," Perez said. "But there's stuff about him you don't know."

Kent plopped his take-out container down on the coffee table. "And you're just telling us about this?" He leaned forward. "He's been beside us the whole time. Did you ever stop to think we should know something's up with him? We work with hundreds of law enforcement officers. We can't investigate them all."

"It has to do with Hazel's background on the PPD," Perez said. "And I didn't mention it because it had nothing to do with missing girls, sexual assault, or any kind of violent crime."

Nina was baffled. "Then what makes you suspect him at this point?" she asked.

"Once Breck narrowed the list to three, everything clicked when I saw his name," Perez said. "I didn't make the connection until now."

"Let's hear it, Perez," Breck said, closing her computer and picking up a set of chopsticks from the coffee table. "What do you know about Hazel that we don't?"

"For starters, he took an early retirement from the PPD ahead of being fired," Perez said. "Two years ago, he failed a urine test."

"Drugs?" Nina asked.

Perez frowned. "He and a small group of officers were juicing. They all went down."

Nina recalled how Hazel had seemed muscular, especially for a man in his fifties. "He was taking steroids." She made it a statement rather than a question.

Perez nodded. "Hazel was a narc before he transferred to robbery. He used his contacts to find a source. No one knows how long it had been going on until he failed a random drug test."

"He could have been compensating," Wade said. "He's a big guy now, but I wonder what he looked like when he was eighteen years old, like most of the victims."

Nina, who had done a temp assignment in narcotics enforcement while she was still a police officer, thought about logistics rather than psychology. "Hazel would be comfortable handling drugs," she said. "He could distill jimsonweed and would know how to properly dose the victims according to their body weight."

Breck straightened in her chair. "He knows all about the surveillance cameras. He could have been sabotaging the video feeds the whole time he pretended to be helping." She touched her fingertips to her mouth. "He could have used the system to select and stalk his victims ahead of time."

Nina put more puzzle pieces into place. "He would be familiar with security protocols, could access any building, and would also know how to cover his tracks after his crimes were committed."

"Remember his reaction when we asked about involving the Phoenix police at our first briefing?" Kent said, catching her excitement. "Hazel blamed it on the chancellor, but I detected some hostility toward his old department."

"There was bad blood when he left us," Perez said. "Hazel thought he got railroaded, and there are some officers who agree."

"Do you know if he's married?" Wade asked Perez.

"Divorced four times," Perez said. "Whenever anyone asked him why he kept walking down the aisle, he used to joke that he liked the taste of wedding cake."

"Inability to maintain a stable relationship," Kent said to Wade. "Works in a male-dominated profession and enhances the hypermasculinity further with the use of steroids."

"Like I mentioned earlier," Wade said in agreement. "He's compensating."

"Are you two saying he fits your profile?" Nina asked, cutting through the psychobabble.

"He does," Wade said. "But I'd like to know more about his background."

"Let's pull him in for an interview tomorrow," Perez said. "I know him well enough to get a good read."

"But he doesn't like you," Kent said. "I can tell."

"I've interviewed plenty of people who don't like me," Perez said.

"I can believe that," Kent muttered.

Wade stopped the debate with a raised hand. "I recommend we wait." He directed this comment to Perez, who technically was in charge, since the PPD had the case and he was the lead detective.

Perez regarded Wade a long moment before speaking. "We don't have probable cause to arrest. Or to get a search warrant. Or even enough to plant a listening device or a tracker on him. Hell, we can't even hold him for questioning at this point." He crossed his arms. "You want to gather some evidence before we approach him."

"Bingo," Wade said. "If we show our hand too early, he lawyers up and hides anything that might incriminate him."

"He's an experienced interrogator," Nina said. "He'll be tough to crack without anything definitive, and he'll smell a bluff from twenty paces. We need leverage."

"And how are we going to get it?" Breck said.

"We need to conduct a search without a warrant," Kent said. When the others looked at him, he added, "Legally."

Nina raised her index finger. "There are no exigent circumstances." She lifted a second finger. "We're not in hot pursuit." Three more fingers went up as she spoke. "He's not under arrest, nothing is in plain view, or in a vehicle." She shrugged. "We're left with consent, and we don't want to ask him." She put her hand down. "I don't see how this is going to happen."

"You've been a Fed too long," Perez said to her. "Forgot what it's like to be a cop."

She expected him to explain, but he simply watched her, apparently waiting for her to arrive at a different conclusion. Finally, it came to her.

"We search his workspace," she said to Perez, who broke into a broad grin.

"Slow your roll," Kent said. "Wouldn't Hazel have a reasonable expectation of privacy, especially if he has a private office or a locker at the campus police building?"

"That's what he was hinting at." Nina tipped her head toward Perez. "When I joined the police, I signed a form acknowledging that I had no expectation of privacy with any department-issued equipment, including vehicles, lockers, desks, offices, and cell phones." She spread her hands wide. "Internal Affairs, or any supervisor, could search stuff assigned to me any time they wanted—and they didn't need a warrant as long as it was department property."

"Hold on," Breck said, setting down her chopsticks and picking up the laptop again. "I remember seeing something in the AIT personnel files that might do the trick." She tapped the screen and rotated the computer. "There you go."

They all leaned in close. Hazel had signed a form very similar to the one Nina had described.

"I want this buttoned up tight," Wade said. "If we find something, it's got to survive a legal challenge." He directed the next comment at Perez. "You should have the chancellor go on record granting you permission."

"Smart," Perez said. "The chancellor of a public university would have the legal standing to authorize the search, and we would be acting on her behalf."

They were both being cautious. Despite the fact that Hazel had effectively forfeited his right to privacy as a condition of employment, it would be better if someone in control of the property granted formal approval for them to go through it.

Wade turned to Breck. "We'll confiscate his computer if it was issued to him by the university, but don't access it until we get a search warrant."

Nina understood that Wade was hoping to find something incriminating enough to put in an affidavit and take to a judge.

"When do we do this?" Nina asked. "I thought we didn't want to show our cards to Hazel yet."

"We don't have to," Wade said. "Perez will see the chancellor first thing tomorrow morning when she gets to her office. Meanwhile, I'll come up with something to keep Hazel busy." He turned to Perez. "Are your fellow Homicide detectives finished with the crime scene at the mine?"

"They cleared the park about an hour ago," Perez said.

"Could you talk to someone on your squad who might be willing to interview Hazel tomorrow morning?"

"Of course." Perez gave Wade a shrewd look. "What's really going on?"

Wade gave him a rare smile. "Lieutenant Hazel oversaw the investigation for several months before any other law enforcement agencies were called in," he said. "That means his campus police detectives and officers gathered a lot of details that went into their reports."

"And my squad has been reviewing those reports," Perez said, apparently catching on. "They might have questions that could only be answered in a one-on-one interview with the supervisor who oversaw the whole investigation. Hazel, having been a former PPD detective, would understand perfectly."

"We're on the same page." Wade inclined his head in acknowledgment. "I'll ask Hazel to meet with one of your partners first thing tomorrow."

"The Homicide Unit is part of the Violent Crimes Bureau," Perez said. "It's at the headquarters building on West Washington Street, which is only a few blocks away. Hazel will know exactly where to go."

"And while Hazel's doing that, we'll be going through his office and his locker," Nina said.

"I like it," Perez said. "Then, when we interview him later, we'll already have something incriminating to use as leverage."

Wade looked around the room. "Ladies and gentlemen, we have a person of interest, and we have a plan."

Chapter 37

He took a moment to consider his circumstances. Alone in the darkness, as he had been so many times in his life, he reflected on his most recent loss. How had he misjudged Melissa so badly? Did he need to alter his training techniques, or was she just another pretty little liar, playing him all along? He took a sip of his Jack and Coke and recalled another pretty liar from his past.

At seventeen, he still hadn't hit puberty, delaying the development of height and deepening of his voice that would begin over ten months later. His sister, Tabitha, had told him how much she and the other cheerleaders regretted what they had done to him the year before.

Tabitha was a freshman in college and explained that she and her friends planned to go to the homecoming dance at their old alma mater. The gorgeous Kara had just broken up with her boyfriend and had no date. Kara, too, felt bad about teasing him in the past, and hoped he would escort her.

He had been skeptical, of course. What if Tabitha was lying to him—as she often did. But his sister had been so convincing on the phone. It sounded as if she was crying when she explained that taking Psych 101 had taught her how much damage her taunting had done to him during his formative adolescent years. She understood the error of her ways and wanted to make it up to him.

Then Kara had called him. She had been so sweet when she apologized. He imagined himself strutting into the dance with the stunning leggy blonde on his arm. The boy everyone called a geek would go to homecoming with the most beautiful girl.

Head swimming with images of his public triumph, he had agreed.

The warning signs had been there, but his addled teenage brain hadn't processed them. His fantasy had been so pervasive that he hadn't wanted to suspect anything.

He had been about to leave to pick Kara up at her house when Tabitha called to tell him she was already at the dance with Kara and the others. He should bring the wrist corsage he had bought for Kara and meet them there.

Palms sweating on the steering wheel all the way to the school, he had little memory of the drive over. Carefully adjusting his boutonniere, he checked his hair one more time in the car's side mirror before walking into the gymnasium.

He searched the swell of students milling around until he found his sister and her gaggle of friends. He strode toward the group, trying to hide his nerves.

Tabitha finally saw him and gave him a big smile. "Look who it is, everyone," she called out.

He stood rooted to the spot, looking around for Kara. Not seeing her. The small sense of unease that had plagued him began to grow.

"You're looking for your date, right?" Tabitha said in a booming voice designed to capture everyone's attention.

He began to back away.

"Now, don't be shy. She's right here." Tabitha beckoned behind her, and one of her friends opened the side access door at the back of the gym. "She got all dressed up just for you."

He heard the shrieks of laughter before he could make out what was going on. The other students parted to reveal Kara striding in. Her right hand held a rope, which was around the neck of a huge, filthy, snorting sow.

His feet were welded to the floor as he looked on in horror. The other kids were all laughing. Kara kept coming, her lovely face lit with amusement. "Her name is Bessie," Kara said, then angled her head. "Is that corsage for her?" She looked around, addressing the crowd. "Now, isn't that sweet? It matches the bow around her neck. Of course, he'll have a hard time convincing his date not to eat the flowers."

He turned and ran, tears stinging his eyes as hoots of laughter followed him. He cursed his stupidity throughout the entire drive home. Once again, a beautiful young woman had lied to him. Made a fool of him. This time humiliating him in front of the entire school.

And yet he could not settle for a homely, unassuming girl, although he'd tried many times after that night. He had even gone so far as to go on a date with a plain Jane who sat behind him in history class; but in the end, he couldn't bring himself to kiss her. Even with his eyes firmly closed, she repulsed him.

When he was eighteen, his latent masculinity finally asserted itself. He grew eight inches in the space of two and a half years. His voice deepened, finally settling into a rich baritone. Only a few pockmarks remained from the adolescent acne that had ravaged his face and shoulders. He joined the Army, and military training added layers of muscle to his tall frame, hardening him into a man no one would recognize. After a little over four years, he transferred from active duty into the reserves, dividing his time between his chosen profession and his monthly military obligations. His life became more settled, and his time was filled with interesting pursuits.

But he still only coveted the most desirable females. Unfortunately for him, everyone else did too. Even with his newly sculpted physique, women who met his qualifications seemed to sense his insecurity when he asked them out. Despite suffering countless rejections, he would rather remain celibate or pay for sex with someone attractive than lower his standards.

Last summer, he had faced humiliation again when he was deceived by another gorgeous face. That final insult had changed him. In sheer desperation, he found the solution to his problem. He needed to find his soul mate. His other half. That was what was missing. He would use the training provided to him by the military, as well as his own research and skills, to bring it about. Excited beyond anything he had ever felt, he set about making preparations.

First, he would search for her in his environment, which provided plenty of potential candidates. Once he spotted her, he would either bait a trap or lie in wait. Carefully, he would capture her. When he had her under his control, he would train her. He had studied the process. After a time, she would realize she loved him. She would be his fully and completely and would never so much as glance at another man. They could emerge together as a couple. Get married. Build a nest.

Unfortunately, selecting the right mate had proven more difficult than he had imagined. The birds tended to be flighty. It took far more effort to shape their minds, and, as he had found out on more than one occasion, they sometimes still tried to escape long after their training period was over.

Disappointment haunted him, but the military had taught him— among many other useful skills—to never surrender. Adapt, improvise, and overcome. A new plan was the path to success.

And so, he would soldier on.

Chapter 38

An odd sensation gripped Nina as she sat beside Lieutenant Hazel in the think tank the following morning. Was she seated next to a serial killer? He seemed so normal. Then again, she had learned that some people could project a veneer of respectability when their minds were a chaotic tangle of violence.

"Are we waiting on Perez to get started?" Hazel asked Wade, who sat at the head of the conference table.

"Perez is in a briefing with the rest of his Homicide squad," Wade said. "He'll join us later."

They had agreed on the drive over not to tell Hazel that Perez was meeting with the chancellor. He might get concerned that the detective was talking to his boss without his presence and insist on sitting in.

Instead, Wade and Kent had worked out a strategy designed to push Hazel's buttons and test his reactions when provoked in a particular way. They would study his body language to determine whether he had the characteristics Perez had described that might lead him to act out. Nina and Breck had prepared in advance to play their parts in the scenario.

Wade gestured to Kent. "Why don't you brief everyone on the additional profiling you completed last night?"

Kent opened his notebook and glanced down at the top page. "I believe the unsub we are dealing with suffers from sexual inadequacy."

Hazel, who was taking a sip of coffee, spit some of it out and cursed.

"You okay?" Nina handed him a napkin while she gave Kent a surreptitious wink.

Hazel dabbed droplets of brown liquid from the table. "I've heard you profilers come up with extremely specific details about suspects, but how the hell would you know anything about that?"

Kent, who had rolled his shirtsleeves up to his elbows, steepled his fingers. "I spoke to the ME after he finished the final autopsy late last night. According to Dr. Pendergast, some of the victims show signs that inanimate objects were used for sexual penetration."

This wasn't true at all, of course. Wade and Kent wanted to see if Hazel might object or defend the suspect's ability to complete the sex act. Nina studied Hazel but could not tell whether his pinched features expressed anger that someone would do such a thing to the victims or irritation that his own sexual prowess had been thrown into question.

"That led me to conclude that the killer used something more substantial as a substitute for his own underwhelming . . ." Kent hesitated as if searching for the best word. "Manhood."

She knew Kent had chosen that particular term for the same reason he had rolled up his sleeves to put his well-muscled forearms on full display. He was undermining Hazel's sense of masculinity in an effort to provoke a response.

"Or maybe he has a medical problem," Breck said. "Maybe he couldn't . . ." She deliberately trailed off.

"A guy at my gym abused anabolic steroids," Kent said. "He ended up with low testosterone, testicle shrinkage, and erectile dysfunction." He gave his head a small shake. "Poor bastard."

Hazel flushed a deep crimson. "We're getting way off topic. Why don't we discuss how we're going to catch this guy instead of evaluating his sexual performance?"

"Or lack thereof," Kent said, stretching and arching his back until his expansive chest strained the buttons of his shirt. His physique was impressive, and the overt display seemed to annoy Hazel, who glared at him.

Wade's cell phone buzzed, and he glanced at the screen. "That's Perez. Hopefully, he'll have news from his squad." He held it to his ear and listened for half a minute. "Thank you, Detective," he said. "I'll let him know."

He turned to Hazel. "Perez told me they've been going through several months of investigative reports from your detectives. They have some questions and would like to talk to you directly, since you ran the whole operation."

Nina appreciated how Wade had appealed to Hazel's now slightly damaged ego. He would want to be seen as someone in charge.

"Could you head over to the Violent Crimes Bureau?" Wade asked him.

"I'll go there right away," Hazel said, getting to his feet.

Nina noticed he seemed anxious to leave.

As soon as the door closed behind him, Breck raised an inquisitive brow at Kent. "Testicle shrinkage?"

He lifted a shoulder. "It's been known to happen when steroids are overused. The good news is that things usually go back to normal once the guy stops juicing."

Nina looked at Wade. "What did you think?" She wanted a profiler's take on Hazel's behavior.

"Kent scored some hits," Wade said. "Hazel's sense of masculinity is just as fragile as we supposed. I'll be interested to hear from the PPD detectives how he responds to questions about his investigation into the disappearances. With an already bruised ego thanks to our discussion, he may feel threatened, like he's being second-guessed."

"You think he'll still go?" Breck asked.

Wade responded without hesitation. "They're his former colleagues. He'll want to make his case to them as a matter of professional pride."

He cut his eyes to Kent. "And he couldn't get away from the think tank fast enough."

"Did you get a read on him?" Nina pressed. "Is he our unsub?"

"He's at the top of my list," Wade said before delivering the news he'd been holding back until Hazel's departure. "Perez told me the chancellor granted us permission to search anything and anywhere we want," he said. "Time for the second phase of our plan."

Chapter 39

"How much time do you think we have?" Nina tossed the question over her shoulder to both Perez and Kent as they walked into the AIT campus police building.

"I told my partner to make sure they kept Hazel busy for at least an hour," Perez said. "He'll send me a text when Hazel leaves, so we'll have plenty of warning."

"Sounds good," Kent said. "And he'll go back to the think tank when he's done. He'd have no reason to come here."

"Unless one of his officers texts him to let him know we're in his office," Nina said. "We need to get this done fast." She strode to the front desk and pulled out her creds. "Special Agent Nina Guerrera, FBI."

A young woman Nina figured for a rookie officer straightened in her seat behind the plexiglass. "How can I help you, ma'am?"

Nina took full advantage of the imbalance of power. "We need access to the building. The chancellor is expecting a report back from us within the hour."

Flustered, the officer hit a button, and Nina heard a loud buzz, followed by a metallic click.

"The door's open," the officer said. "I have to stay at the front desk, but I can call someone to show you around."

"That won't be necessary," Perez said as he followed Nina through the door. "Thanks."

They walked into the common area, and Nina scanned for a corner office. "There." She looked at her companions. "I'll go through his office. You two can check in the back." She wrinkled her nose. "I have zero interest in seeing what's in a men's locker room."

"We'll both help you first," Kent said. "There will probably be a key in his desk since the lockers are AIT property."

They followed her to the corner office, which had Hazel's name on the open door.

Perez headed for the desk. "We'll look at the other two officers who weren't eliminated by the profile after we're done with Hazel."

"If we have time," Kent muttered as he began pawing through the bookshelf. "They both work the midnight shift, so they're not here right now."

"What's the final decision on his computer?" Perez asked as he looked at an older-model desktop with a connected monitor.

Nina slid out her phone and called Breck. "Do you want us to bring you his computer or leave it here?"

"Bring it to me," Breck said. "I'll work my magic after we get a warrant. In the meantime, he can't erase anything or reformat the hard drive." She paused. "I was just getting ready to call you guys. Something's up with Hazel."

Nina made sure they were alone before putting her on speaker. "We're all listening. What's going on?"

"I've been using the cam system to monitor Hazel's movements. He headed to the parking lot, got into his SUV, then got back out without leaving. He's walking back toward the campus again."

"What was he doing in his vehicle?" Kent asked.

"Couldn't tell," Breck said. "Those windows are tinted super dark."

"Is he headed our way?" Nina asked.

"No," Breck said. "Looks like he's walking toward the north side of the campus. He's moving like he means business."

"Wonder what that's about," Perez said. "He seemed totally on board with going to meet with my squad."

Nina was uneasy. Hazel had seemed eager to meet with PPD Homicide detectives downtown. Perez had arranged to put a tail on him after he left the headquarters building to see if he went anywhere before returning to the AIT campus. Now that Hazel had unexpectedly changed his plans, she was grateful Breck could monitor his movements using the surveillance system.

"Make sure you have eyes on him wherever he goes," Nina said into the phone. "Call me back if he starts heading toward the campus police building." She paused a beat. "We'll expedite our search here."

She disconnected and pulled open the top drawer of the filing cabinet. "Hazel is going to know we were in here, so there's no need to be stealthy. Dig through everything. We're looking for anything from a small telemetry device to an ostrich plume."

They had been searching in silence for several minutes when the young officer from the front desk appeared in Hazel's doorway. "Um, Agent Guerrera?"

Nina glanced up. "What is it?" She hoped Hazel hadn't already gotten wind of their search and rushed to intervene.

"Someone's in the lobby," she said. "When he told me why he was here, I thought he should talk to you guys."

Nina flicked a glance at Perez and Kent, who had stopped what they were doing. If Hazel had returned, the officer would have referred to him as her lieutenant, so this was someone else. Without another word, Nina followed her back through the main area, down a short hallway, and through the locked door that led to the lobby, where Professor Dawson was pacing back and forth.

"It's Bianca," he said as soon as he saw her. "She's missing."

Chapter 40

Nina had to fight the urge to grab Dr. Dawson by the lapels of his tweed jacket. "Bianca?" She heard the burgeoning hysteria in her own voice. "What do you mean she's missing?"

"We were supposed to meet this morning so I could take her on the tour of the campus," Dawson said. "But she never showed."

"When was this?" Kent asked from behind her.

Dawson checked his watch. "About thirty minutes ago."

Nina had already pulled out her cell and tapped the speed dial for Bianca. The call went straight to voice mail. A weight seemed to plunge into the pit of her stomach. She texted a message for her to call back immediately.

"Was she supposed to come to your office?" Perez asked Dawson as Nina put her phone away.

Dawson shook his head. "I told her to meet me at the medical sciences building. I wanted to show her the cadaver-storage unit. I had originally intended for her to tour the grounds, but Bianca had been most interested in seeing our on-site morgue. It's a key component of the research she wants to help with."

Dread filled Nina's mind as she looked at Perez and Kent. "The medical sciences building is on the north side of the campus." She licked her lips, her mouth suddenly dry. "He's there."

She didn't say any more. Didn't need to. Breck had spotted Hazel walking in the direction of the medical sciences building, which was precisely where Bianca had gone at the same time. Now she was missing.

Nina strode to the front door and pushed it open, her shoes clacking on the steps as she headed north. She heard Kent and Perez behind her, urging the professor to accompany them.

"Tell us everything you know," Perez said to Dawson.

"I was running late, grading papers in my office, so I texted Bianca to go inside and wait for me." Dawson lengthened his strides to keep up with the team as they made their way across the quad. "I couldn't find her when I got there, so I went inside and looked around. I called her phone, but it went to voice mail, and my texts were never answered." His voice grew strained. "Someone's out there kidnapping students. Figured I'd better make a report just in case."

She heard Kent talking into his cell phone. "It's me. No, we're not done. Listen, is Hazel back at the think tank?" He waited a beat. "Okay, I can't talk freely right now, but let me know if he shows up. Can you put Breck on the phone?" After another moment, Kent spoke again. "Pull up video feeds from all cameras going back over the last hour," he said to her. "Focus on the medical sciences building. Call me back when you've had a chance to review the footage, and tell me if you see where Bianca went." He paused. "All I can say right now is that she's missing, and that was the last place she was supposed to be." He disconnected.

Nina could see the building coming into view and quickened her pace. She swallowed another wave of fear. "Did you see Lieutenant Hazel?" she asked Dawson.

"No," he said without hesitation. "Do you think he's with her?"

The remark was made lightly, as if Hazel might be chatting with Bianca over a cup of coffee in the student union. Nina's thoughts, however, went to a much darker place as a similar question ran through her mind.

Did Hazel have Bianca?

Chapter 41

Nina had thanked Dr. Dawson and sent him on his way after exchanging cell phone numbers and instructing him to call if he heard from Bianca. They were close to the medical sciences building when Kent halted to tug his buzzing cell phone from his pocket.

"It's Breck," he said.

Torn between a desire to rush headlong into the building and a more sensible need to learn whether Breck had spotted Bianca somewhere else entirely, Nina forced herself to stop.

Breck's southern accent, always stronger when she was under stress, was pronounced. "Y'all are on speaker. Wade's here with me."

"The other person who was with us is gone," Kent said. "You can speak freely. It's just me, Guerrera, and Perez. Have you found any sign of Hazel or Bianca?"

"Hazel's walking toward the think tank now," Wade said. "Breck picked him up a minute ago coming from the direction of the med-sci building."

"There's no continuous video coverage between the two locations," Breck said. "So I can't be sure whether he made any stops in between."

"What about Bee?" Nina asked.

"I can't find her anywhere on campus now," Breck said. "But I reviewed the video from forty minutes ago when she arrived at the med-sci building. I'm sending you an edited file, and you can watch it."

Nina and Perez crowded around Kent, who tapped the icon. Within a second, Nina saw Bianca walk into frame. She moved to the front of the med-sci building, then entered.

Nina recalled that Dawson said he'd texted Bianca to go inside and wait for him.

Nina's stomach lurched when Hazel strode into view, walking along the same trajectory as Bianca. Like her, he entered through the front of the building. Breck had edited the footage, which sped ahead several minutes, slowing to normal speed when Hazel reappeared. He left the main entrance and made his way around the outside of the building. He appeared to be looking for someone. He repeated the process around the cadaver-storage facility, which was attached to the main building. He walked off in the direction he had come, his steps unhurried.

The feed sped up again, slowing when Dr. Dawson walked into frame. He went inside the med-sci building, exiting a short time later and heading in the direction of the AIT police building.

"We just watched it," Kent said into the phone. "Is that all?"

"Affirmative," Breck said. "Bianca never left the building."

Nina had heard all she needed to. "She's still in there, then. I'm going to get her."

"We're requesting assistance from PPD to help search the building," Wade said. "And the rest of the campus. We'll lock everything down."

Like they had done when Melissa disappeared. And none of it had done a damn bit of good.

"Tell the PPD we're already inside," Nina said. "I'm not waiting for them to arrive."

"Hazel's almost at the front door of the think tank," Wade said. "Breck will continue to monitor the cameras for any sign of Bianca while I interview the lieutenant. You three go ahead and start the search; we'll advise PPD you're in there."

Nina was already marching up the steps leading into the building before Kent disconnected. She reflected on how they had analyzed the killer's patterns and behavior. She had convinced herself not to worry about Bianca, who did not fit the suspect's target demographic. She was not an AIT student, was almost never alone, and didn't hang around campus after dark.

None of it had mattered.

Then another thought occurred to her. A truly disturbing thought. The team had deliberately upset Hazel in the think tank. They had challenged his masculinity, riling him up until he was red in the face; then they had sent him out.

The guided missile they had armed and activated had found its own target.

Bianca.

Chapter 42

Field Notes

Day	Observation	Water 💧	Food 🍎	Strategy 🧭
Melissa Campbell				
1	Capture went smoothly; nausea from sedation; no other ill effects	None	None	Withhold all stimuli and continue observation
2	Very distressed; may have minor injury to left index finger	None	None	Observe how she moves finger; plan for first contact; attempt drinking
3	Accepted water from mouth after minimal hesitancy; is learning to trust	8 ounces water	None	Wait another day to introduce feeding
4	Feeding by mouth initially successful. Subject displayed overt signs of rejection.	8 ounces water	3 chicken nuggets	

Bianca Babbage			
1	Capture went smoothly; adjusted ziptie, subject is smaller than the others	None	None	Active search ongoing; move up timetable or wait 24 hours for initial contact.

Chapter 43

Bianca moaned, the noise reverberating off the walls in what sounded like a crypt. Her systems were slowly coming online, and she felt cold and nauseated. She forced her eyes open, but the impenetrable darkness would not subside. A moment later, she sensed pressure around her head. She was blindfolded. Shoulder aching from lying on her side, she tried to sit up, only to realize her hands were secured behind her.

When she squirmed, plastic strips bit into her wrists. A sensory memory surfaced from a dark place in her past, and she recognized the feeling.

Someone had zip-tied her hands behind her back.

She had been thirteen the last time she felt the pinch of reinforced nylon digging into her flesh. Her foster father had tied her hands together and locked her in the basement after police caught her sleeping on the street. Every time cops showed up to take a missing juvenile report or bring her back, her foster parents risked discovery of their illegal grow operation. They had promised her she would meet with a fatal accident if she ran again, which she did the very next night.

The night she had met Nina Guerrera. The night everything had changed.

The total isolation, the bone-chilling cold, the abject terror—all of it took her back to the time she had spent in her foster parents' basement. Panic closed in, and she screamed for help, her voice echoing off the walls until silence descended once again. With a gathering sense of dread, she realized Nina could not rescue her. This time, she was on her own.

Head bleary, she struggled to focus her thoughts. The last thing she could clearly recall was walking toward the medical sciences building. Had she gone inside? She couldn't remember. Aware she had been drugged, and that some substances caused memory loss, she realized that whoever had been kidnapping and killing students must have taken her, and her pulse kicked into overdrive.

She willed herself to calm down. Nina had taught her panic was the enemy. She recalled how Nina's dark eyes had glittered with rage when she'd seen the flex-cuff marks on Bianca's wrists. Nina had promised to teach her how to escape so she would never be tied up and helpless again.

Later that week, Nina had come home with rope, duct tape, and flex-cuffs. She had explained each of their weaknesses, and they had not stopped practicing until Bianca could defeat all of them.

That had been five years ago. Could she still do it now? First, she had to sit up to move her arms freely. She tucked into a ball and rolled her body around until she was perched on her knees. She knew that pulling against the nylon cord binding her hands was useless. Instead, she had to do what Nina had taught her and break the zip ties at the locking mechanism, which was their weakest point.

She steadied herself, experimentally lifting her arms higher behind her back and lowering them. Fortunately, she was flexible, and could raise her bound hands about ten inches. That was all she needed. The rest came down to physics. She would leverage velocity and momentum to generate force.

Sucking in a breath, she clenched her hands into fists, raised them away from her body, and then mustered all her strength to bring them down hard against her lower back. A loud *snap* rewarded her effort as the plastic lock popped open, freeing her wrists.

She immediately whipped off the blindfold and blinked rapidly, forcing her eyes to focus. Finally, she made out a room—no, a cell—made of bare cinder block walls and a poured-cement floor with a circular drain the size of a CD in the center. A bare bulb dangled from the ceiling overhead, providing the only light.

The room spun. She reached out to steady herself and saw that her pale slender arm was bare. She was completely naked.

Just like the missing girls. The dead girls.

Her clothes, book bag, watch, and cell phone were gone. She was completely isolated, with no idea where she was or how much time had passed. There was no escape. She was the prisoner of a murderer.

Terror bloomed, and she felt as if the air around her had thickened until she could barely get enough into her lungs. She opened her mouth wide and sucked in another gasp. A blast of hot bile shot up through her throat, and she leaned forward to expel it onto the drain. The sickening sound of liquid splattering onto the perforated steel made her queasy stomach seize again.

She scanned the room in search of an exit, and her eyes fell upon a metal door. She scrambled toward it and was stopped short by something around her ankle.

She glanced down to see a leather band with a metal ring attached to a braided-leather cord secured to an eyebolt in the cement floor. Tethered within about a six-foot radius, she couldn't reach the walls or door. Instead, she scrutinized its surface. There was no doorknob, latch, or handle. No way to open it from the inside. She looked along its edges. No visible hinges for her to remove. She was trapped.

Perhaps her fate was already sealed. Whatever substance had rendered her unconscious might yet kill her if it was a type of slow-acting poison.

She searched her memory banks and came up without any pertinent data. Besides, she seemed to feel a bit better with each passing minute, not worse. The logic reminded her that her captor had taken everything from her, but she still had one tool at her disposal. Her greatest weapon.

Her mind.

Chapter 44

Nina, Kent, and Perez had searched the entire medical sciences building to no avail. The halls and rooms had been eerily empty and silent.

"We don't know what's happened to Bianca yet," Kent said in a soothing tone. "We can't jump to any conclusions."

But Nina already had. She knew the killer had taken her. She felt it in her bones.

"I got a text from the Violent Crimes Bureau commander," Perez said. "He's coordinating with patrol to have this campus flooded with officers and detectives shortly."

For all the good it would do.

"We should check the cadaver-storage facility," she said to him and started down the hall in that direction.

She heard them in her wake, neither making any comments. Perez and Kent both seemed to understand that she needed to conduct this initial search in her own way, aware that the PPD would take over soon enough.

She reached the door to the campus morgue and tried the handle. "Locked."

Perez stepped beside her and held out a keycard. "Found this in Hazel's desk. It's probably an extra. Figured we might need it at some point."

He waved it in front of the reader and was rewarded with a loud click. Nina wanted to hug him but pushed the door open instead.

They split up as they had done in each room before, searching every corner and crevice.

Nothing.

Nina found herself staring at the steel drawers where donated bodies were housed.

Swallowing her fear, she walked to the first compartment and pulled it open.

Empty.

She slid the second one out.

Empty.

The men joined her, and they opened each drawer in the cold storage room. Bianca was nowhere to be found.

"She's not here," Kent said gently.

Nina couldn't give up.

She began to pace. "I have to keep searching for her." She heard the rising hysteria in her own voice but could not seem to tamp it down. Her reserves of self-control had evaporated, and she felt panic creeping up on her.

Kent stepped in front of her, forcing her to halt. He wrapped a large hand around each of her arms and squeezed. The sensation jarred her out of her spiraling thoughts, as she was sure it was meant to do.

"Look at me, Nina." His words were calm yet firm—a gentle command.

She tilted her head back, meeting his steady gaze.

"Breathe with me," he said. "I'm going to count, and you're going to match my respiration."

Suddenly aware she'd been sucking in ragged, shallow gulps of air, she closed her eyes and struggled for control.

"Look at me, Nina." His voice was soothing and sharp at the same time. "Keep your eyes focused on mine."

When she complied, he demonstrated his breathing technique, then waited for her to do it with him. Forcing herself to focus on what they were doing pulled her attention away from the prospect of Bianca being brutalized or murdered. Bianca needed her, but she had to regain control of her emotions, or she would be of no use.

After four or five cycles of respiration, Nina's racing thoughts and hammering heart settled. "I know what you're doing," she told Kent. "And I'm grateful."

"It's a quick calming technique I learned in the military," he said, releasing his grip on her arms. "When you're on a mission, you don't have the luxury of stopping to meditate. We do this in the field to keep our minds sharp and on task."

Perez looked impressed. "I'll have to remember that trick."

With oxygen now flowing freely to her brain, Nina refocused on the case. "Buildings on campus are all normally unlocked," she said, resuming her pacing as she considered the facts. "Students don't need an ecard to enter. Bianca clearly went inside the main building, but she would have needed a keycard with special access to enter this unit." She spun around to face them. "We should go back and search the main building again."

As she pivoted, the toe of her shoe kicked a dime that had been lying on the floor, sending it skidding along the slick tiles. Nina watched it slide onto a wide circular drain the size of a manhole cover. She didn't want to think about the things such a large floor grate would be needed for in a morgue setting. The dime slowed and finally slipped between the slots and disappeared.

Nina waited a long time to hear the tinkling of the dime hitting whatever was below.

Too long.

Chapter 45

Nina looked at Kent, then Perez. "That coin didn't just drop a few inches. There's a lot of empty space below this room."

Perez pointed at the side of the slotted circular cover. "There's a hinge on one side."

She followed his gaze. She hadn't noticed it before because the grate was in the corner of the room, but he was right.

Kent bent down to put his fingers through the holes and pulled the cover open. "I don't know what this is, but it sure as hell isn't a drain." He glanced up at them. "Which makes sense because the drain is over there." He jerked his chin at a round metal grate the size of a dinner plate set into the floor in the opposite corner of the room.

Nina peered down into the exposed hole to see iron ladder rungs bolted to the interior wall below the floor descending into darkness below. "I'm going down."

"Maybe we should wait for—" Perez began as Nina started climbing down the ladder. "Never mind," he finished on a sigh. "I'll let my commander know we're going down below the cadaver-storage unit."

By the time her shoes hit the bottom, she was surrounded by inky blackness.

"Bianca!"

The echo of her own voice was the only response Nina received. She pulled out her cell phone and turned on the light.

"Looks like some sort of tunnel down here," she called up to the others.

Moments later, her light glinted off Perez's polished shoes as he came down to join her. Kent followed next. They all shined their cell phone lights around the smooth rounded walls that surrounded them.

"Let's go," Nina said, making her way down the tunnel.

A strong hand gripped her arm. "I'll go first," Kent said. "We don't know what's down here."

"I'm hoping like hell that it's Bianca," Nina said. "And I intend to find her." She forged ahead, ignoring the stream of obscenities coming from Kent, who remained behind her.

After an oddly disorienting walk in near darkness, Nina came to a bend in the tunnel. She shined her light upward to see another metal ladder that appeared to lead to a grate.

Perez held his phone out around the corner. "Looks like we can either go up or turn and keep going," he said.

Nina made her decision. "I'm going up. If this leads to another room somewhere, that's where Bianca could be."

She scaled the ladder and put her phone away once there was enough ambient light coming down through the grate so she could see. Reaching up, she shoved at the round metal cover. With only a slight amount of protest, she managed to push it open.

"Careful," Kent said to her in a harsh whisper from below. He grasped her hips, ready to pull her back down to safety. "Tell me what you see."

She poked her head up to the surface and looked around at an empty room they had already searched. "This is the main medical sciences–building utility room," she said, then climbed back down. "And I'm guessing that other fork will take us to a different building."

A heavy silence stretched as they all digested the implications.

Kent broke the silence. "There could be an entire network of tunnels connecting every structure on this campus."

"For months, victims have disappeared without a trace," she said. "This is how he's been doing it."

Chapter 46

Nina jerked her chin toward the dark passage leading in the opposite direction. "We need to explore that tunnel."

Kent shook his head. "We've got to call the rest of the team and let them know what we've found and where we're going."

"Small problem with that." Perez was looking at his cell phone's glowing screen. "No signal down here."

"Then we go up and call," Kent said.

Nina pointed down the tunnel. "Bianca is in there somewhere. Every minute counts. You go up to the surface and call." She turned on her phone's flashlight. "I'm going to find her."

"No." Kent moved to block her. "We go together. As a team."

Images of Bianca in the hands of a killer filled Nina's mind, blending with flashbacks of the time she had spent bound and helpless in the same predicament. Desperate to get past Kent, she laid her palms against his chest and shoved, unable to move him in the slightest. The walls of the tunnel began to close in around her as she fought for control.

Again.

A part of her realized she cared too deeply for Bianca to be detached and methodical while conducting the search.

Kent softened his tone, gently prying her hands away. "Perez went up the ladder," he said, continuing to hold her hands in his. "He's calling Wade and Breck right now. Then we'll search for Bianca."

"He has her," she whispered. "You know what he's doing to her. He's the falconer. She's the falcon."

Nina knew the same images would be flooding Kent's mind. Bianca—blindfolded, wrists bound, naked, tethered by a leather strap around her ankle.

She straightened. "The jess." Without another word, she yanked her hands free from Kent's grasp and began to climb the ladder to join Perez.

"We'll be going dark," Perez was saying into his phone. "Let the PPD commander know how to access the tunnel."

"Will do." Breck was on speaker; her clipped response carried in the utility room. "I'll check the AIT database for schematics of the tunnels, but I'm surprised there was no mention of underground passageways in any of the materials I've looked through so far. I might have to hand search the archives at the library. Those tunnels are probably original to the construction of the campus."

Nina scrambled to the surface and snatched the phone from Perez's grasp.

He stared at her. "What's going on, Guerrera?"

She put the phone to her mouth. "Breck, he'll have a tracker in a jess on Bianca's ankle. Can you locate the signal to find her?"

There was a long pause on the other end. Kent gazed up at them from the floor, where only his head and shoulders were above the surface. Nina saw the two men look at each other in apparent agreement.

"Smart," Perez said to her.

"I'm not sure," Breck finally said. "Without knowing the exact frequency being used, I won't have anything to latch on to, but I'm damned sure going to give it a whirl."

"Where's Hazel?" Nina asked.

"Wade took him to a small conference room off the lobby of the computer science building as soon as he got here a few minutes ago,"

Breck said. "I've been watching through the video system, and Hazel's denying any involvement."

"At least if he's in there with Wade, he's not with Bianca," Nina said. "You've got to find a way to hang on to him while we search."

"The interview is consensual," Breck said. "You know we have no legal basis for holding him here."

Nina knew. "Just try," she said. "And call us back if you get a lock on the tracker or if Hazel makes any admissions."

"Perez told me you can't get a signal underground," Breck said.

Nina hesitated. Did she stay here and wait for Breck to scan for an emission from a transponder or start searching the tunnels immediately? Either choice could mean a waste of valuable time. And time could be running out for Bianca.

As she had done countless times before in her career, she made a split-second decision with minimal information at her disposal.

"Leave a text or a voice mail message," she said to Breck. "We'll get it when we come back aboveground. Right now, we're going down to search for Bee."

Chapter 47

Naked, cold, and trapped, Bianca beat back a fresh wave of panic. Fear and desperation had slipped in, trying to suck her down into a black hole of paralysis. A madman was coming for her at any moment, and she had spent what felt like the better part of an hour trying to free herself from her tether without making any headway. First, she had tried to loosen the thick leather binding around her ankle, but she couldn't pull it off and had nothing sharp to cut through the thick hide. Then she'd pulled on the other end of the rope, trying to free it from the steel bolt set into the concrete floor. Finally, in an act of sheer desperation, she had sunk her teeth into the braided cord, pulling and twisting in an effort to chew her way through it. She hadn't even made a scratch. She might as well have bitten the hide of a rhinoceros.

When he came, she had no intention of waiting here, docile like a sacrificial lamb tied to a stake. Refusing to succumb to the encroaching tide of helplessness and despair, she sat back down on the cold floor and recommitted herself to using her brain. Physical force was not working anyway, so she would marshal her mental abilities to figure a way out of her predicament.

She bent to study the strap around her ankle again. The leather seemed impenetrable, the thread used to stitch it together looked like fishing line, and the ring connecting the strap to the braided cord appeared to be made of steel.

She crouched, narrowed her eyes, and scrutinized the metal ring more carefully. She turned her foot one way, then another, trying to get a better look in the dim light provided by the lone overhead bulb.

She recognized the dark gray coloring of the metal, which was the size and shape of a men's wedding band. That thought led her to the next. This was not stainless steel, as she had first thought. This was tungsten carbide, an alloy far stronger than steel or even titanium.

Her captor had made it a point to select the strongest materials possible to hold her in place, but he was no metallurgist. She had initially fallen into the trap of trying to defeat the leather, when in reality the metal ring was the weakest part of the equation. Tungsten carbide was used for rings because it was one of the hardest metals. She had studied enough science to know that its hardness also made it extremely brittle.

She slid her body closer to the steel eyebolt and lifted her leg above it. Carefully, she positioned the metal ring so that it stuck out at a ninety-degree angle from her ankle. She dropped her leg down, letting gravity help her deliver more force to the blow as she smacked the tungsten ring against the steel.

Nothing.

Reaching down, she spun the ring a fraction and repeated the process.

Nothing.

Patience was her only option. This could take many attempts. She kept repeating the same steps, each time rotating the ring a tiny bit before smacking it down against the bolt.

She had lost track of how many times she had tried when she was surprised by a loud popping noise. She reached down, and this time, fragments of the ring that had split in half fell into her hand.

She was free. At least, she was free to walk around. She spent the next several minutes inspecting every millimeter of her prison. She walked the perimeter, her hands tracing the walls and the locked metal door.

Why had her captor left her here alone? When would he return? Nina had refused to share information about the investigation, but Bianca had gleaned details from the media. Based on his prior behavior, he did not kill his victims immediately. He kept them for some period of time before doing so.

She suppressed a shudder at the thought of what he might do during the days or weeks when he had a young woman at his mercy.

Forcing her mind away from dark thoughts that would do nothing but feed her worst fears, she concluded that he either had to go back to cover his tracks, or he wanted her awake and conscious for whatever he had planned. He would return to deal with her when he could take his time. Given that premise, he would not want her dead at this point, so he would need a way to be certain the toxin he had exposed her to would not kill her. How would he do that?

She scanned the room again, this time lifting her eyes to study the exposed ductwork along the unfinished ceiling. Metal pipes ran horizontally across the space, disappearing into perfectly cut holes in the cinder block. She visually traced the swirls of a circular vent and the black electrical tube that supplied power to the lone light bulb. She moved to the side to look from another angle and saw a tiny red dot glowing.

A determined smile lifted the corners of her mouth.

Chapter 48

"Slow down, Agent Guerrera."

Nina glanced over her shoulder at the hulking figure whose boots pounded the ground behind her. "Maybe you should speed up, Sergeant."

The PPD had arrived in force, blanketing the campus and sending a group of tactical officers from their Special Assignment Unit into the tunnels, where they met up with Nina, Kent, and Perez. The SAU operators had split into teams and spent the last fifteen minutes charging through the underground labyrinth. Each time they came to a ladder leading upward, a contingent had climbed up to check while the rest continued on. The search had been efficient but not fast enough for Nina, who was with the team's leader.

"It's pitch dark down here," the sergeant said. "If we go too fast, we're going to miss something."

He was right, but Nina had felt an extra measure of urgency when Breck had been unable to locate any signal that might have come from a transponder on Bianca's ankle. It had been a long shot, and perhaps Bianca wasn't even wearing a jess at this point, but Nina still felt it as a palpable blow after she had gotten her hopes up.

She forced herself to slow down. "Who's got the FLIR?"

The tactical team had brought a forward-looking infrared thermal-imaging camera with them. They had been scanning the space for any human-size heat source hidden within the tunnel.

"One of the operators is checking out another fork in the tunnel. He'll catch up to us soon."

Perez was trotting beside them. "What about the GPR?" he asked the sergeant.

After getting a feel for the extent of the search, the sergeant had requested a Ground-Penetrating Radar scanner to determine whether there were hidden chambers recessed behind the walls of the tunnels or if there were subterranean rooms even farther down below.

"That will take a bit longer," the sergeant said. "It's been deployed, but it's going to take hours to get through this maze."

Nina had seen GPR used, and she knew he was right. The process involved rolling a large piece of wheeled equipment over the ground, and it was slow and methodical at best. Rushing would not yield a clear picture of what lay beneath.

"Our com systems don't work down here," he said. "I can't be sure what anyone's found until we go back up. In the meantime, I've asked my team to let me know if they hear anything important on our channel while they're searching one of the buildings."

This was the best way to search without the benefit of a police K-9, which could have tracked Bianca if the dog got her scent. The PPD, however, had made it clear they were still unwilling to risk having another one of their dogs poisoned.

Kent, who had been silent for the past several minutes, had his own question for the tactical sergeant. "Did you know there were tunnels under AIT?"

"Not a clue," the sergeant said. "There are tunnels under a bunch of the older buildings downtown. In fact, we use them for training sometimes." He looked around. "But I never heard a word about anything like this under the university."

Nina could understand why Kent had posed the question. A police SWAT team would most likely know about anything within their city that could pose a threat to public safety. A vast network of underground passageways certainly fit the bill. And yet one of their supervisors didn't know.

She thought of Lieutenant Hazel. He had overseen the investigation into the disappearances, yet he never mentioned the existence of the very means by which the kidnapper could have pulled off his crimes. As a campus police supervisor, it would be hard to imagine that he didn't know about them.

She could think of only one reason he would withhold such critical information. And she hoped like hell Wade was getting a confession out of him right now.

Chapter 49

Bianca squinted, lifting a hand to shield her eyes from the glare of the bare bulb. The asshole had set up a camera to either watch her in real time or record her movements to view later. Or both.

The ceiling was too high for her to reach, but she'd spotted a small housing around the glowing red dot.

How can I get to it?

She jumped and grasped with her outstretched hands. Not even close. She considered the pipes.

Will they hold my weight?

Only one way to find out.

She looked down at the braided-leather rope lying on the floor. The cord was about six feet long, which would be more than enough for her purposes. If she could get it loose from the bolt in the floor.

She opened her palm and studied the two broken pieces of tungsten, picking the one with the most jagged edge. She walked to the steel bolt, squatted down, and began scraping the leather with the exposed edge of the ring. Unable to get through the hide, she changed tactics, setting the sharp edge against the fishing line used for thread, which was also braided to reinforce its strength.

After a considerable amount of cursing and dropping the ring fragment through her sweaty fingertips, she managed to cut through the line. She stood and took a breath. Now she had both a tool and a weapon. If all else failed, she would do her best to strangle the asshole with the braided leather he had tried to use to imprison her.

She considered using the sharp edge of the ring to cut the strap from her ankle but saw no point in wasting precious time and potentially slicing into her foot. Her priority was figuring a way out or preparing to ambush her captor when he returned. To do that, she would need to deal with the little red light she had seen beside the ductwork immediately.

She tossed one end of the rope up and threw it over a pair of pipes attached to the ceiling. She grasped the other end, tugged experimentally, and the pipes held. She stuck out a leg and placed her bare foot against the rough wall. Grasping the leather rope, she pulled her other leg up until her body was parallel to the floor. The pipes groaned slightly but held.

Grateful for the rough, unfinished surface of the cinder block, she began to walk her feet up the wall as she went hand over hand. She got higher and higher, closer to the ceiling.

When she neared the top, one of the pipes gave an ominous screech, and she stopped for a full fifteen seconds. Muscles burning, she realized she could not hold her position forever. She would either succeed or fail, but she had to go on. She pulled herself higher, finally reaching up to grab one of the pipes with her hands.

She used her abs to tuck her legs up, then let them down. She did it again, gaining momentum as she swung her legs like a gymnast on the uneven bars. When she calculated she had enough momentum, she swung her feet up to hook her ankle around another pipe. This one was much wider. The bolts looked bigger.

She stretched her body until she got both knees over the pipe, then let go with her hands and hung upside down. If she fell from this height, the cold cement floor would be unforgiving. She bent her waist again, this time doing a full-body crunch to latch on to the pipe with both hands. She hauled her body up and lay atop the rounded metal shaft like a leopard on a tree branch.

She inched forward until she was next to the glowing red dot, which was in a small black box clamped to the vent. She reached out and pried it loose. Turning it over, she saw the tiny, rounded lens. She had guessed correctly. It was a camera.

She turned the lens to face her, then held up her middle finger before breaking open the camera's plastic housing.

Chapter 50

Nina played the flashlight the tactical unit sergeant had given her over the tunnel's thick walls. "Even with the best lighting, I feel like we could be missing important clues," she said to no one in particular.

"We've been down here over an hour, and I feel like we're no closer to finding Bianca than when we started." Kent's words reflected her deepest doubts.

"It's tough because of the way we have to communicate," the sergeant said.

Without the means to speak over the com system or use their cell phones, they had resorted to climbing up to the surface every time they came across wrought iron rails bolted to the wall leading up to a hatch.

Unfortunately, the hatches were not always easy to spot. They all led up to utility rooms, storage closets, or dead-end corridors in the basements of buildings where the lights were turned off most of the time. They would have to clamber up and search the immediate area to determine which campus building they were in and whether Bianca was there. Nina was grateful for the manpower brought to bear by the PPD to help with the arduous and painstaking process. The command post tracked the progress of each search party as they worked their way through the maze of tunnels, making sure they didn't mistakenly go through an area that had already been cleared or, worse yet, skip over a place believing it had already been searched.

Each time they surfaced in a different location, the sergeant would make contact with his team and his commander while Nina reached out to Breck for updates on Wade's interrogation of Hazel and any other developments in the investigation.

"I don't think that nut is going to crack," Breck had told Nina during their last communication. "Wade's doing everything short of pulling out the psychological thumbscrews, and Hazel is not coming off his story. He maintains his innocence. Period."

Nina's thoughts warred between her desire to search the tunnels and her wish to be in the room with Hazel, forcing him to tell her where he had stashed Bianca. She felt confident he had kept her alive, because he had never killed anyone before he had a chance to use his mind games on them. But how long would that last? Especially if he was under suspicion for the first time.

Nina heard something and stopped short.

Perez collided with her from behind, knocking her into Kent's back.

"What's going on, Guerrera?" Perez said.

She stilled. "Everybody be quiet."

She heard it again. A faint noise coming from the end of the passageway in front of them. The last portion of the tunnel system they had not searched.

She pointed straight ahead. "That way."

Without another word, they all moved as a group, as silently as they could, shuffling forward. They reached a dead end, each of them swinging their flashlights in every direction while they listened in complete silence.

"I hear it," Kent whispered.

"Me too," Perez said.

"Shhh," Nina said, bending down toward the floor of the tunnel, tilting her head this way and that, trying to zero in on the sound.

She got down on all fours, and the men did the same. Nina thought the noise sounded like someone picking at something. Was it Bianca trying to escape from a chamber inside the tunnel? Was she tapping on the walls because she had heard them?

Excitement surging in her chest, Nina began rapping her knuckles on the lower portion of the wall.

An unearthly shriek emanated from just below Nina's hand. She pulled back to better angle the flashlight, which glinted off glossy black hair.

Only it wasn't black hair with a streak of blue, as Nina had desperately hoped.

It was black fur. And a bare pink tail. And small, sharp bared teeth.

Kent's muscular arm circled her waist, and he yanked her back against him. "It's a rat," he said. "Stay back. It could have rabies."

The creature reared, squealed a loud warning, then turned and retreated into the crevice from which it had emerged.

Nina slumped, her back against Kent's chest. A hot mix of disappointment and frustration rushed through her. They had reached the end of their search. Instead of finding Bianca, she had flushed a rat from its nest.

"We're done," she said, hearing the hollowness in her own voice. "That was the last place that hadn't been cleared." She choked out the next words. "I can't find Bee."

Bianca was truly lost. She thought back to the day she had chased down the juvenile runaway. Nina had known Bianca needed a loving home, and that her own traumatic past had rendered her incapable of providing it. That very night, she had taken a girl who had also survived abuse in the foster system into her care. Nina had made a vow to herself, promising to do whatever she could to shield this girl from danger and give her a loving home. She had recruited Mrs. Gomez to provide the love she could not, instead making it her mission to protect Bianca from harm. Mrs. G had loved her foster daughter with all the warmth and affection any child could want.

But Nina had not held up her end of the bargain. Bianca was in the hands of a serial killer. And it had happened on her watch. She was responsible. As before, she had been so caught up in her duties that she had put the job before her family.

And Bianca was family. She knew that now in a way she never had before.

Nina thought about the rat she had frightened from its hiding place. Clearly terrified and desperate, the creature had bared its sharp teeth, hissing a threat at them before fleeing to safety.

A cornered rat was a very dangerous thing. And right now, Hazel was cornered.

Chapter 51

Fifteen minutes later, Nina, Kent, and Perez made their way toward the computer science building.

"I'm going in with Wade," she told the two men. "I want a shot at Hazel."

Perez frowned. "This is a PPD case. If anyone's going to assist Wade with the interrogation, it should be me."

Kent cut in before Nina could respond. "Wade's been in with him for well over an hour. He's probably wrapping up soon anyway."

After their fruitless search of the tunnels, Nina wanted to focus her effort on the one remaining lead they had.

"Don't care if I only get sixty seconds with him," she said. "I want to look him in the eyes. He's going to tell me what he's done with Bianca."

They had reached the sidewalk in front of the main entry.

"This is a voluntary interview," Perez said. "We don't have enough to charge him, so Hazel can walk out at any point. You can't force him to talk."

"Good point," Nina said, walking through the automatic doors. "He's not under arrest, which means he's not in your custody. Which means he's fair game for me."

Perez followed her into the lobby. "Guerrera, you know better than to interrupt an ongoing interrogation. We can watch from the think tank with Breck." He put a hand on her arm. "Do not go in there."

"She's not good at taking orders," Kent said. "I've tried."

Nina pointedly looked down at Perez's hand, then slowly raised her eyes to level a hard stare at the detective. He heaved a sigh and released his grip. Without another word, she turned and strode toward the small conference room off the lobby just outside the think tank. She pressed down on the door handle and entered without knocking.

"How many times do I have to tell you?" Hazel was saying. "I haven't even set eyes on Bianca since yesterday and I—"

Both men's heads turned in her direction. Wade sat on one side of a Formica table, and Hazel occupied the chair opposite him.

"What the hell is this?" Hazel demanded, then directed a sneer at Wade. "I'm not making any confessions, so you're bringing in the muscle to work me over?"

Wade ignored the sarcastic remark, his attention on Nina. "Agent Guerrera?"

The question held a great deal of nuance. Wade had to be careful what he said in front of Hazel. He would assume the interruption was due to a critical development in the case but had to allow her to either redirect the conversation and adapt on the fly or ask him to go outside to speak with her in private. During a consensual interview, the latter could provide a reason for the subject to leave and prematurely end the conversation.

Nina opted to keep the discussion going. "We just finished searching the campus," she said to Hazel, deliberately leaving out any mention of tunnels. "We haven't located Bianca yet, but we're not stopping until we do."

According to Breck's latest update, Wade had not brought up anything about underground passageways yet. Nina had used similar tactics when interviewing persons of interest. The idea was to keep the subject talking for an extended period. During a mentally draining and stressful session, the person might slip and reveal information only the perpetrator of the crime would know.

Such as the existence of an extensive subterranean network that would allow the killer to move around without being detected.

Nina sat down beside Wade, who appeared content to let her take over, and considered her options. Hazel's comment when she'd entered the room told her Wade hadn't made any progress. Time to broach the subject and watch for any signs of recognition or surprise. A subject's reaction to information could reveal whether the facts were new to him or not.

Before she got to the main point, she decided to let him make the same round of denials once again. It would bring her up to speed and lull Hazel into a false sense of security.

She opened with something that had been on her mind all the way back across the campus. "Why didn't you go downtown to talk to PPD Homicide?"

Hazel let out a groan. "Do you people talk to each other at all?" He glanced from her to Wade and back again. "I got an urgent text message to come to the med-sci building."

"A text that conveniently vanished," Wade said before turning to Nina. "He pulled out his cell phone to show it to me, but there was no such message. Breck came in here for a few minutes and tried to pull it up, but she couldn't locate a trace of it anywhere on his device."

Nina raised a skeptical brow at Hazel. "Convenient." Before he could launch into a defensive tirade, she leaned across the table. "What did this mysterious vanishing message say?"

"I don't remember the exact words." Hazel waved a dismissive hand. "Whoever it was wanted to show me something they would only share with me because they didn't trust the FBI or the PPD. They said it would solve the case."

"And you didn't think to let us know about this hot new lead?" Nina asked in a deliberately derisive tone.

Wade answered for him. "He wanted the glory of solving the case by himself." He paused for effect. "The case that had been taken away from him."

"Or there never was any message at all," Nina said. "Take your pick."

Hazel reddened. "I'm telling you, there was a text. And I went there because I don't trust the FBI or the PPD either." He gestured around the interview room. "I think I've got a pretty damn good reason to feel that way."

"Why didn't you go downtown to meet with Homicide when your mystery texter didn't show?" Nina asked, keeping Hazel off-balance with rapid-fire questions.

He leaned forward in imitation of Nina's earlier move, and they were almost nose to nose. "Because it occurred to me that you were getting me downtown to arrest me, so I decided to come here and confront you people before I went anywhere."

"Why would we arrest you?" Nina asked, refusing to back away. "What did you do?"

Hazel jabbed a finger at her. "You're so desperate to solve the case that you're framing me. I realized what was going on." He raised his voice. "But I didn't do it."

Nina let his words hang in the air a moment. She leaned back, adopting a more considered approach, and changed the subject again, keeping the conversation shifting under him, never allowing him to compose himself.

"When I said we searched the campus just now," she said, studying Hazel's face, "I mean we also went down into the tunnels."

Silence met her words.

Hazel's eyes widened in apparent surprise, then narrowed in suspicion. "What tunnels?"

If he was acting, he was good.

"An underground network connecting most of the buildings on campus." She leaned forward again. "Which is how the victims disappeared without a trace."

Hazel crossed his arms. "I never knew about any damn tunnels. I've been working at AIT for less than two years; how am I supposed to know everything about this place?"

Their search hadn't given them anything to use as leverage, and Hazel's mulish expression indicated he wasn't about to offer anything but flat denials.

"You ran the investigation into the disappearances," she said. "Wouldn't you have made it your business to find out everything you could about the campus where the crimes took place?"

"You guys were investigating too." His volume went up a notch. "How come you didn't know until now either?"

"We have been assisting on this case for a grand total of five days," she said. "You ran the whole show for months. There's no comparison."

"Are you accusing me of not doing my job?" Hazel asked. "Or are you accusing me of killing those girls?"

"Which one is it?" she said. "Incompetence or murder? You tell me."

"Fuck you," Hazel said. "I'm done talking." He pushed back from the table. "If you have any more questions, you can ask my attorney."

Hazel had invoked his right to counsel, effectively ending the interview.

"You two are assholes." Hazel stood and walked to the door. "I know you think I did it, but I didn't." He opened the door, then turned and directed his last comment to Nina. "I hope you find Bianca," he said quietly.

Nina and Wade watched him leave the building before heading into the think tank.

"That didn't end well," Perez said. "Now that he's got a head full of steam, we'll see where he goes." He patted the pocket containing his cell phone. "My guys will keep me updated."

Perez had requested the same plainclothes team who had originally been detailed to follow Hazel from headquarters. Now they were strategically positioned in multiple vehicles so the lieutenant would not see the same car behind him when he left campus. Nina could only hope he would lead them to Bianca. The thought came on a wave of anxiety. She had deliberately challenged Hazel, and now hoped she hadn't interrupted an impending confession.

She gazed up at Wade, who appeared to be studying her. "There was no time to strategize ahead of time," she said with a note of apology. "I went straight to the underground system hoping to get a reaction out of him."

"He wasn't going to come off his story," Wade said. "Didn't matter. I was getting ready to bring up the tunnels myself, but I wasn't optimistic. He'd been uncooperative from the beginning."

Nina tilted her head in question. "How so?"

"I asked him before you arrived, and he refused to provide a sample of his DNA or consent to a search of any of his private property," Wade replied. "I doubt he's going to talk to us again, and without evidence, we've got no legal reason to hold him."

Nina was curious to get Wade's opinion of Hazel's overall demeanor. "What did you read in his body language?" she asked. "Was he being deceptive or just hostile?"

"Hard to say." Wade looked thoughtful. "He's spent a lot of years on the other side of the table, asking the questions. He would know what signs to exhibit and what to avoid."

"I was watching for microexpressions and autonomic responses," Kent said. "Couldn't detect anything one way or the other. A polygraph would have been nice, of course."

"Summing it all up," Wade said, "the interview was inconclusive."

Nina glanced at Breck, who was keeping an eye on the monitors. "What's Hazel up to now?"

"Went straight to his SUV and drove out of the parking lot," she said, then turned to Perez. "I'm assuming the clunker I saw behind him was an undercover PPD vehicle?"

"That's one of them," Perez said. "There are three more."

Nina followed up on the story Hazel had given them. "What about the disappearing text on his cell phone?"

"The technology exists," Breck said. "It's possible to send someone a message that disappears a few seconds after it's been received and opened." She frowned. "He let me have his phone for a few minutes, and I couldn't find any sign of it. Either whoever sent it was good, or—"

"Or Hazel is full of shit," Nina said. Annoyed by the lack of any hard conclusions about Hazel, she shifted her gaze to the wall screen, which displayed the image of a yellowed map depicting a network of tunnels underneath AIT campus grounds.

"Where did you find that?" she asked Breck.

"I went through everything I could find in the AIT database and came up empty." Breck blew a wayward tendril of auburn hair from her face. "I was getting ready to walk over to the library and start pulling some of those dusty old books you and Kent looked through down from the shelves in the basement; then I finally found this little gem. Fortunately, it had been converted from microfiche and uploaded into AIT's virtual archive."

"Damn," Perez said. "You got lucky."

"No luck involved," Breck said. "Skill and pure pigheadedness on my part."

"Sounds about right," Nina said. "Is there any sign of a hidden chamber or holding cell in that schematic?"

All the state-of-the-art equipment and manpower the PPD brought to bear had failed to turn up any sign of Bianca or a place she could have been hidden.

"Sorry," Breck said. "I got zip." She gestured toward the wall screen. "If you look in the lower-left corner, this diagram dates back over a hundred years ago."

Nina looked. The map had been drawn in 1917. "I wonder when it was last used."

"I called the chancellor," Breck said. "She didn't know about the tunnels either. From what I found out, the university stopped using the tunnels before World War II."

"Makes sense," Perez said. "The same thing happened downtown."

"What do you mean?" Nina asked.

"Tunnels were also constructed in the heart of the city to cool large buildings back before air-conditioning was invented," Perez said. "Don't forget that summers here are insanely hot. The first place in Phoenix to get air-conditioning was the Hotel Westward Ho in 1929. As more buildings converted to air-conditioning, their old tunnel systems became an attractive nuisance, and people were discouraged from using them."

"That must be why info about the AIT system is hard to find," Nina said. "They didn't want students to know about them, so they deliberately hid all mention of the underground network back in the 1930s. Eventually, they fell into disuse and were forgotten."

"Until someone ran across them and realized there was a perfect way to commit crimes," Kent said.

"Someone like Hazel," Nina said.

"Speaking of the lieutenant," Perez said, looking at his phone. "Got a text from the surveillance team. Hazel parked his SUV and went inside Arcadia Mall."

"Odd time to go shopping," Breck said.

Nina groaned. "He's not shopping," she said. "He's losing the tail." She exchanged glances with Perez, who nodded his agreement, before explaining. "Hazel must have spotted the team, which isn't surprising considering his experience. He chose to leave his car and walk into a crowded shopping center to make it nearly impossible for anyone to follow him."

"Arcadia Mall has hundreds of stores on three levels," Perez said. "With multiple exits, it would be easy to ditch a tail as long as he didn't get back into his own vehicle."

"He could catch a cab, a city bus, or walk to the nearest light-rail station," Nina added. "We've essentially lost him."

"For now," Perez said, thumb typing on his phone. "I'm redirecting the team to set up on his house. We'll catch up to him when he goes home."

Nina wasn't reassured. What could he be doing in the meantime? She wished they could have put a tracker on Hazel, but the Supreme Court's rulings about planting devices without permission had been quite clear. Even if they tried to get a warrant granting permission, it would take hours to go through the US Attorney's Office to a federal judge. And they still might not be successful.

She felt the constraint of abiding by the law while criminals did whatever they wanted.

"I wish we could locate Hazel and hold him until we find Bee," she said. "At least that way, we would know he wasn't hurting her."

Wade's grim expression conveyed equal parts sympathy and reproach. "There's this thing called the Constitution," he said. "We uphold it. Always. We can finish searching his university-owned equipment, but that's the extent of it unless we uncover something incriminating."

"Besides," Kent said, "we can't be one hundred percent sure he's the unsub."

Nina thought about Hazel's parting words. He had seemed sincere. Then again, she had been lied to by the best. Many of them had been quite convincing. Part of the challenge of the job was to separate lies from truth. Fact from fiction. Had her concern for Bianca clouded her judgment, or was Hazel simply good at deception from his own experience?

A part of her realized she was clinging to the notion that Hazel was the killer because if he wasn't, it would mean they were no closer to finding Bianca.

Knowing what she had to do next, Nina felt a sense of sickening dread. She pulled her phone out. More than anything else, this would make her failure real.

"I can't put this off any longer," she said to the others. "I have to call Mrs. Gomez and tell her Bianca is missing."

Chapter 52

He had fallen for Bianca hard, in a way he hadn't with the others. When he had seen the edge of a scar she tried to hide on her pale slender arm, he knew she was the one he was waiting for. The sight sent his mind back to the months he had spent in Egypt. The day he had found a wounded bird. The moment he had become a man.

He had joined the US Army at eighteen, taller and a bit more filled out but still thin and pasty compared to the others in his unit. He had been tapped to do a rotation on the Sinai Peninsula as part of the Sinai Multinational Force and Observers. The US was transitioning responsibility for the MFO to National Guard troops, but the Army had sent him there after his ordnance-disposal training when they discovered his prodigious computer skills.

Everything had changed the day something flew into an electrical wire strung between two buildings. He'd been walking nearby and rushed over to find a magnificent female golden eagle lying on the dusty ground. He had never seen such a creature up close and had no idea they could be found in Egypt. He carefully approached the bird, who surprised him by allowing him to examine her injured leg. He'd gazed into her amber eyes, and their bond was instantaneous.

At first, he had hidden the eagle while he researched online how to nurse it back to health. Within two weeks, she'd been able to fly again. By then, he had run across information about falconry and suspected she belonged to an Egyptian falconer. He'd tested her by attempting to place a hood over her head. When she had stood still to allow it, he was convinced.

Realizing he had acquired a trained raptor, he decided to convince the base commander to allow him to keep her. He had asked the commander to meet him on the outskirts of the base. When he walked out from behind one of the huts with an eagle perched on his forearm, the commander was leery.

"That thing is a wild animal," the commander had said, eyeing her sharp beak. "It's dangerous. I won't have it threatening anyone on my base."

Anticipating pushback, he had made arrangements ahead of time with one of the few men he considered a friend.

"She can protect the base," he had told the commander. "Watch what she can do."

Before the commander could object, he raised his arm, and the bird soared into the air. He pulled his radio from his belt, mashed the transmit button, and gave the signal.

Moments later, an enemy drone they had shot down the previous week buzzed out from behind one of the nearby buildings. He had disabled the spy software and repaired a broken propeller, enabling it to fly around without sending signals to any unfriendlies.

His eagle had circled high above, and he could see the moment she locked on to the new kind of target he had trained her to hunt. She'd made a beeline for the drone, snatched the device out of the air, and brought it safely to the ground.

The commander, suitably impressed, had allowed him to continue with what he referred to as a new counterterrorism asset.

Falconry had taught him patience, wisdom, and self-mastery. He carried his bird on long runs in the hot desert before letting her fly, ensuring she had ample space to hunt away from the base and its array of wires, poles, and equipment that could present a hazard for her.

After a few months, he had looked in the mirror and been shocked at what he saw. His formerly sallow, pimpled face had become sun bronzed and chiseled. His legs bulged with muscles from running in the sand, and his body rippled with musculature he had never dreamed possible a scant two years earlier.

When the time had come for him to rotate back to the States, members of his unit begged to take over the care of his eagle. He worked with the friend who had helped him with the drone, but his eagle flapped her massive wings, opened her beak, and screeched whenever the man approached.

His friend shook his head. "She's chosen you," he'd said. "She won't have anyone else."

The wonder of it staggered him. This gorgeous creature had bonded with him and would not leave him. Something deep within him responded. For the first time, he had not been found wanting. He had a partner for life.

After endless red tape, the military finally cleared him to take her with him to his next assignment in Arizona. The base commander there had agreed to let her continue her job of guarding the installation against unwanted aerial invasion. The decision had sent his career path in a different direction. His new mission was cyberterrorism with a subspecialty in biological-weapons defense.

He had transferred to the Army Reserves two years after his return but had continued with many of his duties and had been allowed to keep his bird. Everything had gone perfectly.

Until last summer.

Field Notes

Day	Observation	Water 💧	Food 🍎	Strategy 🧭
Melissa Campbell				
1	Capture went smoothly; nausea from sedation; no other ill effects	None	None	Withhold all stimuli and continue observation
2	Very distressed; may have minor injury to left index finger	None	None	Observe how she moves finger; plan for first contact; attempt drinking
3	Accepted water from mouth after minimal hesitancy; is learning to trust	8 ounces water	None	Wait another day to introduce feeding
4	Feeding by mouth initially successful. Subject displayed overt signs of rejection.	8 ounces water	3 chicken nuggets	
Bianca Babbage				
1	Capture went smoothly; adjusted ziptie, subject is smaller than the others	None	None	Active search ongoing; move up timetable or wait 24 hours for initial contact.
1	ADDENDUM: Incredibly bright. Defeated ziptie, blindfold, and tether. May attempt forcible resistance or escape. Destroyed remote viewing capability within habitat.	None	None	Activate notifications for proximity alerts, tracking, and containment. Wait an additional day prior to first contact.

Chapter 53

Bianca's bare sweat-soaked skin slid along the wide metal pipe. She shimmied forward until she reached an oblong vent she had spotted in the exposed ductwork hanging from the ceiling. Two small sheet metal screws held the cover in place. She took the jagged piece of tungsten ring she'd been holding in her teeth and set to work, picking at the corners.

After what seemed like an eternity, she pried it loose enough to get her fingertips underneath the edge. She pulled up, making her fingers raw and sore, until the tiny screw popped off, dropping to the floor some ten feet below. The second screw was less of a challenge now that she could twist the cover. She laid it inside the air duct. If her plan worked, she would either replace the vent cover after she crawled inside or leave it where her captor couldn't find it without taking time to search. He would eventually figure out how she'd escaped, but she wasn't going to make it easy for him.

The rectangular opening was barely large enough for her to squeeze her head and shoulders through, but she managed to wedge herself into the shaft that would take her out of her prison. If it didn't crash to the floor in a heap of twisted metal.

She wasn't claustrophobic, but the confined space around her felt suffocating. She called a picture of Nina to mind. She knew what her mentor had suffered in the past. Understood the lengths Nina had gone to while fighting for her life. If she were in this situation, what would Agent Badass do?

Whatever the hell it took to survive.

Gathering strength and channeling Nina, Bianca began inching her way through the ductwork, heedless of the groaning metal and occasional popping bolt. She was grateful her bare flesh didn't catch on anything as she made her way through the tight space.

The inside of the shaft was so dark that she was able to spot a ray of light far ahead. Light meant there would be another vent in another room. She figured she could either drop into a place from which she could escape or she could fall directly into the killer's arms. She slowed, trying to crawl ahead noiselessly so he wouldn't hear her if he was in the room ahead. She could peek through the metal slits to see if anyone was there.

It seemed to take an eternity before she reached the light that slanted through the vent. She angled her head down, scrutinizing the space below. It looked like some sort of utility room. She saw buckets and mops, metal shelving, and a pile of old rags, but no people. She still had no clue where she was, but anything that put distance between her and the cell she had been held in was progress.

Her gaze landed on a computer monitor sitting on a desk, its screen glowing. Everything else in the room appeared ancient, but the computer was new. Squinting, she could see that the computer's screen was divided into quadrants, each with a live video feed of a different part of the campus. Thirty seconds later, images in the four quadrants flipped to a different view featuring other sections of the university's grounds. This had to be the killer's control room. This was the device he had used to tap into the security feed.

Her original idea had been to drop down and find her way out, counting on dumb luck to avoid bumping into her captor, but now she had a new plan. A better plan.

She pushed at the slotted cover until it popped free and sailed into the air before clattering to the floor. Without the ability to use the braided cord to climb down as she had done to climb up, she would have to drop down and land on her feet. Aware she may not have much time, she stuck her feet through the narrow opening and began pushing her sweat-slick body through.

As before, the metal edges scraped her skin raw and cut her in places, but she simply repositioned herself and kept going. A few minor injuries would heal. Whatever the madman had planned for her would end in death.

She finally dropped to the ground, bare feet smacking hard onto the cold cement floor. She headed straight for the computer and eased into the wheeled ergonomic office chair in front of it.

The killer had used this computer to send a power surge interrupting the feed from the security cameras. She recalled her conversation with Breck, who had coded a program to detect future surges and send an alert to her cell phone. She had recommended a virus that could be used to piggyback on the signal in order to trace it back to its source. There was no way to know if Breck had succeeded, but she was willing to spend an extra two minutes in this room to increase her odds of survival.

She found the program that implemented the surge and typed in a command that would make it as strong as possible. She would completely overload the system to the point that Breck's detector couldn't miss it. Leaving it on would make it like a beacon that would lead the FBI team directly to her location, wherever the hell she was.

She stood and glanced at the door, considering her options. She could wait here and barricade herself in as best she could, hoping the cops would find her before a murderous lunatic did. She could leave this room and make a run for it, but she had no idea what was behind the door. Attack dogs? Land mines? Other nasty booby traps?

Scanning her surroundings again, she noticed a peg in the wall with a black Arizona Cardinals hoodie dangling from it. Pulling it over her head, she noticed that it fell to her knees and was quite roomy. The killer was a big guy. Big enough to break down the door to this room even if she pushed the desk and flimsy metal shelving unit in front of it.

Then her eyes caught the flicker of red light up in the ceiling. Another camera. A shudder went through her as she felt him watching her. He knew where she was now. That settled it. She could not afford to wait to see if Breck's surge detector alerted and if she managed to trace the source of the disturbance. The killer might catch her if she ran, but it was better than waiting here, where he would definitely find her. She crossed the room and opened the door, which led to a dimly lit hallway. She put a tentative foot outside, then broke into a run.

She had to assume everyone was rushing in this direction, and it was a race to see who would get to her first.

Chapter 54

"I will bring Bianca home to you," Nina whispered to Mrs. Gomez before ending the worst phone call of her life. Gripping the cell hard enough to whiten her knuckles, she battled the tears that threatened to overwhelm her.

She turned away from the others, taking a moment to compose herself. Perez was using one of the think tank's landlines to coordinate with his fellow Homicide detectives, who had taken over the search of Hazel's office and were writing affidavits to access his AIT computer. The chancellor had granted permission, but Perez was jumping through extra hoops, not taking any chances of a legal challenge in court.

Wade and Kent were talking, no doubt comparing theories about how best to approach Hazel a second time with his attorney present. Breck was still toggling between her laptop and the control panel as she monitored both sets of security cams for any sign of Bianca.

A warm hand rested on her shoulder. "It wasn't your fault." Kent had crossed the room to offer a quiet word of comfort.

"Some asshole took her on my watch." Nina tapped her chest. "That means it's my responsibility. I should never have let her come here while all this was going on."

"She's an adult," Kent said. "She makes her own choices. You couldn't have stopped her."

"You didn't hear Mrs. G's heart breaking," Nina said, dragging a hand through her short-cropped hair. "She's going to catch the first nonstop flight out of Reagan National." She began to pace. "I can't stand around any longer." The others watched her warily while she tried to think of something constructive to do. "I'm going back to search the tunnels again. Maybe we missed a clue."

"We used experienced people and the best technology down there," Kent said. "Going back isn't going to help."

Something he said made her stop pacing. "That's right," she said, turning his words over in her mind. "We used technology down there but not all of it."

Wade walked over to them. "What are you talking about, Guerrera?"

"I should have thought of it sooner, but I got distracted. The unsub put telemetry devices on the victims." When they all agreed, she continued, "Our cell phones didn't work in the tunnels. How could he use a tracker when we couldn't get a signal down there?"

Silence met her question.

"Interesting point," Wade said, turning to Breck, who was still sitting at the control panel and watching a patchwork quilt of video feeds on the wall screen. "Any ideas?"

Breck kept her eyes riveted to the screen while she answered. "My area of expertise does not extend to telemetry." She considered the problem briefly. "You might try some online research."

Wade shifted his gaze to Nina. "Why don't you use one of the extra terminals to see if there's a way to use a tracker underground?"

She saw through the thinly veiled attempt to distract her but didn't mind. If it would move the investigation forward, she would do it.

"On it," she said, plopping herself down in front of one of the computers that lined the back wall.

She soon discovered that Arizona had a booming mining industry. More than 60 percent of the copper in the US was unearthed in the state, and a substantial amount of silver, other metals, rocks, and minerals could be found beneath the ground as well.

An article about miner safety stopped her scrolling, and she zeroed in on a local company called Underworld that specialized in monitoring underground workers. Within ten minutes, she had convinced the receptionist who took her call to put her through to one of the foremen. Another minute's explanation convinced him she was legit and needed information quickly.

"I'll help in whatever way I can," the foreman said. "What do you need to know?"

Nina put the call on speaker so the others could listen in. "You design equipment that will track the movements of miners, correct?"

"We do." The foreman's gruff voice carried through the tiny speaker on her cell. "Our system can be used to locate machinery or personnel in real time, even three hundred feet down."

They all exchanged glances as he continued to explain. Apparently noticing a growing sense of excitement in the room around him, Perez cut his phone call short and joined them.

"The hardware can be embedded into a miner's helmet or reflective vest so they don't have to carry a unit that can be lost or damaged."

Nina thought about the jesses but didn't want to give too much away. "It's small enough to be sewn into a bracelet or attached to a shoe, then?"

"Absolutely," the foreman said.

"And how accurate is it?"

"The miner's location can be pinpointed within three feet," he said. "It can be used to rescue an injured miner or to send an alert if he enters a restricted area."

Nina figured it could also send an alert if a captive managed to leave a specific area . . . like a locked room. She wanted more confirmation. "Could the system cover a network of mines or tunnels?"

"You could configure it to monitor a five-square-mile area."

Breck, still keeping an eye on the wall screen, interrupted with a question. "This is Agent Breck. I'm working with Agent Guerrera," she began. "How does the client monitor the miners?"

"Our system is internet and cloud enabled and can run on a client's server," he said, apparently unfazed by the introduction of someone new into the conversation. "The user can configure the features for their own needs. It all works through an app we designed."

Breck straightened in her chair. "Someone aboveground or down in the mine can use the app?"

"You bet. There are a series of transponders set up to carry the signal."

"Of course," Breck muttered. "Can the signal be intercepted by a third party?"

"All of our systems are set up with an encrypted access code. In addition, the client chooses the signal's transmission frequency. It's kind of a double safety."

Nina focused on how the unsub could have gotten access to the technology. "Can anyone purchase one of these systems, or do you only sell them to mining companies and other organizations?"

"We only sell to companies," the foreman said.

"Could someone design something like this on their own by tweaking existing telemetry systems?"

"I suppose it's possible," he said. "But they'd have to be pretty damn smart and have access to some good equipment."

"Exactly the kind of person one might find at an elite tech university," Nina muttered under her breath. She thanked him and got his information in case she needed to call with more questions before disconnecting.

"Now we know the tech exists," Kent said as soon as the call ended. "There's a way the killer could be using the same kind of tracker falconers use—with adjustments to make it work in a subterranean setting."

"Does this mean we still think he's trapped Bianca somewhere in the tunnel system?" Nina asked. "Even though we searched it and couldn't find any sign of her?"

Wade broke the momentary silence that followed. "It seems likely that he used the tunnels to abduct all the students," he said. "For that reason, it seems logical that he has a holding cell somewhere off the tunnels that we couldn't find."

Nina was glad he had come to the same conclusion she had. "Can you crack the encryption?" she asked Breck.

"I can sure as hell try," she said. "But first I'll create an algorithm to randomly scan various frequencies. Maybe we can find a signal transmission that matches what he described."

"You're talking about SIGINT," Kent said. When everyone but Breck gave him a questioning look, he elaborated. "Stands for Signal Intelligence. I became familiar with the term in the military. It's one of several types of intel gathered covertly. SIGINT involves intercepting coded transmissions."

"Spy craft," Wade said, summing it up.

"I'd certainly like to spy on this sonofabitch," Perez said.

Nina gave it some thought. "Can you set parameters to seek out the strongest signals first?"

"I see where you're going with that," Breck said, frowning. "If the signal emanates from somewhere on campus or close by, it would register at a higher strength."

She turned toward her laptop and froze.

"What's wrong?" Nina asked.

A red flush crept up Breck's neck. "I was so busy talking to that guy that I took my eyes off the wall screen."

"I was watching," Kent said. "There was no sign of Bianca."

Wade gentled his voice. "I think we should turn our attention to this new lead."

He didn't say that there was no hope of finding Bianca up on the surface of the campus, but he might as well have.

A palpable sense of frustration had descended over the room when the door chime sounded. Nina had nearly forgotten that they had requested Dr. Feldman activate an audible signal before coming from the computer lab into the think tank.

Everyone glanced at the interior door, which slid open to reveal Rick Vale.

He stood there awkwardly until Kent waved him in. "Do you have something for us?"

Rick stepped inside. "I know you guys are busy." He swallowed. "But I found something that might send your investigation in a different direction."

Chapter 55

"Perhaps you'd better tell us what you found," Wade said. "Then we'll be able to figure out what to do next."

"When we first started helping Lieutenant Hazel investigate the disappearances, Dr. Feldman told me to mine the server for information to add more points to our matrix," Rick said. "I downloaded tons of raw data but hadn't had a chance to go through it. When you guys locked down the server and the cloud, that freed up my time from new searches, so I began reviewing the material I'd already captured." He looked at his shoes. "I wasn't looking for stuff about Dr. Feldman, but something kind of . . . popped up."

"Let's hear it, then," Wade said.

"I found a string of communications between Dr. Feldman and an undergrad student," Rick said. "A female. And the conversation was . . . um . . . sexual in nature."

"What communications?" Breck pushed for details. "How were they sent?"

"There's a kind of internal AIT platform where professors discuss assignments, projects, and papers with their students. Professors can also invite students into private chat rooms for one-on-one conversations if they need to give negative feedback or criticism that might embarrass the student in a public forum."

Nina gave Rick a verbal nudge, getting to the heart of the matter. "How long had Dr. Feldman been going into a private chat room to have inappropriate discussions with a student?"

"Once I started reading the messages in that particular chat room, I went back over the past few months," Rick said. "The conversations began with questions from the student about her thesis, then became more suggestive over time."

"I can't imagine why someone with Dr. Feldman's level of expertise with computers wouldn't delete the chats," Wade said.

"They were deleted," Rick said. "But they weren't erased from the server, and I managed to retrieve them." He held up a flash drive. "I put a copy of everything, including the location where I originally downloaded it from the server, on here. Since you guys are the only ones with access, you could probably find it there too."

"Wade's right, though," Breck said, taking the flash drive from Rick. "Feldman would have known how to erase all the history permanently." She tapped her chin thoughtfully. "Unless he was so arrogant he thought nobody would dare to check up on him."

"That would be my guess," Rick said. "Under the circumstances, I thought you all should know. I mean, he's in his fifties, and he's dating a student who's the same age as the victims."

"Is he married?" Wade asked.

"Divorced."

"Dating a student is not illegal," Perez pointed out.

"But it's not allowed," Rick said. "There's no telling what the chancellor would do if she found out."

"So he keeps it secret," Wade said. "Did you find any evidence that he had similar communications with any of the murdered women?"

"No, but I didn't look any further than just the one student."

"We'll talk to the professor and to the young woman," Wade said. "Who is she?"

Rick shifted on his feet. "I don't have her name."

"It's not in the messages?"

"She always used a handle," Rick said. "Even from the beginning."

"She's his student," Nina said, trying to make sense of the incongruity. "Why would she hide her identity to talk to her own professor?"

"I intend to ask him," Wade said. "We'll focus on him until we can ID her." He turned to Breck. "While we look for Feldman, see if you can find out this young woman's name."

She bent to insert the flash drive into a port under the table.

"Where is the professor now?" Nina didn't want him rushing out the back door if he suspected they were focusing on him.

Rick shrugged. "Haven't seen him at all today."

Another thought occurred to her. "Have you ever heard Dr. Feldman mention anything about the AIT Sphinx Society?" she asked Rick. "Was he interested in ancient pyramids?"

Rick looked genuinely confused. "Pyramids?"

Breck popped back up. "Sorry I didn't mention this earlier," she said to Wade and Nina. "But the society turned out to be a dead end."

"What society are you talking about?" Rick asked.

"There could still be a nexus with Egypt," Wade said to Breck before turning to Rick. "Did Dr. Feldman ever travel to Egypt?"

"Not that I know of," Rick said, then cocked his head in thought. "Is this Egypt stuff because some of the bodies were mummified?"

Nina wasn't surprised to hear that part of the case had made its way to the public. The families would have been told about the condition of the victims, and word would have spread.

"Yes," she said, ending that line of questioning without explaining the society and its pursuit of what Kent had termed arcane physics.

"Thank you for bringing this to our attention," Wade said to Rick, then stared at him.

Apparently getting the hint, Rick lifted a hand. "Uh, I guess I'll be going now." He turned toward the computer lab and stopped short. "What if Dr. Feldman calls me or comes to his office?"

"You get in touch with me immediately." Wade crossed the room to hand him a business card. "And you pretend this conversation never took place. But hopefully we'll find him before that can happen."

Rick left the think tank after another apology for interrupting them.

Wade gave Breck a significant look. "Can you pull up the personnel files we got from the chancellor and put Feldman's on the wall screen?" He turned to Perez. "Can you contact the PPD command post and ask them to help us locate Professor Feldman?"

"Of course," Perez said. "But we could be wasting our time on a *cochino viejo* professor who likes to date women less than half his age."

"He may be a dirty old man," Nina said, "but there's enough there to warrant a closer look. He had access to the AIT security cams and an insider's view of the investigation until recently." She frowned. "Besides, we've reached a dead end with Hazel until we hear back from your squad about the searches."

"Everybody be quiet," Breck said sharply. The room fell silent. A series of piercing beeps cut through the sudden stillness. Breck jumped up from her seat and ran to get her phone. "That's the surge-detector alert."

Chapter 56

He had watched Bianca send the signal, unable to remotely shut down the computer. He had thought it wise to install redundant layers of firewalls to prevent anyone from accessing the hard drive from an external system when he configured it, but now he saw the flaw in his plan. What had worked to his advantage had been weaponized and turned against him.

Just like Bianca.

He continued to follow her on the video feed to see where she went next. While he waited, he fished out his small leather notebook and clicked the top of his pen.

Field Notes

Day	Observation	Water 💧	Food 🍎	Strategy ✦
Melissa Campbell				
1	Capture went smoothly; nausea from sedation; no other ill effects	None	None	Withhold all stimuli and continue observation
2	Very distressed; may have minor injury to left index finger	None	None	Observe how she moves finger; plan for first contact; attempt drinking
3	Accepted water from mouth after minimal hesitancy; is learning to trust	8 ounces water	None	Wait another day to introduce feeding
4	Feeding by mouth initially successful. Subject displayed overt signs of rejection.	8 ounces water	3 chicken nuggets	
Bianca Babbage				
1	Capture went smoothly; adjusted ziptie, subject is smaller than the others	None	None	Active search ongoing; move up timetable or wait 24 hours for initial contact.
1	ADDENDUM: Incredibly bright. Defeated ziptie, blindfold, and tether. May attempt forcible resistance or escape. Destroyed remote viewing capability within habitat.	None	None	Activate notifications for proximity alerts, tracking, and containment. Wait an additional day prior to first contact.
1	2ND ADDENDUM: Subject has escaped. Unsuitable.	None	None	

Chapter 57

Nina raced across the room to stand next to Breck, who had snatched her cell phone from the top of a credenza. She sensed Wade, Kent, and Perez coming up behind her as they all peered over Breck's shoulder at the small screen in her hand.

"Can you trace the signal?" Nina asked, breathless.

"Working on it," Breck said. "In the meantime, go check all the security cameras. See if the AIT ones are jamming. If they are, check the FBI cams to see what the bastard is up to."

Nina understood. The killer had always shut the AIT video system down to conceal his movements when he was about to strike. Why was he doing it now? Did he plan to move Bianca somewhere?

She rushed over to the table and brought up every camera on both systems. The wall screen was an amalgam of fifty individual squares. Kent and Perez sat on either side of her while Wade stayed beside Breck.

"All the AIT cams are down," Kent said.

Indeed, half the squares on the big screen were filled with fuzzy gray static. The remainder, which were the FBI feeds, maintained images of the campus.

"I'll let the PPD command post know what's going on," Perez said, pulling out his phone.

Nina continued to scan the feeds but saw no sign of Bianca. She swore. "We let that sonofabitch Hazel go, and now he's doing something."

"I got a lock on the signal," Breck said. "It's strong and steady." She tapped the screen a few more times. "I'm going to use a GPS interface and overlay it on a map."

Nina held her breath, waiting for Breck's next words, but kept her eyes riveted to the cameras.

"Holy crap," Breck said a minute later. "This can't be right." She glanced up at them. "The interference is coming from downtown Phoenix."

"Stand by a second, Commander," Perez said into his phone as he stalked over to Breck. His dark brows snapped together as he glanced down at the screen in her hand. "That's North Central Avenue," he said so everyone could hear. "Near East Van Buren Street."

Breck fiddled with the screen, trying to pinpoint the precise origin of the signal while Perez talked to his commander. He disconnected and glanced up at them. "They're dispatching area-patrol units to check it out."

Nina wasn't happy. "How much do the beat cops know about the situation?" She worried about a hostage situation or worse—a shoot-out.

"They're getting all the pertinent details from the dispatcher," Perez said.

"We should head out there too," she said. "There's nothing showing up on the cameras, and Breck can keep monitoring her phone as we go." She focused an imploring gaze on Wade. "We're not doing any good here, and Breck may get a stronger signal if we're closer."

Wade regarded her for a long moment before he gave the order. "Let's go."

They all scrambled to grab their phones, check their weapons, and rush out the door. Within minutes, they were clambering inside the black Suburban with its tinted windows. Nina jumped behind the wheel and Perez sat in the front passenger seat, giving her directions, while Wade and Kent flanked Breck, who sat in the back seat with her nose almost touching her phone screen.

Perez pulled out his buzzing cell. "It's the command post," he said, lifting it to his ear. "Yes, sir?" His eyes widened. "That makes zero sense."

"What is it?" Nina said, tires screeching as she took the corners hard in the top-heavy SUV.

"The patrol units checked the entire area," Perez said. "There's no sign of anything going on." He swiveled his head to address Breck and put his phone on speaker. "Are you sure about the coordinates?"

Breck nodded. "We're closing in on the location fast. The signal hasn't moved or decreased in strength. There's no glitch. I'm certain of it."

The PPD commander's voice carried through the phone's speaker. "Give us an update when you arrive at the scene, Agent Breck." He disconnected.

Nina took a left turn from East Van Buren onto North Central.

"Stop!" Breck said. "We're here."

Nina ignored honking horns and raised middle fingers from other drivers as she swerved onto the shoulder of the roadway. Traffic whizzed by while they all looked around.

Normal city traffic. Normal city pedestrians. Normal everything.

"What the hell is going on?" Wade said.

"Y'all are never going to believe this," Breck said, eyes glued to her phone.

"What?" they all asked in unison.

Breck turned her phone to face them. "I kept refining the search as we traveled closer to the source, which is represented as a red dot." She pointed at the dot for emphasis. "Look where we are."

Nina, who had twisted her body to get a better view, shifted her gaze from the screen to Breck's wide green eyes. "We're right on top of the signal."

"Exactly," Breck said. "As in about four meters above it."

Perez blinked. "I don't follow."

Realization crashed in on Nina with the force of a physical blow. "The signal is coming from underground," she said. "Directly below us. That's why no one could see anything going on at street level."

"Wait a minute," Perez said, his voice strained with urgency. "The Phoenix tunnels run underneath this street." He pointed downward. "No one uses this system anymore, but it's not a secret, and it's not connected to the one at AIT."

Nina remembered Perez mentioning the tunnels built over a hundred years ago to cool the buildings before the advent of air-conditioning. "How can we get down there?" she asked him.

He scrunched his eyes in concentration for a moment. "The nearest access point is through the Hotel San Carlos in the two hundred block of North Central Avenue." He pointed. "Right there."

She threw the Suburban into gear and gassed it. Another volley of horns sounded a protest as she forced her way into traffic.

"We need a plan," Kent said. "This signal will likely lead us to the unsub's base of operations. Someplace he felt comfortable setting up a computer capable of jamming the security cams. We have to assume he will have surveillance in place and will know we're coming."

Nina knew what was coming next and made her opinion clear. "It could take the better part of an hour if we wait for SWAT to come out, review schematics of the tunnels, and create an ops plan. For the first time, we may know where the killer is. If he's alone, he might take down the signal, and we'll never find him. If he's with Bianca . . ." She let the implication hang in the air.

"I'm with Guerrera," Breck said. "We'd best act now before we lose our chance."

Perez slanted a look at Nina. "Our tactical team is capable of rapid deployment that will cut the normal response time by half," he said. "But we'll be there in less than sixty seconds. I'll advise the commander that we're going in through the San Carlos, and he can coordinate a response with all our other assets."

Nina pulled the vehicle to the curb in front of a stately cream-colored building with blue neon lettering announcing the hotel's name.

As they jumped out of the SUV and rushed toward the hotel's front entrance, Nina held out hope that perhaps Bianca had figured out a way to escape. The girl was brilliant and didn't think like most people. An instant later, a new thought struck her with sickening clarity.

"What's up, Guerrera?" Kent asked, running beside her.

She turned to him. "I followed protocol," she said. "Never discussed the details of the investigation with Bianca."

"And?" Kent said.

"I've been so distracted by chasing the source of the surge, that I forgot the unsub might be chasing a signal of his own."

"Spell it out, Guerrera."

"If he sticks to his pattern, he would have put a jess with a transponder on Bianca's ankle." She saw dawning realization in Kent's eyes as she voiced yet another scenario they hadn't previously considered. "If she somehow managed to get away from him"—her throat tightened around the next words—"she has no idea that he can track her down."

Chapter 58

Bianca raced down another dimly lit corridor, the black hoodie's hem flapping against her bare thighs. The dank smell in the air and the smooth construction of the windowless walls had led her to conclude that she was underground. Somehow, her captor had taken her down into a subterranean labyrinth. This was how he had taken the other girls, hiding them from the world until he was finished with them.

There had to be access points leading up to the surface, but she had found only one so far. At the dead end of a fork, a reinforced-metal door was set into the wall. The only light throughout the dark passages came from widely spaced single bulbs like the one that had been in her cell. Unable to get a good look at the door, she had wasted valuable time trying to open it before realizing that someone had soldered it shut.

Biting back a scream of impotent rage that might have brought the killer to her, she turned and retraced her steps back to the place the tunnels had diverged and took the other route.

The sound of footfalls echoed around her, reverberating off the cement walls. The noise seemed like it had come from behind her, but she couldn't be sure. Was it Nina and her team? The police? Or a madman coming to reclaim his lost prize?

She spotted a recess in the tunnel's smooth wall ahead of her and ran faster. Better to duck into the crevice and hide until she could see who else was down here rather than reveal herself by calling out.

She rushed ahead, running at full tilt, her bare feet smacking the cold floor. When she got close to the recess, she slowed just enough to dart into it.

Her body slammed into a man's hard chest. Instantly, a strong arm tightened around her waist while a large hand clamped over her mouth. He had found her.

She was trapped.

Again.

Chapter 59

He had planned to tackle Bianca as she raced by his hiding place, but she'd darted into the nook, rushing headlong into his arms.

Where she belonged.

He could have simply fled. Could have left the campus, left the state, left the country. But she called to him. He had given up on her. Made up his mind to deal with her as he had with the others. After jotting the quick mark that sealed her fate in his notebook, he recalled the thin, pale scars he had spotted under the edge of Bianca's shirtsleeve, and he had decided to give her one more chance. Unlike the eagle he had found in Egypt, she was not only wounded but also untrained. He sensed a part of her that was wild, even feral. She would need extra conditioning.

Reflecting on this, he concluded that she was the one he had been searching for after all. He would take her with him. They would be together. Once he got her far from this city, he could take his time taming her. Molding her like clay. Forging a lifelong bond.

She bucked and struggled, but he easily overpowered her. She was the smallest of any of his birds, a kestrel with the heart of a falcon.

"Call me Horace," he whispered to her. "I will take care of you from now on."

She tilted her head back, straining to glimpse his face. He knew she would have no memory of their encounter in the medical sciences building. She had merely looked at him in surprise when he sank the needle into her thigh. The injection he'd given her would rob her of any recollection of what had happened. She had no idea whose arms held her tight.

Thrashing with every ounce of strength she could muster, she lifted her bare feet and kicked, throwing him slightly off-balance. He stepped forward, still pinning her against his chest. Now that they had stepped out from the shadows, she tipped her head back again. Their eyes locked.

Her jaw slackened under his hand. Her gaze registered shock, then anger, and finally, hate.

A short time ago, he had watched her slip her jess and use her tether to climb up and dismantle his camera. He knew she was smart but hadn't expected her to be so resourceful. None of the others had managed to escape the holding cell, much less found their way to the control center he had built. And then she had put his hoodie on, signaling that she was his. Acknowledging his claim. Forsaking all others.

Or so he had thought.

Now he read her aversion as plainly as if she had shouted it. He knew what he had to do next, and his heart ached. She wasn't the one, but she could still serve a purpose. He yanked his hand from her mouth, pulling it back. Before she could work up a scream, he drove his clenched fist into her face. Head snapping back, she collapsed into his arms.

He hoped she remained unconscious. Force was not his first choice, but he could be brutal when necessary. If she woke and tried to yell for help, he would hit her again. Harder.

He lifted her easily, slung her slight frame over his shoulder, and started down the tunnel toward his next objective. He had prepared for every contingency months ago, bringing the materials he needed to set up his ideal refuge underground where no one was likely to find it.

In the event they did, however, he had taken certain precautions that guaranteed him an avenue of escape.

Before coming to get Bianca, he had checked his supplies and equipment. Everything was in place. He had a surprise waiting for the FBI, and people would talk about what happened beneath the city today for years to come.

Chapter 60

Nina rushed to the main entrance of the Hotel San Carlos with Breck, Kent, Wade, and Perez close on her heels.

Perez had called the front desk as they drove from the spot where Breck had pinpointed the source of the power surge to ask for the manager to meet them in the lobby.

As soon as they pushed through the rotating glass doorway, a white-haired man dressed in a dark suit with a lapel pin identifying him as Aaron Rayburn met them. Perez held up his gold shield, rapidly outlining the need to access the entrance to the tunnel without revealing much about the investigation.

"I need to see all your badges before I unlock the door to the tunnel," Rayburn said.

The rest of them flipped open black leather billfolds. Rayburn's brows lifted when he saw the FBI credentials, which seemed to spur him to action.

"Follow me." He strode through the lobby, stopping at a hidden entrance set into the side of a corridor. He inserted a key, then led them down two flights of stairs to the basement level. They continued past the laundry and housecleaning-supply areas, ending in front of a metal door painted battleship gray. Rayburn went through the dangling ring until he found another key.

"These tunnels aren't safe," Rayburn said, slotting the key into the lock. "That's why we don't let anyone down here. They're very old, and they're not well maintained. I can't guarantee your safety."

Nina understood that he was ensuring the hotel would have no liability in the event anyone got hurt. "We'll take our chances."

Rayburn opened the door and stepped aside.

"One of the PPD tactical teams will be here shortly," Perez said. "You can stay in the lobby to direct them down here."

After Rayburn left, Nina glanced at Perez. "I'm not waiting for SWAT." She had overheard his conversation with the PPD command post on the drive over. "You can stand by if you want, but I'm going after Bee."

"We could at least check out this part of the tunnel," Wade said. "Perhaps she's nearby."

Grateful they had agreed, Nina started down a flight of cement stairs and came out into a long corridor, its darkness punctuated by regularly spaced single, bare light bulbs attached to the ceiling.

"At least there's some light down here," she said, pulling out one of three flashlights they had taken from an emergency kit before leaving the think tank. She moved forward, prepared to click on the flashlight if it got too dark.

"Do we call out to her?" Breck asked.

"I don't want to advertise our presence if the killer is down here," Wade said.

"We'll do a preliminary sweep," Kent said. "If we come up empty-handed, we can wait for the tactical team to use their FLIR and GPR equipment like they did before."

It was better than sitting on their hands while Bianca could be fighting for her life. They surged ahead, the eerie silence gathering around them in the gloom.

Within minutes, Nina halted. "Now what?" She pointed to her right and then to her left. They had arrived at a fork in the tunnel system.

They began debating their options when a distant scream echoed off the smooth walls, then abruptly stopped.

Everyone froze, trying to determine which direction the sound had come from.

"That was Bianca," Nina said.

Her heart seized midbeat. Bianca was here. So close yet lost in the labyrinth beyond. In her bones, she knew the sudden silence cutting off the scream meant the killer had Bianca. Even when Nina had been tied to a table, facing a gruesome death at the hands of a demented sadist, she did not feel as helpless as she did in this moment.

Chapter 61

Nina looked from one fork in the tunnel to the other, uncertain which direction Bianca's shriek had come from. She had to make a choice and went with her best guess. "I think Bianca is this way." She gestured toward the tunnel to her right.

"The surge signal was emanating from north of the San Carlos," Breck said, pointing toward the corridor that branched to the left. "I'll go that way and try to find the source." She met Nina's gaze. "You can go the other way and look for Bianca."

Made sense. If a computer was at the heart of this situation, Breck was the one best qualified to locate and deal with it. She, on the other hand, was determined to rescue Bianca.

"We can't get a signal down here," Wade said, glancing at his phone before looking up at Breck. "You won't be able to zero in on the location."

"I know which way is north," she said.

Bianca's scream had caused a knot to form in Nina's stomach, and she didn't want to linger. "I'll head that way." She started down the tunnel to her right.

"Hold on," Kent said. "We've got no cell signal this far underground. How the hell are we supposed to communicate?" He paused. "We also have no way to convey information to the responding police who will soon be converging on this hotel."

Nina didn't care. Bianca had cried out. Deep within her, Nina had heard it as a call directly to her. She started down the tunnel.

"We're coming with you," Perez said a moment later.

Kent jogged up to her other side. "Wade is going with Breck to find the signal."

So it was the three of them, racing through the dimly lit corridors, searching for Bianca, her captor, or both.

They ran along in silence, Kent and Perez playing their flashlights along the walls to either side while Nina held her beam straight in front of them. No one spoke as they rushed around a series of bends and passageways.

Nina was in the lead. She had rounded another corner at a fast clip when her flashlight caught a dark shape on the floor in the middle of a long corridor. She stopped short, causing Kent and Perez to nearly crash into her from behind.

"What's that?" Perez whispered.

Kent, with his years of military experience behind enemy lines, kept quiet. He squeezed Nina's arm in a silent signal. When she looked up at him, he motioned ahead with two fingers and pointed at himself.

She understood the tacit communication to mean that he intended to run point and evaluate the threat. As he crept forward, she took a second look at the silhouetted shape. She moved closer, and made out what seemed to be a small human body.

Gasping, she lurched past Kent and dropped to her knees beside Bianca's still form.

Chapter 62

Nina spoke in a hoarse whisper, cognizant the killer might be nearby. "Bee," she said, counting on Kent and Perez to watch her back. "Honey, are you okay?"

She gently shook Bianca's slender arm but got no response. Filled with fear, she pushed the neck of the hoodie open to lay two fingers against the side of Bianca's neck. A strong, steady pulse throbbed against the pads of Nina's fingers. *Gracias a dios.*

"Shit," Perez said, drawing closer. "Is that Bianca?"

"She's alive but unconscious." Nina looked closer and was struck by a fresh wave of rage. "Judging by the blood coming from her nose, I'd say the sonofabitch punched her in the face."

"Might have drugged her too," Perez said. "She needs medical attention."

"You two take her up to the surface," Kent said. "I'm going to do a quick recon."

She glanced up to see that Kent was in Special Forces mode, standing guard over them while they discussed what to do with Bianca.

"This whole situation hinks me out," Kent said, his gaze continuously scanning the corridor. "He incapacitated her, then left her for us to find. I've seen this before. It's designed to either slow us down while he escapes or to set us up for an ambush."

"Or both," Nina said. "But that doesn't mean you should rush forward by yourself and—"

"It's what I'm trained to do," Kent said. "I've done recon behind enemy lines before. Sometimes it's the only way to get accurate intel about what you're facing."

"We have Bianca," Perez said. "Let's take her and go."

Kent shook his head. "This unsub has killed six people we know of. He's not about to stop, and he's a danger to the community. We have a fix on him right now, but if he escapes, he'll take more innocent lives before we corner him again. I'm not going to let that happen if I can prevent it."

Nina noticed Kent had called the killer an unsub. "You're not convinced it's Hazel, even though all the evidence points to him." She made it a statement. "That's why you want to run him down."

Rather than deny it, he focused on Perez. "Get them back to the surface. I'll catch up to you in a few minutes to take up a rear-guard position. If I can figure out which way he ran, we can let the SWAT team know, and they'll flush him out of here quicker."

Without another word, Kent turned and ran toward the far end of the tunnel that ended in another T intersection.

Perez bent down to wrap his strong arms around Bianca. He lifted her effortlessly and turned to Nina. "Let's go."

Nina glanced at Bianca, who still hadn't moved, then to Kent's retreating back. She couldn't abandon either of them. "There's no way I'm letting my partner chase a serial killer by himself," she said. "I can't carry Bee all the way back through the tunnels and get her up to the surface." She took in his athletic physique. "You can."

She watched Kent take the right fork and disappear around the corner. Every cop instinct she possessed urged her to join him. He was her partner, and she needed to back him up. She hesitated as warring instincts demanded that she stay and protect Bianca. It's what Kent had wanted her to do.

"You're coming with me." Perez's harsh words pulled her attention back to him. "I'm not leaving you down here."

"Kent needs backup," she said, coming to a decision. "Bee needs medical attention. There's no time for debate."

Perez opened his mouth, doubtless intending to bark another order at her, when an explosion rocked the tunnel.

A cloud of dust plumed from the right fork at the end of the corridor.

Where Kent had just gone.

Chapter 63

Nina struggled to keep her footing as the walls around them trembled. Perez staggered but stayed upright, clutching Bianca's inert form close against his chest.

"We've got to get going," Perez shouted over the last rumblings. "Now."

The blast galvanized her. Kent had not come back from his recon. "Take Bianca out of here." She pulled out her Glock. "I've got to check on Kent."

"Kent was the one who told us to take Bianca to safety." Perez's dark eyes narrowed. "You think I'm going to just leave you here while I run away?"

"You're not running from danger," Nina said. "You're rescuing Bianca. I'm trusting you with her life, which is more important than my own."

She could see the conflict play itself out on Perez's expressive face. His need to protect clashed with his need to rescue. She knew the only way to resolve his dilemma quickly was to give him no choice.

"When you get to the lobby, tell the SWAT team what happened and where we split up," she said, then turned and began to run in the direction she had last seen Kent, ignoring the stream of expletives in two languages coming from behind her.

She had played her trump card. She knew Perez would not leave Bianca to join her. She also knew he would never carry Bianca toward danger to help Nina locate Kent. She had used the honor of a good man against him, but she had no regrets. Bianca would be safe. Perez would protect her. And she would help Kent.

Nina continued to rush toward the end of the corridor without looking back. She rounded the corner at a dead run and came to a halt.

Motes of gray dust swirled beneath the only light bulb that hadn't shattered in the explosion or its aftermath. As the haze continued to clear, she made out the silhouette of a man pointing a gun directly down at a pile of rubble near his feet.

Was it Kent?

A groan sounded from under the heap of broken cement, and she recognized the voice.

"Kent," she murmured, shifting into a tactical stance. She leveled her gun at the standing figure. "FBI. Don't move!"

His head snapped around to face her, casting his features into sharp relief in the dim light. Their eyes locked.

"You?" She could not believe her eyes.

This was the unsub. This was the man who had taken so many innocent lives. The man who had abducted Bianca. The man who was about to shoot Kent at point-blank range.

And it wasn't Lieutenant Hazel.

Chapter 64

He cursed his luck. Then he remembered that a good plan was better than good luck. And his plan was sound. He simply had to make some adjustments to deal with this new development.

"Special Agent Guerrera," he called out, engaging her to buy time. "The Warrior Girl."

"Drop the gun," Guerrera said to him.

His IED had done its job by taking out the G-man, and he'd gotten the agent's gun as a bonus prize. Now this small woman expected him to hand over all his power? Like hell.

"It's mine now." He kept the Glock trained on the downed agent's chest as he strategized. "Captured weapons are spoils of war."

Mind racing, he reflected on his military training. He'd begun his Army career working with live ordnance. Recognizing his innate intelligence, the Army had moved him into bioweapons research, working on a project funded by dark money hidden in the Congressional military budget. He knew more about the human nervous system than some medical doctors. He had also learned a great deal about the mind—specifically, how to elicit preferred responses in captives.

"Not happening," Guerrera said. "You're done. There's no escape. Lay down the gun, and back away." She injected command into her tone. "Now."

He'd watched Bianca on his computer sending a power surge through the security cams using the technology he had developed. He'd deduced that the only reason she would take time away from her escape and risk recapture to send a surge through the system was that she knew the Feds could track it to her location.

His secret exposed, he'd activated his escape plan, leaving Bianca in the tunnel behind him to slow down pursuers. She was the lure. But somehow, it hadn't worked. Bianca wasn't here, but two Feds were. He realigned the facts until he came up with the most likely scenario. They had someone else with them who had taken custody of Bianca. Someone who was probably rushing her to safety while these two chased him.

Fine. He realized there was another way to accomplish his objective. His new plan required him to lay a few of his cards on the table.

"As you can see, Agent Guerrera, I'm very comfortable with explosives. Uncle Sam taught me how to make things go boom. I've wired the entire tunnel system to blow."

He allowed her a moment to digest this information before continuing.

"Once I press this detonator"—he lifted his free hand to let her see it nestled in his palm—"a series of blasts will go off. Everyone in the tunnels will be crushed in a cave-in . . . including Bianca and whoever is with her right now."

He could see the horror register on the woman's lovely face, quickly replaced by a mask of calm. It didn't fool him. His threat had found its mark.

"What about you, asshole?" Guerrera said. "You'll die too."

Her remark proved to him that she did not question his threat or his ability to carry it out.

"I left out a few details," he said. "The explosions are timed to detonate at set intervals. They'll begin at the entrance to the tunnels and gradually work their way through the entire system."

That had been the genius of his escape plan. He had considered a scenario in which law enforcement would come after him. He'd programmed devices to blow, starting where the police would make entry and successively going off toward his planned exit point. That way, he would have time to run just ahead of the explosions while the tunnels imploded behind him. He would get out. Anyone pursuing him would be buried alive.

He was fit and strong, with plenty of training. More than capable of taking on the petite FBI agent who thought she could arrest him. The big guy still groaning and shifting beneath the rubble at his feet, however, looked like he could be trouble. He certainly couldn't deal with both of them by himself if the man fully recovered.

He was a student of human nature. These two were clearly alone, or reinforcements would have already arrived. He could use a different version of the same tactic he had employed when he'd used Bianca as a distraction.

He would give Agent Guerrera an impossible choice.

"Everyone can survive if you do as I say," he called out to her. "Put your gun down and back off, or I'll press the button right now."

He had no intention of letting anyone leave the tunnels besides himself. As soon as Guerrera laid down her Glock and backed away, he would shoot the man on the ground and press the button. While she rushed to help her wounded colleague, he would escape.

"Many lives hang in the balance," he said to Guerrera. "Choose wisely."

He saw the resolve in her eyes the instant she made her decision and braced himself for what was about to come next.

Before he could fully process what she was doing, Agent Guerrera pulled the trigger.

Chapter 65

The single bulb that lit the corridor exploded in a shower of sparks, briefly illuminating Dr. Dawson's livid face before plunging them all into pitch darkness. The weapon's blast boomed like a cannon in the confined space. Nina ducked, avoiding the responding hail of gunfire. As she had intended, he was shooting at her, not Kent.

She had been stunned to see who her attacker was when his features were revealed from the shadows. The depth of his deception solidified his brilliance as nothing else could have.

How many times had he met with Bianca in his office? Walked the campus with her? Had his fascination begun when he read her thesis? Was that part of the reason he had invited her to AIT? Her high IQ and quirky personality made her stand out, and sometime after his fantasy with Melissa Campbell ended, he had decided to make Bianca his new falcon.

"You bitch!" Dawson's shout sounded closer to her than he had been.

Nina knew Kent was injured but couldn't call out to him. Dawson was stalking her in the dark; any sound would give her position away. The thought gave her an idea. She bent to grope around on the floor until her fingers closed over a chunk of fallen rubble. She threw it, and the cacophonous bouncing of the rock against the cement walls drew Dawson's fire, as she'd hoped it would. Like her own service weapon,

Kent's Glock held fifteen rounds plus one in the chamber. So far, she had counted eight shots fired. Could she rope Dawson into emptying his magazine?

Impenetrable darkness surrounded her, disoriented her, pressed against her eyeballs. The fetid smell of mildew competed with the acrid scent of gunpowder.

Edging toward the place where Kent had fallen, Nina clutched the gun in one hand and held the other out in front of her, fingers splayed, to avoid bumping into anything.

"You want to play, Agent Guerrera?" Dawson taunted. "I don't think you'll like my game."

The tumbling of loose rubble nearby told her the professor was prowling along the wall in her direction. She circled away from the sound, trying to reach Kent before he did. She would place her body in front of her partner's before giving Dawson a chance to surrender. If he made any movement that sounded like he would try to shoot Kent, she would fire in his general direction until she found her target or emptied her clip. Placing each foot carefully behind her, she inched backward, then dropped to her knees and began scrabbling through the rubble.

Crawling painfully over sharp chunks of cement, she finally touched what felt like Kent's arm. One moment, she was trying to find his wrist to check for a pulse, and the next she was thrown onto her back, the wind knocked out of her as Kent pinned her to the floor.

Clearly responding to his training and not yet aware of what was going on, he had reached out to latch on to the first threat he detected. Terror gripped Nina when she realized Kent could snap her neck before fully realizing who she was or what he was doing. He was in survival mode, and his SEAL background made him lethal.

Still afraid to give away their location by speaking, she raised her free hand to his face, praying he would notice the palm touching him was soothing, small, and feminine.

He stopped all movement, apparently evaluating new sensory information. "Guerrera?"

Dawson had clearly recovered enough of his hearing to zero in on the single word. He fired three shots in rapid succession, the rounds coming so close Nina could feel puffs of air coming up from bits of cement around her. Deafened by the fresh barrage of gunfire, she gave Kent a shove, slid out from under him, and got to her knees. She aimed in the direction of Dawson's muzzle flashes and fired blind.

His shots ceased instantly. A round had apparently found its mark.

"Drop your weapon," she shouted, then waited for a response, or perhaps a thud from Dawson's body collapsing to the floor.

Nothing.

The realization that, like Dawson, the brief incendiary flash from her weapon's muzzle had revealed her position came a moment too late. The blast from Kent's stolen Glock accompanied the sensation of a Hornady 9mm Luger +P 135 grain Critical Duty round slamming into her chest.

Chapter 66

Nina clenched her jaw against the scream filling her throat. The sheer force of a small projectile traveling at 1,450 feet per second smashing into her Kevlar vest drove her backward. She sprawled onto her back, eyes blinking in the pitch darkness.

Gulping air, she lurched to her feet, assessing her situation. If she stood still, Dawson would keep shooting until he hit some part of her not protected by body armor. If she sidestepped to avoid incoming rounds, one of them would eventually hit Kent, who was unarmed and vulnerable.

Unacceptable.

It appeared Dawson was forcing her to choose between saving herself and saving her partner. She had to think of a third option. Her training afforded her the ability to sort through possibilities in seconds, discarding each idea as quickly as it formed. All at once, it hit her.

Do the one thing Dawson would never expect.

In a move born of pure desperation, she opted for the element of surprise and went on the offensive. Continuously firing in Dawson's direction, she advanced on his last-known position.

Between spurts of thunderous gunfire in the confined space, she could barely make out Dawson's bellowed expletive, which was followed by a heavy thud. Finger on the trigger, she paused to listen. Echoes from her last shot reverberated through the eerie silence. Had Dawson fallen, or was this a ploy calculated to lure her into point-blank range?

This time, Kent remained silent and still. Clearly, he had recovered enough to understand that any verbal communication would jeopardize both of them. Visual gestures wouldn't work, and they were no longer in physical contact, so tactile signals were also impossible. That meant Kent would have to trust her to take on Dawson single-handedly.

Blinded by total darkness, hearing compromised, she had to rely on her remaining senses to guide her approach. Edging closer to her quarry, she detected a metallic scent through the thick stench of gunpowder hanging in the air like a toxic cloud. Years of experience had taught her to recognize the smell of fresh blood. Dawson had been hit, but was he still a threat?

Crouching into a squat, she held her Glock in one hand while she felt along the floor with the other. Her fingers soon found a puddle of warm, sticky liquid. Sweeping her arm to the side, the edge of her palm bumped against a shoe with its toe upturned toward the ceiling. She shifted her hand and felt the hardness of his shin. Evidently on his back, Dawson lay perfectly still. She continued her tentative exploration, sliding her hand up his body to his neck. She laid two fingers against his carotid pulse point for a silent count of twenty.

"Kent," she called out. "Dawson's got no—"

Her words were cut off by an explosion.

Chapter 67

Nina sprang to her feet as the residual shock wave rumbled through the tunnel system. After several terrifying seconds, the space around her seemed to settle.

Kent groaned in the darkness, and she called out to him, "You okay?"

The response came as a low grumble. "Peachy."

She felt the corner of her mouth quirk up despite their grim situation. Kent's sarcastic response, more than anything else he could have said, reassured her that no additional rubble had fallen onto him.

"That explosion came from the direction of the San Carlos," she said, trying to find her way to his side. "Back the way we came."

Kent grunted his agreement. "If that asshole was telling the truth, he set the IEDs to go off at regular intervals behind him as he fled. The first one must have been a smaller device he carried with him in case he needed a quick diversion or to disable an attacker."

Nina drew the next logical conclusion. "Which means we need to go in the opposite direction of the way we entered and hope we can find an exit. Do you still have your flashlight? Mine's gone."

A small beam cut through the darkness, playing across the ground. For an instant, the light fell on Dawson's inert form. "Did you check his vitals?" Kent asked her.

Before she could answer, another thunderous noise shook walls.

"He's dead," she said quickly. "We need to move. Now."

Kent stooped to retrieve his Glock, and they started toward the far end of the corridor, where a dim shaft of light emanated from around a bend. She noticed Kent had substantially recovered and wondered if he had simply been biding his time for an attack on Dawson.

He broke into a steady jog. After they rounded the corner, single overhead bulbs spaced far apart once again illuminated their way.

"The next one should go off any second," Kent said, stowing his flashlight back in his pocket and picking up the pace.

As soon as the words left his mouth, another explosion—even closer this time—shook the floor enough to make them both stumble.

Kent grabbed Nina's hand and dragged her along at a dead sprint. She was fast, but his ground-eating strides made up twice the distance of her short ones.

They had no idea how to locate the exit Dawson had planned to use for his escape. There were no schematics, and there was no time to call anyone on the surface even if they could get a signal.

The overhead lights began to flicker, and Nina figured the explosions had compromised the electrical wiring. Did that mean the structural integrity of the entire tunnel system was on the verge of collapse? Probably.

Kent pulled his flashlight from his pocket and turned it on as the lights went out. Now scanning the walls with only a small beam, Nina felt the desperation of their situation. They could barrel straight past an alcove with a door hiding steps leading to the surface. The door they had used to enter the tunnels had been in a recess in a long corridor.

Kent abruptly jerked her to a halt. They were faced with yet another T intersection.

"Do we go right or left?" he said, peering first one way, then the other.

"No clue," she said between gasps.

"One way will lead us out, the other way will bury us alive," he said. "There is no time to search both directions. We have to choose."

She hesitated. "Unless."

"What?"

"We split up," she said. "You go one way. I go the other. One of us escapes."

"And the other dies." He gave her a searching look. "I'm not leaving you, Guerrera." He arched a thick blond brow. "Besides, I'm the only one with a flashlight."

"Then it's double or nothing if we stick together."

"Come on." He tugged her to the right, and they raced down the dark tunnel with only a thin beam to guide them.

Another device detonated in the tunnel behind them as they reached a solid wall. In that moment, Nina knew they had chosen the wrong path.

The walls around them began to shake. Small fragments of cement tumbled down from the ceiling. Larger chunks tumbled down in a thunderous cacophony several yards behind them. When the dust settled, Nina saw that the rubble reached from the floor to the tunnel's rounded ceiling, cutting off any possibility of retreat. The next explosion would likely crush them where they stood. Everything she had been through, all that she had done, had not prepared her for the moment of death.

She thought of Bianca and prayed with all her heart that Perez had gotten her to the surface in time. She would gladly forfeit her life if she could be certain she had succeeded in saving the small, maddening, impish girl who had come to mean everything to her. Had she ever told Bianca that she loved her? She looked at Kent and saw the bleakness she felt reflected in his eyes.

They were trapped.

Kent stood still, assessing the situation, no doubt coming to the same conclusion she had. He angled the flashlight up toward his face.

"There's no way out," he said, pulling her closer. "We're not going to make it, Nina."

Distantly aware that he had used her first name, which he rarely did, she made out a softness in his tone that she had never heard before.

"I need to tell you something." His deep voice was tinged with sorrow. "And I want you to look at me."

Chapter 68

Nina tilted her head back to study the ridges and planes of Kent's face, which were thrown into sharp relief by the flashlight he held under his chin. She felt the warmth of his arm tightening around her. His features began to glow brighter, and she noticed a thin shaft of light shining down from above.

Her eyes traveled up to the ceiling. "What is that?"

"Nina, I can't help but feel—"

"No." She pointed upward. "What is that light?"

He followed her gaze. "It looks crescent shaped." He angled his head. "Like maybe from a round hatch."

"If it's a hatch, maybe it leads to the street," she said. "Could be a manhole cover. There should be metal rungs leading up to it."

He shined the flashlight along the walls, which had begun to crumble. When he lowered the beam, she spotted several short metal bars scattered among the rubble on the floor.

"They came loose from the wall," he told her.

She quickly calculated the height of the tunnel's ceiling. "Give me a boost."

He handed her the flashlight and bent down, lacing his fingers together. She put her foot in his hands, and he lifted her up to stand on his broad shoulders. She wobbled briefly, then clutched the edge of a round metal door.

"It's a hatch." She cursed. "But it's stuck."

"Look for a latch. It wouldn't be locked from above. There must be a way to open it from below for safety reasons."

She shined the light around the edge, finally spotting a rusty catch. She banged on it with the bottom of the flashlight until it swung loose. Stuffing the light in her waistband, she pressed both palms against the hatch and shoved. Kent added his strength, pushing her upward.

The metal door groaned upward, then swung wide and clanged open. Without warning, Kent thrust her up with such force she practically shot through the opening. She barely had time to grab the sides of the hole and pull herself into a sitting position on its edge. Glancing around, she saw that she had landed . . . not in a street, but on the floor of what appeared to be an empty warehouse.

She peered down at Kent, who had tilted his face up to look at her.

"Run, Guerrera," he said. "This whole tunnel system is on the verge of collapse. If you stay where you are, you'll go down with it."

He had used his formidable strength to launch her up to safety, sacrificing himself so that she could survive. Now he apparently expected her to simply scurry away and leave him to his fate.

Fuck that.

"You said you weren't leaving me," she told him. "I'm not leaving you either."

Ignoring the stream of obscenities floating up to her from below, she scanned the deserted room. There was no furniture, no cords, no equipment, nothing she could pass down to Kent to pull him up.

"Leave, Guerrera." Kent made it a command.

She didn't do well with commands. "Shut up. I'm trying to think."

She had forced Perez to rescue Bianca when she could not, but she would not allow Kent to save her because she didn't have the physical strength to help him. She might be small, but she had spent her entire life finding ways to compensate for her size. She would damn well figure out how to rescue Kent.

A scan of her environment had revealed nothing useful, so she let her gaze travel down her body. Suddenly excited, she slid her nylon web belt from its loops, lay facedown on the floor, and dangled it down through the hole.

"First of all, that's way too short," Kent called up to her. "Your waist is tiny. Second, even if I could jump up and grab it—which I can't—I'd yank you right back down in here with me. It's not going to work, and we're out of time." His voice sharpened with a guttural shout. "Go, dammit!"

She scrambled to her feet, completely disregarding his barked order, and looked around again. What else could she use to reach him? Another idea occurred to her. An insane idea, but the only one she had.

She unbuttoned and unzipped her jeans, shucking them down to her ankles. After kicking off her shoes, she tugged her pants off and tied the cuff area in a knot around the belt. She lay down on her stomach again, this time lowering the opposite leg of the thick black denim.

"I can reach the pants," Kent said. "But I'm not pulling you down here, Guerrera. No way."

Cursing his stubbornness, which rivaled her own, she knotted the top of the belt around the hinges of the metal hatch. "It's secured to the hatch. I'm not holding on to it. The denim should hold. Go ahead and climb up."

"I'm not going anywhere until I know you're safe."

Aware he would not attempt to save himself until he believed her to be out of danger, she decided to give him what he wanted. She lowered her voice to make it sound as if she were calling out to him from a distance. "I'm running outside to the street. I'll meet you there."

She hunkered down, staying right where she was, and waited. If he got stuck, if he was injured by an explosive, she would be there to haul him the rest of the way out.

Kent's grunts carried up from the opening. She saw a hand grasp the edge, then another, then a blond crew cut emerged. An instant later, a pair of blue eyes fixed on her and turned to chips of ice.

"Dammit, Guerrera, you said you were leaving."

She shrugged. "I lied."

He heaved himself the rest of the way out. "Do you ever follow orders?"

She got to her feet, then stumbled as the floor shifted beneath her. Thunderous rumbling started low before seeming to build.

Kent charged forward, scooping her up in one arm as he raced to the service door without slowing. He used his free hand to slam the metal bar that ran across the door, setting off an alarm as he pushed it open and rushed outside.

Metal shrieked, windows burst, and stucco walls fissured behind them. Shoes thudding along the sidewalk, Kent shifted her in his arms as he ran, shielding her body with his.

"The warehouse is going to implode," she said to Kent, who kept moving.

"Keep away from the building," he shouted to passersby who had slowed to see what was going on.

Moments later, a cacophony of voices cried out as people warned each other to stay back. After barreling two blocks away, Kent finally stopped. They both looked on as the warehouse seemed to fold in upon itself, disappearing in a massive plume of dust that spewed three stories into the air.

"You can put me down now," she said when the thunderous roar subsided.

Kent spared her a glance. "You've got no shoes, and there's broken glass everywhere. Those socks won't prevent your feet from getting cut to ribbons." He hesitated. "And . . . you're not wearing pants."

Nina felt her cheeks warm. "Good point. Maybe you should take me inside somewhere."

He lowered his voice. "Don't think I've forgotten how you lied to me. I've aged ten years in the past five minutes."

Their gazes locked.

"I have no idea what to do with you," he said. "A part of me wants to keep you safe, even if it means barking orders—which you ignore. Another part of me wants to fall to my knees like a knight before his queen, totally at your command." His words grew thick with emotion. "You are the most exasperating woman I've ever known."

He tilted his head down to hers, then froze at the sound of approaching sirens. They both glanced up to see an ambulance and a cruiser blow past them.

Nina's heart was hammering. Had Kent been about to kiss her? Was this what he wanted to tell her when he thought they wouldn't make it out of the tunnel? She had no time to process her feelings about him, which seemed as confused and conflicted as his were for her.

Still cradling her in his arms, he turned his back to the street and strode in the opposite direction. Whatever had been in his mind, the moment had passed.

Chapter 69

Nina barely managed to wait for the PPD officer to hand back her creds before rushing inside the Phoenix Convention Center. She was still in her socks but now wore Kent's button-down shirt, which covered more of her than some dresses she'd worn. Coming to an abrupt stop, she turned in frantic circles, looking for Bianca and the rest of her team. Had they made it out of the tunnels before the explosions began?

The massive convention center, commandeered as a temporary disaster-operations command post, was a hive of activity. First responders of every description had set up workstations marked by hastily written placards within the vast open space. Every minute, more federal, state, and municipal agencies arrived.

After Nina and Kent fled from the imploding warehouse, they had tried to call Wade, but the cell towers were overloaded, and service was down. In sheer desperation, Kent had held up his FBI shield and flagged down a passing PPD patrol car. The officer advised them that a command post had been set up and offered to drive them to the location. On the way over, Nina learned three buildings had collapsed and six more were evacuated pending evaluation for structural integrity. The unstable ground made it impossible for search-and-rescue teams to check some areas for casualties.

Nina finally spotted Perez in the crowd. She heaved a sigh of relief. He had made it out of the tunnels unharmed, and he would not have left Bianca behind. With Kent close on her heels, she threaded her way through the throng to reach him.

He caught sight of her and closed the distance at a run. "Nina." He gripped her arms, eyes filled with concern moving up and down her body, checking for injury. "Are you okay?"

"Where's Bianca?" she said, hearing the desperation in her own voice. "Where's my team?"

"Bianca's on her way to the hospital," Perez said. "I helped load her into the ambulance. The paramedics thought she showed signs of a concussion, and she might have a fractured nose, but she was alert and conscious, and her vitals were good when they took her away."

Overcome, Nina leaned in to give Perez a hug. "Thank you," she said against his chest. "You saved her life. If it weren't for you—"

"What about the rest of our team?" Kent said, his tone sharp.

Before Perez could answer, a pale blur with auburn hair rushed directly at them. Nina barely had time to step away from Perez and brace herself before Breck launched headlong into her arms.

"We thought you and Kent were dead," Breck said, her green eyes glistening.

"How the hell did you two get out of there?" Wade sounded uncharacteristically shaken. "There's no way you should be alive."

"She refused to follow orders," Kent said, jerking a thumb at Nina. "Saved my life. Twice."

"You saved mine too," Nina said. "Not that anyone's keeping score."

Wade's eyes narrowed. "Sounds like you left out a few pertinent details."

Nina realized that in her rush to find out what happened to Bianca, she hadn't shared a critical fact. "After Perez took Bianca back to the surface, Kent and I had a run-in with the unsub."

She deliberately downplayed the nightmarish encounter in the tunnel. Her written account of the incident would include every detail, but for now, she didn't want Kent to face questions about how his service weapon had been taken from him and used to shoot her.

She took in their shocked expressions and realized her woefully understated summary had left out a critical detail. "It was Dr. Dawson."

"The professor we met in front of the computer science building?" Perez frowned. "The one who was recruiting Bianca to be his graduate research assistant?"

"So it wasn't Hazel," Breck whispered. "Or Feldman."

"Hell, for a while there, I was even considering Rick," Kent said.

"We can discuss the various suspects later," Wade said. "Right now, I have one overriding question." He looked from Nina to Kent. "Where is Dawson?"

"That was the first time Guerrera saved my life," Kent began. "Dawson detonated an IED large enough to bury me under some rubble but small enough not to cave the tunnel in. While I was down and barely conscious, he took my Glock." Kent tipped his head toward Nina. "He made the mistake of getting into a gunfight with the Warrior Girl and lost."

Wade turned to Nina. "You shot him?"

"I returned fire," Nina clarified. "When I checked his vitals, he had no pulse, but he must have pressed the button on his handheld detonator before he died."

"He had the whole tunnel system rigged to blow," Kent added. "We managed to find an escape hatch leading up to a warehouse."

"Then Dawson's body is somewhere under the city," Perez said. "And you two were almost buried with him."

"What happened to your pants, Guerrera?" Wade asked.

Kent, now in a formfitting black undershirt, answered the question. "They're back in the warehouse, under a mountain of rubble with her belt and her shoes."

All eyes drifted to her sock-clad feet.

"Nice dress," Breck said, breaking the awkward silence.

Nina looked down at the tails of Kent's gray oxford shirt.

Wade lifted a brow. "This should make for an interesting report."

Nina thought about the paperwork that would take hours to complete. "Can it wait? I'd like to go to the hospital to see Bianca," she said quietly. "I have to make sure she's okay."

Wade nodded. "I need a bit more from you and Kent first. There's a media shitstorm breaking, and I've got to make a joint statement with the police chief and the mayor. The governor is on his way too." He heaved a sigh. "There are widespread blackouts, and communications are virtually nonexistent. We need to reassure the public that the immediate threat is over."

He went on to explain that the Arizona Department of Public Safety and the Maricopa County Sheriff's Office had each deployed officers to help the PPD answer calls for service, direct traffic, and maintain order in parts of the city without power.

Media representatives were flocking to the area to report that the governor had declared a state of emergency due to the scope of the damage.

Listening to the litany of chaos and widescale destruction, Nina could hardly believe it had all been caused by one man.

Chapter 70

Nina had allowed Perez to persuade her to let him take her to the hospital, where he had access to police parking and could badge his way into the overcrowded emergency room. She had wanted to go to the hospital immediately, but he pointed out that she needed proper attire and shoes, or security would stop her at the door. After a fast stop at her hotel room, where she showered and put on her own clothes, he had taken her to Phoenix General. She followed in his wake as he made his way past security to the nurses' station. Apparently familiar with the detective, they had not hesitated to direct him to Bianca's room.

She walked inside to see Bianca lying on a hospital bed covered in a white blanket, her head wrapped in gauze.

Heart pounding, Nina strode to her side. "Bee, honey, how are you?"

Bianca's cobalt-blue eyes, surrounded by purpling skin, peered at her over a bandaged nose. "About time you got here."

Nina smiled. Bianca's sardonic tone assured her she was okay. She was certain Mrs. Gomez, who was currently on a flight from Washington to Phoenix, would have rushed to pull Bianca into a hug, probably loosening tubes and knocking over monitors in the process. Tears would have flowed freely, as would words of love and comfort.

For the thousandth time, Nina felt the sting of inadequacy. The gaping hole left by growing up without a family, and then distancing herself from others as an adult, had left her unable to offer the kind of emotional support Mrs. G would have given instinctively.

Instead, she fell back on what came naturally between them, and answered Bianca in kind. "A shoot-out, a few bombs, and a tunnel collapse delayed my arrival a bit."

"I think we were all surprised by how things went down," Bianca said, taking Nina's recitation in stride. "I have to admit that I've taken my fair share of psych classes, and I never suspected that Dr. Dawson was a complete whack-a-doo." She shook her head. "He told me to call him Horace. What the hell is that? His first name is Paul, and his middle name is Vincent. I saw it on the invitation he sent me."

"Horace?" Nina repeated, perplexed, then moved on. "Listen, Bee, I know this is not the best time, but I need to ask you some questions about what happened. I have to meet with my team, but before I go, I'll have to take you through everything you can recall."

Bianca lifted her chin. "I can handle it."

Nina silently gave Bianca full marks for courage, but knew she had to be gentle with her. Fresh from surviving a near-fatal attack, Bianca didn't fully grasp the psychological ramifications of what she had endured.

Nina knew firsthand. No one on her team ever discussed it, but she was aware her colleagues noticed the symptoms of PTSD she occasionally exhibited.

She would make sure Bianca got proper counseling, hopefully lessening the potential for long-term damage.

Bianca's gaze shifted to Perez, and the corners of her mouth lifted. "By the way, I was kind of out of it before. Can't remember if I thanked you for getting me out of there."

"You are most welcome," Perez said softly.

Nina had forgotten he was standing beside her. She figured he was probably wondering why they weren't clutching each other and sobbing. Perez, however, had not grown up in foster care. Had not learned from an early age to conceal his feelings.

Nina and Bianca had both learned those lessons, but Nina could see Bianca's eyes begin to shimmer with unshed tears. Her heart swelled. This was why she had placed her with Mrs. G. The past five years spent in a warm, loving home had made all the difference. Bianca was hesitant but capable of opening up. Finally, a single tear spilled out to course down her swollen cheek. In that moment, Nina knew she had done right by her.

"I kind of woke up while Detective Perez was carrying me into the hotel lobby," Bianca said. "The last thing I remembered was Dr. Dawson hitting me down in the tunnel."

Nina's muscles tensed at the mention of the professor's brutality. He had come close to murdering Bianca, as he had the others. The thought of losing her caused a physical ache in Nina's heart.

"I asked Detective Perez about you," Bianca continued. "But he wouldn't answer."

Perez looked at Nina. "How could I have told her?"

His piercing dark eyes conveyed what he didn't say, the words that remained unspoken. *How could I have told her I left you down there to die?*

She reached out to give his hand a quick squeeze. "I gave you no choice."

He looked like he wanted to respond, then thought better of it and remained silent.

"I finally got him to admit he didn't know where you were," Bianca said. "That's when I knew you were down there, going after Dr. Dawson. Then, when the ground started shaking, I—"

Nina picked up Bianca's trembling hand. "He's not going to hurt anyone ever again."

She knew she didn't have to say more for Bianca to grasp her meaning.

"I shouldn't have worried," Bianca said, her voice regaining its strength. "Once you were onto him, that asshole didn't have a chance." She glanced at Perez. "Some people find superheroes in comic books." She slanted an admiring gaze at Nina. "I just have to look next door."

Chapter 71

An hour later, Nina sat at the conference table in the think tank with her FBI team and Detective Perez. Wade had just returned from the news conference, looking drawn and haggard.

"You look rode hard and put up wet," Breck said to him.

"Chief Tobias took the brunt of it," Wade said. "Reporters are going with the security threat angle, questioning why the Phoenix police didn't seal off the tunnels under the city long ago."

He turned to Nina. "How's Bianca?"

"She's in good spirits, but she's going to have a couple of panda-worthy black eyes," she said. "They're going to discharge her in a couple of hours. My cousin Alex is on his way to the airport to pick up her foster mother. They'll stop at the hospital and take Bianca back to Teresa's house. Mrs. Gomez will stay there for a couple of days until Bee is medically cleared to fly. The docs say she'll recover completely."

"In other words, she's small but tough," Kent said with a wry smile. "Like someone else we all know."

Wade shifted gears. "Did everyone complete their assignments?"

A murmur of assent went around the table. Before he left to meet Chief Tobias, Wade had asked each of them to investigate part of the case for an in-depth review. Apparently, he was ready to begin the after-action debriefing.

"There are plenty of questions that need answers," Wade said. "And I want to start with Dr. Dawson." He looked at Perez. "Has his body been recovered?"

"It will take weeks to stabilize the tunnels enough to send anyone down," Perez said. "If they can ever be made safe. The body may stay where it is forever."

"You said he was dead before the cave-in, right?" Wade asked Nina, clarifying.

"I'm documenting everything in my report," Nina said, recalling the preliminary notes she'd made. "I returned fire and he collapsed. I found a pool of blood beside him, then I checked his vitals and found no breathing or pulse. It's safe to assume he managed to press the detonator before he died."

Wade addressed Kent. "Was there anything in his background that indicated he had ordnance training?"

When Nina had shared Dawson's comment regarding Uncle Sam teaching him about explosives, Wade had taken advantage of Kent's military background by tasking him with unearthing as much as he could.

"He transferred to the Army Reserves after a four-year hitch in the Army," Kent said. "He was assigned to Fort Huachuca, where he retired last summer after serving twenty years."

"Fort Huachuca's in Sierra Vista," Perez said for everyone else's benefit. "That's in southern Arizona near the Mexican border."

Wade stroked his jaw. "Isn't that where the Army Intelligence Center is?"

"Bingo," Kent said. "The Network Enterprise Technology Command, or NETCOM, is housed there. There's also an electronic proving ground, computer tech, cyberanalysis, and a lot of other secret squirrel shit going on there."

"He would need a security clearance," Breck said. "How could he pass a background check while he was murdering people?"

"Because he didn't start committing crimes until after he retired from military service," Wade said. "I'll get to my profile in a bit, but this plays into his mindset." He inclined his head toward Kent. "Go on."

"He joined the Fifty-Second Ordnance Group after completing advanced individual training," Kent said. "The Army later reassigned him to work with bioweapons. In the last phase of his career, he was heavily into computers, cyber intelligence, and counterespionage."

Hazel and his investigators had developed an electronic spreadsheet listing twenty thousand individuals associated with the university. The task force, including the PPD, had sifted through the data, strategically selecting individuals for follow-up investigation. There had been no indication the unsub was affiliated with the military in any way. In fact, Dawson had flown so far under the radar that he hadn't raised a single red flag. Chagrined, Nina realized that his background in the armed forces—including training with explosives, chemical weapons, and, apparently, psychology—would have surfaced if he had come to their attention for further scrutiny.

But he hadn't. And Bianca had nearly paid the price.

"What about the falconry angle?" Nina asked, forcing her mind away from dark thoughts.

"The sonofabitch trained falcons for the Army." Kent crossed his arms. "Which is why he never showed up in the Arizona Game and Fish Department database."

"Come again?" Perez said. "Why would the military use falcons?"

"They're developing computer programs at Fort Huachuca to hack enemy spy drones. The idea is to reprogram their control systems to make them crash, or at the very least, disrupt their ability to transmit video."

"Let me guess," Breck said, making the connection faster than the others. "By sending a surge to overload the system before taking it over?"

Kent pointed at her in acknowledgment. "You got it. But that technology doesn't always work, especially if it's been developed by a variety of countries using different coding systems. They needed a reliable, low-tech method to intercept spy drones in the field."

"Raptors," Nina said. "I've heard some airports use birds of prey to take out personally owned drones that get into the flight path of airplanes."

"The military uses them for the same reason, among others," Kent said. "And Dawson was the first of three falconers on the base. He helped train the others, who took over most of the routine duties because he lived three hours away. You'll never believe where his bird came from."

"According to the Game and Fish Director, they're usually caught in the wild nearby," Nina said.

"Not this time," Kent said. "Records show he got clearance to bring the raptor stateside from his tour of duty in Egypt."

"Egypt?" she repeated in surprise.

"He was stationed on the Sinai Peninsula with a peacekeeping mission early in his career. A golden eagle flew into a wire and got hurt. While nursing it back to health, he discovered someone had already trained it to hunt. He convinced the base commander to let him keep it to take out enemy drones. The pilot program was so effective they made arrangements for him to continue with it here."

"So that's when he became fascinated with Egypt," Nina said. "And with falconry."

Wade leaned forward, his intense gaze focused on Kent. "What happened to Dawson's bird?"

Kent gave Wade a significant look. "A golden eagle's average life span is twenty years, but it can live past thirty. This one spent a good chunk of her life with him." His expression grew pained. "She finally died of old age last summer. It's one of the reasons he retired a few months earlier than he had originally planned, according to the records I found."

"He couldn't face going on with his career without his partner," Wade said.

"Golden eagles are monogamous and bond for life," Kent said. "I think he was looking for a new mate after she died."

"She?" Nina said.

"His eagle was female." Kent flipped through his notes. "He named her Hathor."

"That's an odd name for a girl," Perez said.

Breck was typing on her laptop. An instant later, she straightened. "Oh hell no."

"Let's hear it," Kent said with an air of resignation.

Breck turned the laptop around, showing them an image that looked like it came straight from an ancient Egyptian tomb. A tall, slender woman was depicted in profile, wearing an orange-red dress. Her long ebony hair was crowned by a large circular headdress that included a pair of pointed cow horns and a cobra's head. She carried a staff in one hand and an ankh in the other.

"Hathor was an ancient Egyptian goddess," Breck said. "She has many roles but is most often recognized as the wife of Horus."

"Hold on a sec." Nina's mind raced. "When I was at the hospital with Bianca, she said Dawson told her to call him Horace." She tilted her head. "You know, the first name that's spelled H-O-R-A-C-E. It's pronounced the same as *Horus*."

Breck sucked in a breath. "That's what I was about to show you all next." She clicked another button. "This is Horus." The drawing of a man with a bird's head atop wide shoulders appeared. "The falcon-headed god."

Chapter 72

Nina turned to Wade. "When you and Breck were doing the research on the jesses, you mentioned the ancient Egyptians worshipping a falcon-headed god."

"Dawson must have identified strongly with Horus," Wade said. "I recall reading that the deity was associated with royal power, which must have appealed to him."

"Looks like Horus could also take the form of a falcon," Nina said, noticing the inset image in the corner of the screen.

Kent pointed to a drawing of a kohl-rimmed eye with a brow above it, a thick line extending down and another sweeping out to the side, ending in a tight curl. "The Eye of Horus."

"That's supposed to symbolize well-being, protection, and healing," Wade said. "Don't think it worked out that way for his victims, but he might have thought he was protected from law enforcement."

"And we can't forget the feather of Maat," Kent added. "Dawson steeped himself in ancient mythology. We'll learn more as we do our psychological postmortem, but I'd guess he developed a rich fantasy life over time as reality continued to disappoint him. Something always broke the spell."

"In other words," Wade said thoughtfully, "he walked among us but lived in his own world."

"There is so much data here," Breck said, scrolling through pages of text and images. "It's going to take a while to get through it all to find out what it meant to Dawson."

"There is a chance that the mythology of Horus didn't have as much significance to him as we think," Wade said. "It's possible that he simply identified with the physical image of a half-falcon deity who was associated with royal power."

"Agreed," Kent said. "This will be part of a long-term study."

"Why don't we table that discussion," Nina said, "and shift our focus to how he executed his plans."

"I've already heard from the detectives and evidence techs serving the search warrant on his apartment," Perez said. "They found a fake campus police uniform he'd probably bought online, a full set of keys, and an extra electronic entry card. Everything he needed to gain his victims' trust and get into locked doors. They also collected several potted plants. Guess what he was growing?"

Nina knew the answer. "Jimsonweed."

Perez gave her a nod. "They haven't found any narcotics paraphernalia or equipment he might have used to make the jesses or restrain the victims, so we're thinking he must have kept that stuff down in the tunnels somewhere."

"Makes sense," Kent said. "The plants needed light to grow and wouldn't cause suspicion if they remained in his home unless someone really knew their botany. Drug paraphernalia and bondage gear, however, might have raised eyebrows if anyone spotted it."

"He was wearing the uniform when he grabbed Melissa Campbell," Breck said. "Which, unfortunately, only made Lieutenant Hazel look more guilty."

"But the uniform and keycard would only get him into the AIT tunnels," Nina said. "Not the ones in downtown Phoenix."

"I can help with that part," Breck said. "Once I got the green light to go through Dawson's personal computer, it was easy pickings. That man planned every move he made. The whole thing was laid out in an encrypted file."

"How did you hack in?" Nina asked.

"He was talented with computers." She winked. "But I'm better."

There were times her colleague reminded Nina of her young neighbor. She would have to make sure Bianca used her powers for good like Breck did.

"I found a recipe for sevoflurane in one of Dawson's files while I was cyber-snooping," Breck said, pulling a flash drive from her pocket. "It's a fast-acting general anesthetic," she added. "I looked it up. It can either be inhaled or injected directly into the muscle." She frowned. "It's known to cause retrograde amnesia."

"Bianca couldn't remember him taking her," Nina said. "He must have used it to knock out his victims." A new worry kicked her pulse up a notch. "Are there long-term side effects?"

Breck gave her a sympathetic look. "I didn't find anything to indicate Bee's in danger going forward."

"Thank you," Nina said, calming slightly. "And I agree with Perez. There was probably a mini lab down in the tunnels where no one would ever find it."

"I'll put everything on the wall screen so you all can see what else he was up to," Breck said, sliding her hand under the table to insert the flash drive into a hidden USB port.

Moments later, the fauxquarium was replaced by an image of Dawson's desktop. Breck opened a file and began sorting through the documents inside.

She skimmed her fingers over the controls in the table. "Turns out the AIT underground system butts up against the one downtown."

The schematic Nina had seen before they searched the AIT tunnels appeared on the screen. Seconds later, a similar 3D diagram of the Phoenix system materialized above it.

"Here's how they line up." Breck worked the controls, rotating the two images until the tail end of one aligned with the farthest point of the other. She moved them closer together until their tips touched each other.

Nina tried to make sense of it. "Dawson must have found the AIT-tunnel diagram buried in the archives on microfiche like you did," she said to Breck. "Assuming he had prior knowledge of the downtown tunnels because that's more widely known, how would he connect the two?"

"According to his notes on the Word doc associated with this schematic, he mapped out both systems and realized there was a point where they were only separated by a thin barrier." Breck zoomed in on the juncture. "He used a controlled blast to make an opening between the two networks."

"I know exactly how he did it," Kent said, excited. "It's called explosive breaching. We used it in Special Forces."

Wade's brows shot up. "How exactly would Dawson be able to blast a hole to connect the two tunnels without causing a cave-in?"

"He has advanced ordnance training," Kent said. "He would also have access to detonating cord, plastic explosives, or strip charges from the military, where he could have gradually pocketed extra supplies over time so no one would notice. He would know how to use the absolute minimum amount of force to accomplish the objective." He shrugged. "To be extra careful, he could have set the devices to detonate after he made it back to the surface so he wouldn't be caught in a cave-in if he misjudged."

"If that's true, the dude had *cojones*," Perez said. "But we searched the AIT tunnels. Between us and the tactical unit, someone would have noticed an opening leading to another underground network."

"I'm not an Explosives Ordnance Disposal expert," Kent said, "but I've worked with a lot of them. In the military, EOD techs are trained to both detect and conceal charges. In other words, he would know how to create a hatch or portal between the two systems and camouflage it to blend in perfectly."

"That's why the ground-penetrating radar didn't find it," Nina said, thinking about the equipment the SWAT team had brought to search the AIT tunnels. "The kind of GPR unit they use is on wheels. You push it like a lawn mower on the ground. There was no way of running it up the side of a wall." Another thought hit her. "And the heat sensors," she added. "The FLIR devices didn't pick up a heat signature at the end of the tunnel, so Bianca must have already been taken past that point."

"Unlike downtown, the AIT tunnels had no lighting," Perez said, clearly coming to the same conclusion she had. "We used our cell phone lights, and SAU had tactical flashlights. We could have easily missed a hatch or some other kind of barrier if it was well hidden."

"He would have to make sure to shut it behind him," Nina said.

"The only problem Dawson would have had was a trained K-9 tracking him or his victims," Wade said. "The dog would have run straight up against the wall and started pawing at it." He frowned. "So he eliminated that possibility early on by poisoning one of the dogs."

"Let's not forget that he had months to do this," Breck said, drawing everyone's attention back to the screen. "This file dates back to last summer."

"Last summer again." Nina gave Wade a significant look. "You promised to fill us in about your profile regarding that time frame."

"Slow down a second." Wade held up both hands. "You're saying Dawson carried Bianca—and presumably all the others—through both tunnel systems?"

"I could do it," Kent said. "It's not that hard if the woman you're carrying is light, and if you're in decent shape, which, according to his military medical records, he definitely was."

Nina recalled how easily Kent had held her in his arms as he ran through downtown Phoenix earlier. "I'm guessing Dawson was pretty muscular underneath that tweed he always wore," she said. "Plus, he was motivated." She waited a beat before asking, "Where's the room where he held the women?"

"Been waiting for someone to ask," Breck said, then activated a pointer on the screen to indicate what looked like a storage room set into the wall of the Phoenix side of the tunnel. "Judging by the size of the rest of the underground structure, that room is tiny."

"All the better to torment his captives," Kent said darkly. "I've been inside a cell less than half that size. It's barbaric."

Nina knew better than to ask for details. Instead, she kept her attention on Breck. "Bee told me she sent the surge from a control center. Did you find that?"

"The tunnels downtown are a hundred years old." Breck expanded the image. "The original plans did not include a control center or technology of any kind. The system was later wired for electricity, but that's about as fancy as it got down there."

"So he set something up himself?" Nina asked.

"That's what I'm thinking," Breck said. "From Bianca's statement, I reckon it was in this area." She moved the indicator arrow to a space near the heart of the underground labyrinth. "Which is the spot where the surge was originating from. This is about the size of a three-car garage. It's a mechanical room with switches to shut off the power in the event of flooding or other emergencies. There are also valves to redirect the water in the pipes that run through some of the corridors."

"Bianca mentioned pipes," Nina said. "That's how she climbed up to escape through the ductwork."

"We may never be able to get down there now that the whole thing collapsed," Breck said. "But his files make it pretty clear Dawson spent months belowground setting things up. He could easily move between AIT and downtown without anyone knowing he had ever left the campus."

"Which is how he must have moved the bodies," Wade said. "He couldn't have taken them through the lobby of the San Carlos, so he must have had several exits from the downtown tunnel system."

Nina considered the logistics involved and concluded Wade was right. "Dawson could have parked near one of the surface exits. Then all he would need to do is put the body in a sack, load it into the trunk of his waiting car, and drive right down Central Avenue to the abandoned mine."

"Could the downtown tunnels be connected to the mine?" Kent asked. "Maybe he never had to take the bodies to the surface at all."

Perez shook his head. "Arizona is known for copper, but the most productive mines aren't in the Phoenix area. I double-checked with the ranger, who told me all the abandoned mines in the park are shallow. They were basically exploration shafts."

Wade gave him a wry smile. "You're saying the mines in South Mountain Park literally didn't pan out?"

"Exactly," Perez said. "Any tunnel connecting the site where we found the bodies to the downtown tunnels would have to be about seven miles long. No mining company would keep digging without anything to show for it."

"So he had to transport his victims by car," Breck said to Perez. "And the park closes at dark, but no one ever spotted him walking the trail with an oversize sack slung over his shoulder?"

"South Mountain Park is huge," Perez said. "And the area around the mine is way off the beaten path; he didn't have much chance of getting caught, even if he did it in broad daylight." He shrugged. "If he saw another vehicle at the trailhead, he could just come back later."

"He may have mapped out different exits downtown," Nina said, thinking about another aspect of Dawson's escape plans. "But once Kent and I started chasing him, he headed toward the AIT-tunnel system. I'm guessing he planned to surface somewhere on campus while everyone was looking for him downtown. That way, he could just get in his car and drive away while we wasted our time and resources elsewhere."

"I've also figured out what he did to Professor Feldman," Breck said. "Once we got our hands on his computer, I could see how he planted those chat messages to an unidentified student for Feldman's graduate assistant to find."

"That's not the only scapegoat he set up for us," Nina said. "Dawson clearly waited until Lieutenant Hazel would be on camera going into the medical sciences building. Bee still doesn't recall going inside the building, but she can remember Dawson telling her to go in and wait for him."

"So that's why she just went in by herself," Breck said. "I was wondering if that part was true."

"He knew about the security cams," Nina said. "So he created a sequence of events for us. We watched Bianca enter the building, then Hazel went in and came out, but Bianca didn't."

"I get it," Perez said. "He used the tunnel to go from the building where his office is to the medical sciences building. No one saw him. He grabbed Bianca, incapacitated her, then hauled her through the hallway to the cadaver-storage unit, probably at the same time Hazel arrived. By the time Hazel completed a thorough check of the main building and headed into the morgue, Dawson had already taken Bianca to the holding cell."

Nina added to the scenario. "All he had to do was run back to his office and walk across the campus like he normally would to meet Bianca. Then he went to the AIT police building to report her missing, claiming he couldn't locate her."

"He knew we'd conclude Hazel took her," Wade said on a sigh. "I spent hours interrogating that man."

Perez cursed. "He kept us distracted by throwing suspects at us."

"Misdirection," Kent said. "A classic military tactic."

Breck opened another screen. "Maybe that part of his background explains why he's so organized and meticulous. He scanned several pages from what appears to be handwritten entries in a field notebook. Take a gander at this."

Nina shifted her gaze to the other side of the display. A handwritten chart showed the names of each captive, including sketches and behavioral observations, as well as notations regarding each individual's care and feeding.

"Sonofabitch," Perez said, summing up Nina's thoughts perfectly.

As Breck scrolled down, each victim's name appeared beside the sketch of a bird. An appallingly small amount of food and water was given to each girl, with their reactions noted.

"Look," Nina said, pointing at a drawing of a black feather at the end of each entry. "He makes a note of when he's done with them."

Each page cataloged the last days or weeks of one or two young women. Nina's heart nearly seized in her chest when Breck scrolled to the last sheet. Melissa Campbell's name was there, along with a black feather, and below that, Bianca's name.

"No notes are entered for Bee," she said.

"I'm guessing he kept his notebook on his person," Kent said. "He probably jotted things down, then scanned and uploaded them later."

"But he never had time to do that with Bianca's notes," Nina said to Kent. "We'll never know what his last few entries about her said."

Wade drew closer, eyes narrowed on the field notes. He turned to Kent. "I believe it's time you shared your thoughts on the demons that drove Dr. Dawson."

Chapter 73

Nina directed a raised brow at Kent. "Where did this creepy chart come from?"

"While you and Perez were at the hospital and Wade was fending off the media horde, Breck and I did a deep dive into Dawson's computer," Kent said. "She found these so-called field notes, as well as details of a recent personal crisis buried in his files."

"Let's start with the chart," Wade said. "It offers fascinating insight into his psyche."

Kent strode over to the display, where he began pointing at each segment of the graph as he spoke. "It's broken down by 'day,' which begins with the first day his victim was captured; 'observation,' in which he documents what he visually observes; 'water and food,' where he lists exactly how much each woman consumes daily; and 'strategy,' in which he plans what he will do the next time he makes contact."

"Looks like he numbered the days each woman was held," Wade said. "The longest was in his custody for twenty-one days. It appears he had a set methodology he would use as an induction process to indoctrinate them into his desired behavior pattern."

Nina tried to connect the theory with what they had uncovered during the investigation. "Dawson devised a technique for mind control based on what he had done with falcons?"

Kent nodded. "He refined his technique as he went, adjusting it to the personality of each captive. Some would naturally be more compliant than others."

Nina figured Bianca would be the least compliant of anyone. Then she noticed the sketches beside each of the names. "Haley Garrett has a swan next to her name, and Melissa's name looks like it's next to a songbird. I see that Bianca is the only one with what looks like an eagle or some other bird of prey next to it." She glanced at Kent. "What does that mean?"

"I can't be sure," he said, regarding the diagrams. "But I believe he gave each girl a representation of how he saw her personality. I'm not certain about his victim-selection strategy, because none of them were his students, but he must have known things about them before he grabbed them."

"I can help with that," Breck said. "While Kent was following up on another part of the investigation, I found some video files and decrypted them."

A few seconds later, they were all watching footage of the AIT campus. A lovely young woman whose glossy black hair contrasted with her fair skin strolled across the quad, laughing with friends.

Nina noted the time stamp. "That's midafternoon last November fifteenth."

"This is Sandy Owens," Breck said. "His first victim. He abducted her on December second."

"He had her under observation for more than two weeks," Wade said. "Could have learned a lot about her in that time frame."

Nina knew Wade was always highly interested in a killer's first crime. He had explained that their learning curve altered their MO as they progressed through a series, so the first scene tended to be more revealing.

"There are video logs containing footage for each victim," Breck said. "He had basically hijacked the AIT security cams and was piggybacking onto them to follow these poor girls around for days or weeks before he took them."

"That's how he knew where Melissa would be," Nina said, another piece finally slotting into place. "He knew her schedule and watched her patterns. The night he kidnapped her, he probably watched her with her date and lay in wait for his chance."

Kent scowled. "He had probably seen that prick of a boyfriend of hers leave her to walk back to her dorm alone in the dark on other occasions. Posing as a campus police officer would be the perfect ruse to catch her off guard."

"He couldn't have had Bianca under observation for an extended period of time, though," Perez pointed out.

"I believe he gradually became fascinated with her as he got to know her," Wade said. "It appears the others held a strictly physical appeal for him; Bianca is not only beautiful, but she's also highly intelligent."

"All of these girls were smart," Breck said. "Or they wouldn't be attending AIT."

"True," Nina said. "But Bianca is on a different level. The other students were the same age, but they were freshmen, while Bee was applying for grad school. Plus, she was helping to develop cutting-edge research."

"Agreed," Kent said. "We'll know more as we go through our post-mortem on this investigation, but it looks like Bianca was special to him."

"He recognized her as a potential threat," Nina said, wading into the unfamiliar territory of psychoanalysis. "He could tell she would challenge him at every turn."

"Based on what you've told us about her," Wade said, "she would be difficult—if not impossible—to tame."

Nina felt a fierce sense of pride at his assessment. "You're damn right she would."

"She learned from the best," Kent said dryly, then turned his attention back to the chart. "Dawson used operant conditioning and reinforcement. This guy studied B. F. Skinner."

Breck's brows furrowed. "Wasn't he the Harvard psychology professor who worked with pigeons?"

"He experimented with other animals as well," Kent said. "But he became famous for training pigeons. The techniques could be adapted to other birds, but raptors would present more of a challenge because—as the falconer we met with pointed out to us—they're predators."

"Humans can be predators too," Wade added. "They can also be unpredictable, although conditioning has been known to be highly effective on people."

Kent moved across the graph to point at the orderly columns. "Notice the way he makes a careful note of their food and water consumption, like a scientist conducting an experiment."

Wade gave his head a disgusted shake. "I remember reading similar charts when I was working on my dissertation in psychology. Only those studies were on the behavior of rats—not people."

"Exactly," Kent said. "I think you've gotten to the root of the problem. Dawson sets out to make a woman fall in love with him, but he has no conception of what love is, so he creates a relationship based on dependence and manipulation. Obviously, that will never work."

"He's desperate for a woman he finds beautiful to love him," Wade said, excitement growing as he fleshed out the pieces with Kent. "But he treats his captives like animals in an experiment because he can't understand them at all. He tries to control what he cannot understand. The frustration mounts as he repeatedly fails."

"He keeps choosing a new victim after every disappointment," Nina said, trying to keep up. "He never realizes that *he's* the problem, not the woman he selects."

"I get it," Breck said. "He doesn't realize there's no fox in the woods, so he keeps switching hounds."

Perez heaved a sigh. "If he weren't a homicidal maniac, I'd almost feel sorry for him."

"Wait until you hear the next part," Kent said. "It's all about what happened to him last summer. It seems that as soon as his eagle died, he was desperately trying to fill the void." He tipped his head toward Breck, who took the cue.

"Dawson started an online relationship at the beginning of June," Breck said. "By the end of the month, his virtual girlfriend agreed to meet in person. Flight records show he went all the way to Connecticut to see her."

"Let me guess," Nina said. "He's into gorgeous women, so she didn't measure up to his expectations." She hesitated a moment, rethinking. "Or he didn't measure up to hers."

"Worse than that," Kent said. "He was catfished."

Nina inwardly cringed. Someone with a fragile ego like Dawson being humiliated and deceived could have caused the precipitating stressor Kent and Wade often mentioned that sparked a serial killer to violence.

"The photos she sent him before they met were on his hard drive," Breck said. "She looked like a supermodel, which should have been his first clue. Then there was a picture he took with his cell phone at the restaurant when they met in person for the first time." She grimaced. "Turned out to be a middle-aged man who wanted to blackmail him."

Nina's mouth fell open. "For what?"

"The guy threatened to send copies of all the sexting threads to AIT," Breck said, her cheeks coloring. "I saw some of them. Dawson and the person he believed was his virtual girlfriend got hot and heavy. He sent a couple of naked pics and some spicy videos of himself too." She shook her head. "I can't imagine that would have gone over well for a respected professor at an elite university."

"He could safely fantasize about a virtual lover." Wade appeared to consider his analysis. "The reality of finally meeting in person after a few weeks of dating only to be humiliated would have triggered him."

"What happened to the catfisher?" Perez asked. "Is there a murder in Connecticut that needs to be investigated?"

Nina imagined a middle-aged man dead under mysterious circumstances on the other side of the country and thought Perez had a fair point.

"There was a cash withdrawal from Dawson's bank account in the amount of ten thousand dollars," Breck said. "He clearly paid the guy off."

"We'll have to follow up on that with authorities in Connecticut," Wade said. "Blackmailers don't usually stop at one payment." He stroked his jaw. "Getting back to our profile, Dawson ends a twenty-year career in the military, which is disruptive in many ways. His eagle, which he's spent a great deal of time training and bonding with, dies. Finally, he believes he's found love, only to be made a fool of." He paused for emphasis. "All at the same time."

"To use a highly technical term, he snapped," Kent said. "He used his background and training to create a situation where his ideal woman couldn't reject him. He held his captives in a cold cell, naked and bound, inducing a state of fear and powerlessness. Then he systematically deprived them of food and water until they came to him willingly out of desperation, which he deluded himself into believing meant they wanted him. As he took care of them, they learned to depend on him. He became their whole world. He controlled whether they lived or died. They were eventually drawn to him and were grateful to him."

"Stockholm syndrome," Wade said. "That's how it happens. A human coping mechanism to ensure survival by bonding with whoever is keeping you alive. The interesting thing is that it works on both the captor and the captive."

"That's why some groups who take hostages rotate who is in charge of their prisoners," Kent added. "They also keep bags over their heads and tape their mouths to prevent themselves from relating to their captives as human beings." He paused as if recalling a distant and disturbing memory. "Makes it harder to kill them. A fact I used to my advantage once."

Nina regarded him thoughtfully. "You were captured on one of your covert missions, weren't you?"

"Held for a month," he said quietly. "Don't want to talk about it."

She had always suspected that had been the case. Kent had mentioned his scars, comparing them to hers. Their eyes locked for a long moment. Unlike the others in the room, they both knew what it felt like to be held prisoner, to be dehumanized, to be tortured. She knew Kent had admitted it for her benefit, and she was grateful.

He had made it clear he did not want to delve into the matter further, so she changed the subject to one very close to her heart.

"I'm just grateful he never had a chance to do that shit to Bee," Nina murmured.

Perez folded his arms. "So Dawson uses a combination of falconry and Stockholm syndrome to manipulate his captives. Why does he kill them after putting all that work into programming them?"

"I stand by my earlier assessment," Wade said. "Something destroys the fantasy. The victim has an unguarded moment where a flicker of revulsion shows in her expression, or she does something he sees as a betrayal. This creates cognitive dissonance, which he resolves by ending her ability to reject or betray him. Permanently."

"And then he goes on the hunt for his next candidate," Nina said.

"There's enough here to keep us busy for quite a while," Kent said.

"Agreed." Wade regarded Nina thoughtfully. "We may need a volunteer to stay in Phoenix until the end of the month."

Thinking of her newfound family, Nina shifted in her seat. "I could wrap things up here."

She couldn't ask her team to stay longer than they already had.

"If she's going to follow up on Dawson's online activity, she'll need a cybercrime specialist," Breck said.

"And a criminal profiler," Kent said.

"Or two." Wade sighed. "I'll call SSA Buxton and talk it over with him."

Her team was stepping up for her again. They had already extended their stay in Phoenix to investigate the AIT disappearances after the conclusion of their last case. At the time, Nina had been fully aware that any team of agents could have been detailed to assist. Buxton had gone out of his way to make arrangements for her to stay in town and get to know her newfound family.

Now it appeared her team was prepared to prolong time away from their homes, friends, and personal lives again.

Nina lowered her gaze. "I couldn't ask you all to—"

"No, you couldn't," Kent cut in. "It's something a team does without being asked. And we're your team."

Breck strolled over to rest a hand on Nina's shoulder. "You're stuck with us, sugar."

Nina reached up and placed her hand on top of Breck's. "Thank you."

She did not trust herself to say more, hoping the heartfelt look she gave each of them in turn conveyed the gratitude in her heart.

Chapter 74

That night, Nina sat at the hotel bar on the mezzanine of the Phoenix Royal Suites, swirling red liquid in her glass. "Perez told me I should try a prickly pear margarita, and he was right. This is the nectar of the gods."

Wade had suggested the team meet in the cocktail lounge before turning in. They were ensconced in a quiet corner away from the other patrons, drinks in hand, blowing off steam.

Breck laughed. "The good detective might have had an ulterior motive for getting you to imbibe." She winked. "Which is not a bad thing. He's definitely easy on the eyes."

Kent muttered something under his breath that Nina couldn't make out.

"Before we stray too far into personal concerns," Wade began, "I have business to discuss."

Nina wasn't surprised. Wade had been on the phone with Supervisory Special Agent Buxton for the last hour, filling him in. She was interested to hear what the boss thought about how things had turned out and whether he would join them in Phoenix for the final stage of the investigation.

"Buxton's getting promoted," Wade said, interrupting her thoughts. "He's going to be the Assistant Special Agent in Charge of the Miami field office."

"Miami," Nina said. "Palm trees, putting greens, and sandy beaches sound like a nice change of pace."

They all shared a chuckle, aware their boss was the last person who would lounge on a beach or play golf in his spare time. Mostly because he never seemed to have spare time. As an ASAC, he would probably have even less than he did now.

"You never know," Breck said. "Maybe a tropical climate will mellow him out. He's certainly earned a break."

"I should've known when they kept him in DC for so long," Kent said. "They were probably negotiating a spot for him, and it might have involved a lot of jockeying for position."

"While I'm thrilled for Buxton," Wade said, bringing the conversation around to what apparently had been his original subject, "this leaves our team without a supervisor for the time being."

"What about you?" Nina said without thinking. "You've been doing the job since Buxton flew back to DC."

They all turned to him.

"It's under discussion," Wade said. "But I'm close to retirement, so my name's not on a list for promotion right now. If I want to go for it, I'd have to get on the first flight back to get the ball rolling."

Nina suddenly realized why he had asked them all for an impromptu gathering. "You want to know if we'd support you becoming our boss." She made it a statement rather than a question.

Their eyes met. A few months ago, Nina would never have believed she would come to view Dr. Jeffrey Wade as a partner, an ally, and a friend.

"It would be my honor to work for you," she told him, then added, "sir."

Breck lifted a mojito. "Same here."

"It'll be a huge step down from Buxton," Kent said, grinning. "But I'll make sure you don't screw things up too badly."

Chapter 75

Nina sat on the armchair, watching Breck scroll through websites with blurring speed. Every few seconds, she would stop and scan the page, then move on. They had returned to their shared hotel room ten minutes earlier, and Breck hadn't wasted any time dragging out her ever-present laptop and propping it open on the coffee table in the center of a cluster of chairs in the corner.

"What has you so engrossed?" Nina asked her.

"Ancient Egypt," Breck said. "It's fascinating. The culture, the rites and rituals—everything about it."

Nina chuckled. Breck was the type to go down a rabbit hole for hours, which was probably what made her such an outstanding cyber-crimes investigator.

A soft tap on the door that separated their suite from Wade and Kent's interrupted them. Nina stood and crossed the room to open the door.

"Can I have a word?" Kent said. "In private?"

His penetrating expression made her wary. "What's up?"

"I want to show you something," he said, offering no further explanation.

She stood aside, and he walked past her into the room. Breck had a hotel pad and pen beside her, jotting down notes before her eyes returned to the screen.

"She's in the zone," Kent said dryly. "I doubt she'll even notice you're gone."

"Kent and I are heading out for a few minutes," she called out to Breck, who waved without looking up from her computer.

"She's doing a deep dive on ancient Egyptian culture and symbolism," Nina said to Kent as they walked into the hallway and closed the door behind them. "Probably won't come up for air until midnight."

Kent refused to answer any questions about where he was taking her, and she resigned herself to wait and see, following him into the elevator, where he pushed the top button. When the doors hissed open, he led her out onto a rooftop patio that overlooked the city.

Dawson's obsession had laid waste to several blocks. In silence, they looked at the damage he had wrought. Crews of municipal employees worked in tandem with their state and federal counterparts under the glow of portable lights. Nina knew the reconstruction would continue for weeks, if not months. After several minutes of quiet contemplation, she turned to Kent, wondering why he had wanted to show her this tableau of devastation, to find him gazing down at her with an intensity she had never seen.

"This city has suffered tremendous destruction," he said. "But it will rise from the ashes like its namesake. It won't be the same, but it can come back stronger. More beautiful than before."

She cast a glance at the mountainous piles of rubble below before turning back to meet his piercing gaze. "It takes a lot of work to repair that kind of damage."

His voice dropped to a hoarse rasp. "When I was down in the tunnels, there were a couple of times I was sure I wasn't coming out alive—or coming out at all."

She shuddered. "Don't remind me."

"No." He moved in close. "There's something you need to know."

"Kent, I—"

"When Dawson had that gun pointed directly at me, I accepted my death, but I didn't make peace with it." He lifted a hand to her face, gently stroking a knuckle down her cheek. "Because I had one regret."

Sensing where this was going, Nina stilled.

"I never told you how I feel about you," he said quietly.

She could guess why he hadn't shared his feelings. "Because you know I'm not . . . not capable of a relationship."

His hand fell to his side. "What the hell makes you say that?"

She looked him up and down. He was whole, healthy, and handsome. The kind of man women fantasized about. She was physically and emotionally scarred—the kind of woman men kept at a distance.

"Because it's true." The only way she could make him understand was to be totally honest. "You're hot." She glanced down. "I'm a hot mess."

"No," he said sharply. "You're—"

She silenced him with a raised hand. If he wanted to have this discussion, she would end it quickly. And she knew exactly how.

"The Cipher," she said, letting the two words hang in the air between them. "The night he attacked me—back when I was sixteen . . ."

Her heart pounded. Perspiration prickled her scalp. She was about to share something that she had never told anyone. Could she get the words out?

"I was a virgin," she whispered. "Before he . . ." Her throat constricted, cutting her off midsentence.

Kent regarded her in silence. She knew he had seen the video of what the Cipher had done to her. How he had assaulted her, degraded her, devastated her. Apparently sensing more was coming, he gave her time and space to continue.

Unable to meet his gaze, she stared resolutely at his broad chest and spoke around the lump that had formed in her throat. "I've never been . . . intimate with anyone since."

There. She had said it. Now he would know how broken and damaged she truly was. This was why she had walled herself off years ago. The emotional distance had kept her heart safe, but it had also made her incapable of showing Bianca the love she needed, and she had recruited Mrs. G to fill the void. Now that Kent understood, he would walk away.

And she wouldn't blame him. Who would want to take on a relationship with someone whose sole sexual experience had consisted of a brutal rape at the hands of a killer?

He reached for her, but she took a step back, and he withdrew his hand. "Oh hell, Nina. I didn't know."

Of course he didn't. And he still wouldn't know if he hadn't made it clear he was interested in pursuing something more. Something she didn't think she could give him.

He reached out again, and this time she let him gently lift her chin with his finger. "Are you trying to scare me off?" he whispered.

She looked into his blue eyes and saw no trace of apprehension. "I am," she said frankly. "Can't believe it's not working."

"I'm a SEAL." A slow grin crept across his face. "I don't scare easy."

He slowly bent his head toward hers, taking his time, giving her every chance to pull back. For whatever reason, damaged as she was, this man wanted to be with her. He stopped, his lips a hairbreadth away from hers. His message was clear. She would have to come to him. She would have to be willing to open her heart and take a chance at love.

She froze, heart pounding, unable to move closer, unwilling to move away. After an eternity, he straightened and gave her a sad smile.

"Whenever you're ready, Nina, I'll be here."

Chapter 76

Nina sat at an extra-long picnic table in Teresa's backyard the next day, stunned at how quickly her aunt had managed to create a gathering place for the team and the family. Teresa had called half an hour earlier to invite everyone over for a hearty lunch, and Nina had accepted on her team's behalf.

She had been anxious to see Bianca again to make sure she was recovering emotionally, as well as physically, after her ordeal. She would have spent the night at her aunt Teresa's, but Mrs. Gomez had flown in from Springfield. Teresa had insisted Mrs. G stay at her house, which was now full to bursting with family and guests. Nina figured she would only get in the way while the two women fussed over Bianca as only a pair of doting Latina mothers could.

Nina's uncle John called out to the group, "A little help here?"

He was holding tongs in one hand and a platter of burgers fresh from the grill in the other. Nina jumped up to grab a second platter filled with patties, this time covered in melted Monterey Jack cheese, and everyone else pitched in to carry side dishes and condiments out from the kitchen.

"Do you have any sweet pickles?" Breck asked Teresa.

"No, but we have jalapeño pickles." Teresa gave her a mischievous grin. "Want some?"

"I'll pass," Breck said quickly. "Thanks anyway."

Soon the FBI team, along with Bianca, was clustered around the table with Teresa, John, Alex, and Mrs. G. The only thing they all had in common was Nina, who felt as if her worlds had collided.

When Bianca, wedged between Nina and Mrs. G, darted a glance at Alex, his normally tan complexion grew ruddy. Nina would have to keep track of that situation if Bianca decided to attend AIT in the fall.

Thoughts of her precocious neighbor gave Nina a peculiar feeling. The three schools Bianca was considering for her master's degree were all far from DC. No matter which one she chose, she would leave town. Leave Nina and Mrs. G behind.

"What's wrong, *mi'ja*?" Teresa said, eyeing Nina.

"Nothing." Nina used the tongs to lift a burger patty from the platter. She placed it neatly on the open bun on Bianca's plate, then went back for another for herself.

Teresa rose from her seat. "I need some help in the kitchen."

Nina understood it for the summons it was. She dutifully got to her feet and stepped over the bench. She felt all eyes on her as she followed her aunt into the house.

Teresa got straight to the point as soon as the patio door closed behind them. "I saw you looking at Bianca," she said. "I know that look."

Nina opted for honesty. Her aunt deserved that much. "Bee told me she still plans to start her graduate program in the fall." She gave her head a small shake. "After everything that happened, I assumed that . . ." Nina's throat constricted, cutting off the end of the sentence.

"That she would stay with Mrs. Gomez and keep living next door to you?" Teresa said quietly. "That she would give up her dreams and her future so you could watch over her and keep her safe?"

"That's not what I meant," Nina said, a little more sharply than she'd intended. She wanted Bianca to reach her full potential. To realize her goal of helping people with spinal cord injuries walk again. To use her unique gifts to change the world for the better. "She needs time to recover from what happened."

"You told me you found a therapist for her, and she has months before September."

"But she'd be . . ." Nina struggled to find the right words to express her feelings. "All alone."

"Vulnerable?" Teresa asked.

"Yes." Nina looked down. "Exactly."

"And she's small, too, right?"

Nina nodded, relieved her aunt finally seemed to understand her misgivings.

Teresa rested a hand on her hip. "You're describing yourself at her age, *mi'ja*."

Nina's head snapped up. "What?"

"Only you were far worse off," Teresa said. "It was long before we met, but I know your story."

Like just about everybody else who had internet service. Thanks to the Cipher, only a few short months had passed since her background in the foster system had become public knowledge. Very public knowledge.

"When you were emancipated at seventeen, you had no one to care for you," Teresa continued. "No friends. No family at all." She dropped her arms and took a step closer. "You're small, but you're still the strongest person I know." She paused. "I sense the same strength in Bianca. She will be fine."

Nina remembered the frightened thirteen-year-old she had taken from an abusive foster home environment five years earlier. An unnamed emotion bubbled close to the surface.

Teresa lifted her hands to frame Nina's face. "What you're feeling for her is love."

Unable to look away from the warm brown eyes that reminded her so much of the mother she had never known, Nina felt a single tear slide down her cheek.

"I'm not good at love," Nina whispered. "Don't have much experience."

"You have more than you realize," Teresa said. "What do you think you've felt for Bianca, Mrs. Gomez, and everyone on your team? Love comes in many forms."

"It also sucks," Nina said.

"I won't deny it, *mija*. Love means letting go. The reason I had an empty room in my house for Bianca and Mrs. Gomez is because my daughter left to start her own family. My son will leave for college soon. We can't keep everyone dear to us safe forever."

"But I swore to protect her." She didn't add that she had recruited Mrs. G to provide the love she didn't believe she could. Somewhere along the way, Bianca had burrowed into her heart. The kid sister she'd never had.

"You taught her everything you could," Teresa said. "Now it's time for her to leave the nest."

Nina turned the words over in her mind. *Time for her to leave the nest.* And then it hit her. Bianca was ready to fly. She was a rare and special creature—a falcon who could not be tamed.

In the same moment, Nina realized she had known how to love all along. Not in a traditional maternal or sisterly way, but in the way of a warrior, a protector. That was the gift Bianca had given her years ago when she had placed her trust in another trauma survivor.

Nina may have saved Bianca's life that night, but Bianca had saved Nina's soul.

A childhood spent in abuse and neglect had taught Nina to wall herself off. A madman's brutal attack when she was sixteen had only served to harden her internal defenses. Finally, as an adult, she'd become a guardian, protecting those who were as vulnerable as she had once been.

She had spent her entire life feeling alone, separate from others. She had let a precious few into her inner circle, but still maintained a barrier around her innermost core.

She turned to look out the sliding glass doors at the picnic table crowded with everyone dear to her. Kent glanced up, and their eyes locked. Despite everything she had been through, despite all her physical and emotional scars, he was offering her a chance at another kind of love. A few days ago, she would not have thought it possible. She had considered herself too damaged, but now she understood that scars could be beautiful.

It was time to tear down the walls. Time to open her heart and live.

ACKNOWLEDGMENTS

My husband, Mike, has been incredibly supportive through all my endeavors. The best partner and friend anyone could want, he is my rock.

My son, Max, brings me joy and laughter every day. How blessed I am.

So much more than an agent, Liza Fleissig shares my vision and makes miracles happen. Her advice, support, and outstanding professionalism have been life changing for me and many others.

My other agent, Ginger Harris-Dontzin, is always there to lend her sharp eyes and equally sharp mind as rough ideas struggle to take shape.

The law is complex and ever-changing, and retired attorney Martin B. Richards is my go-to legal eagle to keep me on the straight and narrow. I am always grateful for his sage advice.

Ancient Egypt has a rich and fascinating culture. Malayna Evans generously provided me with her expert insight and advice regarding its history and traditions. Any inaccuracies are strictly my own.

The men and women of the FBI work without expectation of fame or fortune. They dedicate themselves to upholding their motto, "Fidelity, Bravery, Integrity." A special thanks goes out to Ret. Special Agent Jerri Williams, who shares their stories in her FBI Retired Case File Review podcast.

Senior editor Megha Parekh, my acquiring editor with Thomas & Mercer, has been with me through every part of the process. I am grateful for her support and willingness to work through unexpected challenges . . . and there were plenty of those.

My developmental editor, Charlotte Herscher, put her considerable talent toward making this story better. Her incisive observations and keen eye for details were invaluable.

The amazing team of marketing, editing, and artwork professionals at Thomas & Mercer is second to none. I am incredibly blessed to have such talented professionals by my side.

ABOUT THE AUTHOR

Photo © 2016 Skip Feinstein

Isabella Maldonado is the award-winning and *Wall Street Journal* best-selling author of the Detective Cruz series and of *The Cipher* and *A Different Dawn* in the Nina Guerrera series. Before turning to crime writing, she wore a gun and badge in real life. A graduate of the FBI National Academy in Quantico and the first Latina to attain the rank of captain in her police department, she retired as the Commander of Special Investigations and Forensics. During more than two decades on the force, she served as a hostage negotiator, department spokesperson, and district station commander. She uses her extensive law enforcement background to bring a realistic edge to her writing. Maldonado lives in the Phoenix area with her family. For more information, visit www.isabellamaldonado.com.